Praise for *Big Cactus*

"It's a rollicking literary road trip which, like any great trip, is fun but also illuminating, full of poignant insights. Aunt Lucy in an indelible character, a person who might require her own glossary."
—**Leon Capetanos**, whose films include "Moscow on the Hudson," "Down and Out in Beverly Hills," and "Fletch Lives"

"When I finished reading *Big Cactus*, I wanted to go back to page one and start all over again. That's because I didn't want to part from these three amazing travelers: Benny Foushee, Aunt Lucy Lucy Williams, and Tennessee Gentry (to say nothing of the dog). Sylvia Wilkinson's ear for southern speech is pitch perfect, and she uses it to create a genuinely American Odyssey, wonderfully funny and tenderly wise."
—**R. H. W Dillard**, author of *The First Man on the Sun*, *What is Owed the Dead*, and *The Greeting: New and Selected Poems*

"Benny's and Aunt Lucy's voices in *Big Cactus* are the soul of this story, a story as American as the landscape they pass through to get the old woman to the Big Cactus. From North Carolina to Arizona, like Huck and Jim on the river, they learn about themselves. Benny learns what he wants to become and Aunt Lucy, what her life in one place has amounted to. They both discover what they love and why, revelations that carry the reader along with them. Wilkinson's sense of the human heart is unerring."
—**Jane Gentry**, Poet Laureate of Kentucky and author of *A Garden in Kentucky* and *Portrait of the Artist as a White Pig*

BIG CACTUS

OTHER BOOKS BY SYLVIA WILKINSON

NOVELS
Moss on the North Side
A Killing Frost
Cale
Shadow of the Mountain
Bone of My Bones
On the Seventh Day, God Created the Chevrolet

NON-FICTION
The Stainless Steel Carrot: an Auto Racing Odyssey--Revisited
Change: a Handbook for the Teaching of English & Social Studies
Dirt Tracks to Glory

YOUNG ADULT FICTION by "Eric Speed"
Mexicali 1000
Road Race of Champions
Gt Challenge
Midnight Rally

CHILDREN'S NON-FICTION
World Of Racing (Series)
- *Can-Am*
- *Trans-Am*
- *Stock Cars*
- *Endurance Racing*
- *Formula One*
- *Super Vee*
- *Karts*
- *Champ Cars*
- *Formula Atlantic*
- *Sprint Cars*

I Can Be a Race Car Driver
The True Book of Automobiles

BIG CACTUS

A Novel

Sylvia Wilkinson

Owl Canyon Press

First Edition, 2014

Library of Congress Cataloging-in-Publication Data

Wilkinson, Sylvia.
Big Cactus—1st ed.
p. cm.
ISBN978-0-9911211-2-0
2014944421

Owl Canyon Press
Boulder, Colorado

Manufactured in the United States of America
1 3 5 7 9 10 8 6 4 2

"You've always got to go with your imagination over your previous plans. It isn't about where they start out but what they become."

Louis Rubin

1

"What are you doing in the floor, Aunt Lucy?"

"Benny, look at the pretty dress I wore for Rupert's wedding," she answered.

Rupert is my daddy. Aunt Lucy, his old sister, was flat on her back in her living room floor, wearing a blue dress big enough for my fat sister Ethel. If I had on something that wrinkled, Mother would ask me if I slept in it, knowing I really hadn't.

"Sure glad I could find it in time to wear to yours."

"Aunt Lucy, I'm not old enough to get married. I just finished tenth grade. I'm here to get you for church."

She didn't answer and swatted me away like I was a fly when I stooped to help her up. I put the macaroni and cheese Mother sent in her refrigerator, while Aunt Lucy crawled up in her rocker.

I already explained twice that the rented white coat I showed her last week was for the prom not my wedding. I tried a new answer, talking real loud: "Not going to be a wedding, Aunt Lucy. Me and Valinda busted up. She got mad because my new dog got mud on her prom dress. I'll tell you about it after church. Now go hurry into your Sunday dress. And either put on two brown shoes or two black shoes."

She stood up, grabbing the *Arizona Highways* out of my hand that Mother told me to bring her. I forgot I was holding it. "You got it, Benny. That's the one. The one with the big cactus I got to go see real soon. You can take me."

The cactus on the front looked like it was holding the sun between its green fingers, like a cowboy movie without the cowboys. I don't think there's anything like that cactus over in Duke Gardens. "Mother finally found the magazine in the attic, Aunt Lucy." I don't think she heard me.

"There's a lot more tadpoles in the sea, Benny," Aunt Lucy muttered as she shuffled back towards her bedroom with the magazine open in front of her. "I always figured that Valinda girl wasn't good enough for my favorite nephew," she added after she walked into the wall, said "Shit!" and backed up like a windup toy. Her only nephew. And she never even met Valinda. But as Mother would say: Remember Benny, it's the thought that counts.

"There's some chocolate covered cherries hid in my cedar chest. Help yourself," Aunt Lucy yelled from the bedroom. "Least you asked my opinion before you tied the knot. Wish Rupert had. This is the book I been looking for, Benny. How about this? A cactus tall as a five-story building that's two hundred years old. I'll make you a deal. You drive and I'll cook."

"Aunt Lucy, please, read that magazine later. Mother is going to have a fit if we make her late for church." I think Aunt Lucy has about as much interest in church as I do. I'd whole lot rather work on my truck but Mother would give me that "working on the Sabbath" stuff. Or I could go in to McDonald's where that friendly cheerleader with the big boobs works the drive-through and get Aunt Lucy some fries. Got to wash my truck first.

"Papa couldn't stop talking about that big cactus, Benny. He come home from out there with nary one of them turquoise baubles they show in here. Cost too much. Stole a little biddy ring off a drunk Indian. I still got it somewhere…"

"Aunt Lucy, get your church dress on right now."

I finally got her ready and up in my truck, her nose still in that magazine. She didn't even notice my new plaid seat covers. "Listen to this. It's got thorns to keep stuff from stealing its water." Some things she says are so goofy, they really tickle me. She sure was crazy about a plant she never met in person. I don't think Aunt Lucy has any idea how far away that cactus is.

I used to imagine going out west too, but I didn't imagine being a cowboy anymore. Didn't interest me that much now that I got a truck, but I wouldn't mind taking a trip. According to Aunt Lucy, Grandpa did have a big time out west. But something killed him here in Summit long before I got to meet him and she won't tell me about it no matter how many times I ask. Daddy says he was too little to remember and Uncle Tendall just grunts and shakes his head and says he doesn't want to talk about it. Mother tells me: "Leave well enough alone," whatever that means. It means I'm going crazy until I find out what happened. I only knew one person ever who got killed and it was Sammy Barefoot who rolled over his tractor and mashed his head.

After church I heard Mother tell Daddy in the kitchen: "Rupert, you are delaying the inevitable. One of these days your sister Lucy is going to fall down and break her neck and who'll get the blame? Me, that's who." I never mentioned about Aunt Lucy falling down. "Rupert, didn't you notice she had on a black shoe and a brown shoe at church? I was embarrassed to tears. Benny, don't you let that filthy dog in here. Why on earth you brought something like that home. Look at your complexion. Have you been sneaking chocolate down at Lucy's again?" Mother could fuss at two people at once.

"You know, Mona," Daddy said, "Black and brown look pretty much alike to me too." Then he added one of his look how funny I am chuckles: "I bet Lucy has another pair of shoes in her closet just like them." He went running out to the porch pretending she was going to pop him with the pan she was drying.

After we ate, Daddy, who has white hair and looks old enough to be my grandpa; my big sister Ethel who just graduated from high school; and Daddy's real old brother and sister: Uncle Tendall and Aunt Lucy were sitting on our porch like they always were on Sunday, Uncle Tendall already three sheets to the wind. Most people figure they're my grandparents since they're old and we take them everywhere. We all live in different houses on the farm, ours about twice as big as Aunt Lucy and Uncle Tendall's houses put together. I wanted to go out and drive some, maybe just go get Aunt Lucy some McDonald's fries because she couldn't stand Mother's fried chicken, but I didn't have any money left to get gas. I had to spend all I made last week working at the filling station on two used tires for the front. I was kind of stuck on the porch.

When I took a swig of my Coke, Uncle Tendall tossed out the first piece of red meat to his sister: "Bet you didn't know Co-Cola used to be green?"

"It wont green," Aunt Lucy growled back. "It come in a green bottle. Tendall's color blind anyhow. If they turned the stoplights upside down, he'd kill hisself." Her legs stuck straight out from the porch chair, one foot wearing a brown shoe and the other a black one. She got her dress changed OK but I should have made sure she got her shoes right. They appeared to both be for the same foot.

"Tendall lies so much he's got to pay somebody to call his dog."

"Talk about lying, Lucy, I ain't even got a dog."

I petted my new dog Polar. I couldn't ever forgive Uncle Tendall for shooting my last dog when he got drunk hunting and mistook him for a bear. He wouldn't have an excuse with this dog. This dog is white not black like Bear was and there aren't any polar bears around here. Uncle Tendall had forgotten to button his fly, his polka dot old man under britches poking out like a flower in his crotch. "Co-Cola was so green," he snorted. I would take Aunt Lucy's side if I knew for sure it wasn't ever green.

"Just one Sabbath," Mother said, taking a Kleenex out of her pocket and wiping off her porch chair seat, "I wish to witness a civil conversation between adults. Eighty-four and eighty-two years old respectively," she shook her head and sputtered, "Oh me. Ignore me. There is no respect for anyone or anything in this family."

"You must have that number written down somewhere," Aunt Lucy grumbled. "I don't remember eighty-four."

"Don't even know how old you are," Uncle Tendall sneered, wobbling down the steps holding his arms out like he was on a tightrope. He disappeared around the house.

"You are eighty-four years old, Lucy," Mother insisted. "And Tendall is eighty-two." They fussed until Mother said: "Now, can we change the subject? Let's find something agreeable."

"The mother cactus looks after the baby cactus until it grows up and kills her."

"Lucy, I don't know how on earth you see that as something agreeable. Tendall! Oh my Lord Jesus Christ! Tendall Foushee!"

I couldn't believe it. My own mother said Jesus Christ Tendall Foushee. Running back in the house, she squealed loud enough to bust a eardrum and let the screen slam shut so hard behind her the windows rattled, which would have got me sent to my room. My sister Ethel turned white as a bed sheet. Even Aunt Lucy got awful quiet.

Uncle Tendall stood at the top of the porch steps, holding a red and black snake. The snake stretched about three feet between his fists, its tongue flipping out of his right fist and the tip of its tail whipping up and down out of his left. All I could hear was Daddy switching between chuckling and coughing, like something went down the wrong pipe.

"Red next to yellow will kill a fellow," Tendall recited like he just got called on at Sunday School, then added with a nod towards his snake, "Red next to black is a friend of Jack." He shook the snake's head at Aunt Lucy before he took it down the steps and turned it loose in Mother's garden.

"Jack Shit!" Aunt Lucy yelled and spit snuff at him, missing him a country mile.

"Lucy!" Mother's voice was muffled because she was behind the screen door. I'd never have the nerve to say shit in front of Mother but I could say it at Aunt Lucy's when I felt like it.

"OK, little brother," Aunt Lucy said to Uncle Tendall. "You've got our attention. Now what you going to do with it?"

Well, what he was going to do with our attention was start telling his same old World War II story again that we have all heard about a hundred times about how his parachute got caught on a church steeple in France on D-Day. His war story was pretty good the first time: a paratrooper in his company sucked like a moth into a building our bombers set on fire, dead men hanging in the trees, Uncle Tendall swinging till he took his pocketknife and cut himself loose. He hid in a clump of trees and got surrounded by cows. He started shooting Germans and cows till they got him in the shoulder. The Germans, not the cows. Then he got a Purple Heart. I don't even like to see the same movie twice.

Later in the afternoon, when I walked Aunt Lucy back to her house, holding her arm with her trying to pull away from me, I asked: "Do you think that the cows mooing was why the Germans found Uncle Tendall in the bushes?"

"Cows ain't got good sense when they need milking. Tendall was one sorry milker."

"Did he really get shot?"

"Yep."

"How come he never shows us his bullet hole?"

"Because it's in his butt."

"He said it was in his shoulder."

"Nope," Aunt Lucy repeated: "The hole's in his butt."

"Why didn't you tell on him for lying, Aunt Lucy?"

She didn't answer, pulling away from me and shortcutting through the garden, stepping across tomato rows on ground rough enough to turn a man's ankle. And she did it carrying her big black purse, a fist full of chicken scraps for her cat, Elijah, with one shoe on the wrong foot. I wanted to holler for my mother. Look at her. She's OK on her own. Nobody around here listens to me or Aunt Lucy either. I believed her about the bullet Uncle Tendall must of got when he was running away, not being a hero. She had just told me something important that nobody else knew. But what I was about to find out, no matter what Aunt Lucy did good from now on out, nothing was going to change the way things were going to go for her.

"Rupert, the macaroni and cheese was rotten in the refrigerator. And she had paper towels hanging all over the house to dry. Like they were cloth, Rupert."

Daddy shrugged but I was afraid to move. "Oh, you think that's nothing? Benny and I took her a banana pudding and you know what she said?" I didn't want to hear this again. "She said you shouldn't have killed the banana." Daddy snickered.

"Oh, you think that's funny? On her table was a bowl of what appeared to be cereal with milk. But you know what that was, Rupert? It was Lux flakes. And she was flat on her back in the kitchen floor with disgusting bubbles coming out of her mouth, cussing hateful things at me about buying cereal that wasn't fit to eat."

Daddy cleared his throat, maybe to keep from getting tickled.

"Benny, go get me four medium tomatoes. If you men think I'm going in that garden with that snake, you have another think coming."

I felt like such a coward, picking those tomatoes. Why couldn't I just explain to Mother that that was the way Aunt Lucy was? About half the time anyway. She would have figured out how to get up and dip some snuff to get the bad taste out of her mouth. Mother was making a mountain out of a molehill. But there was no stopping her this time.

The next Saturday Mother made me and Ethel drive Daddy's truck back over to Aunt Lucy's. We had moved her furniture out all day and were dead tired. Picture ghosts spots were on the wall and Aunt Lucy was in her rocker which was the only furniture left in her living room. She glared at me and Ethel like a cat in a corner. I couldn't stand to face her.

"Help me pull out her stove," Ethel snapped. We tugged on Aunt Lucy's old fashioned stove with the big hot plate on top where she made pancakes that you always had to lift up to make sure a fly wasn't cooked spread eagle in the bottom. Aunt Lucy kept rocking and cussing at us. She was mad, but she had a scared look too. Behind the stove was lost stuff, each thing rolled in so much fuzz, it looked like it ought to have legs and a tail.

While we inched the stove towards the door, Aunt Lucy started a story about terrapins in the cornfield, how Grandpa set them up on top the fence posts to paddle in the air while he plowed. I knew what she was up to but Ethel didn't. Since I begged her a million times to tell me what killed my grandpa, she was doing her best to make me think she was finally going to tell me. And make me stop moving her stuff and listen.

"'Terrapins,' Papa told me when he set them back down at the end of the day, 'keep right on going where they were going in the first place. Even if where they're going is going to get them squashed.'"

"So is that the moral of this story?" Ethel interrupted real loud, "You're not getting put on a fence post, Aunt Lucy. The real moral is you're a bull-headed little old woman who can't live in this house by herself any longer." Ethel didn't have to say something that ugly even if it was obvious. That ended Aunt Lucy's terrapin story.

"If I wasn't a little old woman, I'd bust your fat mouth," she yelled. "But I'd rather bust your mama's mouth. I don't have to live up in that house with her. I'm going to live right here with me."

Ethel gave up on the stove. She decided to drag Aunt Lucy and her rocker towards the door, nodding at me in that way of hers that said I either did what she intended or I better duck. While we wobbled outside down the steps carrying her in the rocker, Aunt Lucy bent over and stuck her fists in her eyes like she was trying to plug up two holes that wouldn't quit dripping. Her hair was twisted into a tight knot on the back of her head, one of those things that women can do without looking. Anyone who could still take their three foot long hair, comb it through every day, do all that perfect crisscrossing and tie up the end with the matted mess left in the comb; she ought to be allowed to live by herself. Now who could I tell that to who would listen to me? Nobody.

On the porch railing, her cat Elijah licked his lips, chicken bones turned to white toothpicks on the floor beneath him. Polar would be chewing off my leg if I was Aunt Lucy, which is why I like dogs. I couldn't stand to think how bad it felt, that poor old woman too weak and too old to stop two kids from changing her life for good. Then before we got halfway to Daddy's pickup, Aunt Lucy did something neither one of us was ready for.

"In the name of our Lord, Aunt Lucy, why did you do that?" Ethel dropped to her knees like she was having one of her religious experiences. Aunt Lucy threw herself out of the rocker, face down in the dirt. Ethel felt her tiny skint-up arms and legs. "You're useless as a football bat, you know?" Ethel yelled at me. She tried to gather Aunt Lucy up, folding her arms and legs like she was a square tablecloth.

All of a sudden Aunt Lucy tore into my sister like a animal you're trying to let out of a trap. Ethel turned her face away; her farm girl training taking over. "You're acting like a chicken going to the chopping block, Aunt Lucy. Cut out your flapping." I imagined Aunt Lucy's skinny ankles wrapped by one of my sister's bricklayer hands, her tiny white neck stretched out across that blood stained stump behind the house, ready for me to drop the ax. I looked just long enough to make me push Ethel out of the way and remember who was the man around here.

"Get out of the way, Ethel."

I must have sounded pretty good because old Ethel hopped to the side like I'd kicked her butt. When I squatted to pick up Aunt Lucy, the old lady quit kicking. But she didn't get any quieter.

"You think you can just do as you damn well please, Benny Foushee. I got rights." She wiggled so much when I lifted her, I was afraid I might drop her again.

"Open the goddamn pickup, quick," I hollered at Ethel. She ran ahead of me and never said one word about me using the Lord's name in vain, which I wouldn't have done in front of Ethel if I had thought two seconds about what was coming out of my mouth. That's what working at a filling station will do to you.

It usually made Aunt Lucy laugh when I cussed but she wasn't laughing now. I set her on the pickup seat, expecting to get a wad of snuff between my eyes. A red dot on the tip of her nose oozed down over her upper lip.

"Go get my pocketbook, Ethel," Aunt Lucy snapped. As Ethel went back in Aunt Lucy's house, I swear I thought I heard my sister say something she wouldn't say if she had a mouth full of it. After I scooted the old woman over on the seat and got in beside her, she popped me one on the knee, a solid hit I didn't expect. She left dirt stuck on my jeans.

"Benny, you got to help me." I heard the voice, but it didn't sound like Aunt Lucy. "You got to help me out of this," she repeated real quiet. I still couldn't make myself say anything. I was starting to shake. I don't know what I was afraid of. "Benny, don't you see what's happening? Them women going to put me in the county home." Fresh tears cut streaks in the dirt on her face. "Do you hear me, Benny?" I don't think she could hear herself.

"I hear you, Aunt Lucy," I answered finally without thinking, which I guess must have sounded like a promise. I wiped around her eyes with a shop rag out of my pocket and pressed it on her bloody nose.

Ethel threw Aunt Lucy's big black purse and her rocker in the bed and got in behind the wheel. Then she drove too fast over the rough road, which wasn't like Ethel. Aunt Lucy's little body bounced up and down so hard on the seat, I thought she might fall apart, like the petals coming off a bloomed out flower.

I didn't know this at the time because too many feelings were coming at me too fast. Just like that big old white dog riding in the back, dodging the sliding rocker, I was meant to save this little old white lady. There wasn't anybody I could talk to about it because Aunt Lucy was the person I always talked to about everything. She was never going down the path to her own house again. I couldn't go down to see her and the two of us tell stories and cuss and eat chocolate covered cherries. That was hard to take, for me and her both. From now on, she was going to hold onto my arm and let me lead her anywhere Mother saw fit for me to take her. As long as it wasn't back to her little house and that was where we both wanted to go.

I had a feeling right then that I couldn't make come out in words. Aunt Lucy still had a mind of her own, though it wasn't always all there. Even though she had a big mouth of her own, her body had got too old and too weak for her to get her way anymore. I never saw her scared of anything before. I didn't think I could stand to make her do what she hated.

I didn't want her to get her hopes up either, but I knew right then it was me and Aunt Lucy. Me and Aunt Lucy against the world was the long and the short of it. I couldn't think of a single person who was really on our side. And I couldn't stand to let her down.

2

Dear mother and daddy

Dont be to mad at me for leaving like this out asking you about it but I made a promise to aunt Lucy that I would take her to see the big cactus. Only trouble is the big cactus is pretty far away. Little farther than going to Durham to see the Christmas lights or down to Carolina beach Ha. Like it is all the way out west if you didnt know - Arizona. May be you should have started a fire with that Arizona Highways Mother Ha Ha. I will feed the chickens ever day in stead of ever other when I get back Ethel so dont you be mad at me to. You can use any of my stuff you want to while I am gone. Probably nothing you want to use since my truck is all I got worth any thing and its going with me. May be I can get you a pretty ring with a blue stone from those Indians out there. Aunt Lucy wanted me to ask you Ethel to give Elijah some chicken scraps now and then in case he cant get a mouse. I quit my job down at the Exxon at least till I get back.

Love Benny

P.S. I got Polar with me in case any body missed him. I took his food out of the pantry and the old can opener. I left fifty cents to buy a new one. Can opener that is. This is the longest letter I ever wrote. Good thing I didnt try to get it on a post card Ha Ha.

May be you are glad we are gone.

Well, here we go in my truck, off to the big cactus: me, Polar, Aunt Lucy and Aunt Lucy's rocking chair. After Aunt Lucy said something ugly about me planning to take Polar, I put her rocker in the back of the truck, hid in a big garbage bag, if you can put that together. I'm guessing Mother had been doing a lot more for Aunt Lucy than I knew about. She missed the sleeve on her sweater three times until I just decided to button it at the neck and up the front, one arm in, one arm out. I never dressed a person before but me, not even someone I could boss around like a baby, and it wasn't easy.

After I got one-armed Aunt Lucy up in the truck cab, pushing up on her butt with my shoulder with her giving me about as much help as a sack of potatoes, she started trying to get her sweater on right, looking like I had her in a strait jacket like they put on crazy people in the movies. She worked on that for about ten miles then punched me good when she got her arm free.

"Ouch! You better cut that out before I put you back in the strait jacket."

"Put me back in the attic?"

"Never mind."

Actually I guess we did pretty good. I stuck my going away letter on the refrigerator with a Band-Aid out of the bathroom because of the noise I'd make opening the junk drawer for the Scotch Tape. As Aunt Lucy, who's got a old saying for everything, put it: "We got out of there quieter than two mice peeing in a ball of cotton."

Now that we were going up the North Carolina mountains in the dark, I had to yell for her to hear over the hole in the muffler. I used to especially like the noise when I could pretend I didn't hear what my old girlfriend Valinda was complaining about which was everything.

"What kind of job did Uncle Tendall get after the war, Aunt Lucy?"

"One with short legs and brown spots that barked all the time."

Oh boy. Well, I used to like the noise my muffler made. My old truck, that used to be Daddy's plumbing company truck, sounded like a racecar to me. Benny Foushee, fastest NASCAR truck out of Summit, North Carolina. Trouble was my muffler wasn't a glass pack and noisy on purpose. It was about to fall off was what it was. Can't wait till I can afford to get my truck painted. It's that ugly slimy green. I asked Daddy why he bought green and he said because everybody bought a green truck, like that makes sense.

"Now, I wanted to go west to where Papa saw the big cactus," Aunt Lucy said. I could still hear her talking, which she did most of the time. "And Tendall, he wanted to go east. Maybe I didn't know much but I knew which side the sun come up on. When it gets up, Benny, I'll let you know if you're heading the right direction. Tendall didn't fool me but he was doing the driving and I was doing the cooking. How soon you think we'll make it to the big cactus?"

I didn't answer her because I didn't know the right answer. Days. A lot of days.

She told me about cooking potatoes on the engine, tied on with baling wire, when she and Uncle Tendall left home during the war to go work on the Liberty ships in Wilmington. I shouldn't have wished out loud that I'd taken a cold biscuit or at least a few slices of loaf bread with us. Big mistake. She started asking for food like a stuck record. "I'd give five smackers for some McDonald's fries."

"Don't you even think about cooking potatoes on my engine," I yelled at her. "After I put on new valve cover gaskets, I got my engine clean as a whistle."

"I'm so hungry I'd eat anything don't eat me first."

"Shows you what a woman cares about a engine." I swear we were already starting to sound like Aunt Lucy and Uncle Tendall, yelling at each other and talking about two different things and acting like we weren't.

"Ain't this the cat's pajamas, Benny? Money in our pockets and nobody named Mona telling us to watch our mouths. Except her damn starchy drawers feel like I'm setting in a paper bag." Aunt Lucy didn't want to bring any extra clothes because Mother had made them scratchy with starch. I picked out a few things from her chest anyway. One was her Sunday dress and a clean nightshirt. Aunt Lucy wore her nightshirt under her dress, which really drove Mother crazy. I left her brown shoes in the closet after I made sure she got her black ones on the right feet.

Soon as it got light enough to see a little, Aunt Lucy reached in her purse, pulled out the *Arizona Highways*. "Papa said to me, wait'll you see it for real, Lucy." She held the cover in front of my face until I pushed her hand down, trying to keep my eyes on the edge of the road. One of my headlights shot too high up; I could cut it off now. Lucy took a flashlight out of her purse and pointed it at the cactus on the front. "It don't look like much here because there ain't nothing to measure it by." With one flip, she opened the magazine straight to the big cactus pages.

Her snuff and all her money that we got at the bank and who knows what else was in that purse. Aunt Lucy said she made thirty dollars a week back when she was Rosie the Riveter during the war. I never saw her rivet anything. She always took her money out, one coin at a time and studied it before she let go of it. Daddy said she pinched a nickel until it squealed. She gave me ten bucks yesterday which wasn't going to last very long with my truck getting nine miles a gallon.

"Aunt Agnes, Papa's baby sister, raised your daddy till he got to be five. Then I mostly took over till me and Tendall went to Wilmington. Agnes was such a good old soul. Taught me to read and to dip. When we gonna eat?" I ignored her. After I figured we were far enough away for them not to catch us, I'd find us a place to eat breakfast. I needed to slow down because my engine was getting hot. Haven't had a good flat stretch in a long time. "Sorry old fellow," I said to my truck. "Didn't mean to push you so hard."

"That's OK," Aunt Lucy answered. "You meant well."

Benny Foushee will be ready for the Camp Butner loony bin before this trip is over, I can tell you that already. Aunt Lucy was happy as a pig in a mud puddle and I was feeling like as big of a worrywart as my mother. We were both running away from home I guess, but I had a lot more in my head than cooking a potato and Mother not fussing at me. I had both of us to take care of by myself plus Polar and my truck. I hadn't even thought about getting a new girlfriend since Aunt Lucy decided on this trip.

"I want some McDonald's fries."

"Would you stop it, Aunt Lucy? I'm trying to find us a place. I've never been here before. I'm not used to going this far before breakfast neither. Not a light on out there anywhere. I wish the golden arches would just pop up out of these trees."

"Remember this, Benny. If wishes were horses, peasants would shit in your hand."

Sometimes I can tell she gets her old sayings messed up. I decided not to waste my time explaining it ought to be wish in one hand and shit in the other and see which one fills up first. I don't know where the one about the peasants and horses came from. I'll ask Mother when I get back and not tell Aunt Lucy who I asked. I'm hoping Aunt Lucy's old brain will still be there by the time we get to the big cactus. And she can still get around well enough to take a look up close. At least a cactus wasn't something she needed to hear.

By full sunup I found a eating place: Libby's Finger Lickin' Good Café with the twenty-four hour, dollar ninety-nine cent, breakfast special I saw for about twenty miles on signs that leaned on every rock from Persell to Samton, North Carolina. I dumped some of Polar's dry food out in the truck bed. It smelled good enough to eat myself. Polar crunched it up like it was fried chicken. That dog made me feel like a million bucks. I needed to get him a bone and some water.

After we finally made it inside the door, the waitress pointed towards a table. Wow, she was something. First good thing I'd seen in a while. She had on a t-shirt with a tiger face on the front with this little ruffly apron over her short shorts so you'd know she was the waitress. I'm telling you, I felt a tickle in my crotch that went all the way back to the monkey bars on the grammar school playground. Any man alive had to believe the way her boobs poked out under that tiger's eyes meant that she was ready to jump him; the tiger I meant was ready to jump. Now, I'm not really sure what I meant. Damn she was good looking. I meant that.

We followed her to a table, Aunt Lucy leaning on me like one of the road signs to Libby's Finger Lickin' Good. I made a muscle in my arm around Aunt Lucy in case Libby happened to look back. Libby's butt might have been a little wide by some standards—Valinda would have compared it to a barn door—but it looked pretty darn nice to me, slipping out of her shorts a little in back. Lot better than Valinda's ever looked. Valinda was so much trouble to please, it could get you off girls for a while.

"Your name Libby?" I asked as Tiger-Eye-Boobs turned around.

"Huh? Libby? Who? Oh, never mind," she laughed. "Her. That her. Naw, she's old and dead. I'm Sue Faye. You like these tiger eyes, don't you, honey?" She bent her back and poked her boobs out fast, then took them back. Made my face get hot, I can tell you that.

"Yeah. Uh. Nice shirt."

"Not a face man, honey?" she laughed real loud and slapped two menus on the table.

"I like faces too," I said like a dumb ass while I was pulling out Aunt Lucy's chair, centering her shoulders and butt over the chair before she dropped down.

"I figure this shirt was made by one of them men who hates women," Sue Faye started telling me, "so a man don't hear nothing you say. You know the kind of man I mean, the kind that makes them shoes with toes that go out to a point? Feet don't point. Only a man who hates women real bad could make them shoes. Probably a queer. What you want?" She put one hand on her hip and laughed a short laugh, "What you want to eat, I mean."

Boy, she could talk a blue streak and she didn't even know me. I forced my eyes off the tiger eyes and looked down at the front of the menu. I didn't mean to act like such a jackass, but I must have been. Her perfume was so strong I could have been at Aunt Agnes' funeral.

"Two specials," I said like I knew what I was talking about. "Eggs over easy. No runny whites." No runny whites. That always ended with "Mona". No runny whites, Mona. Really glad I stopped that Mona slip from falling out of my mouth. Damn, how far did I have to get away from Daddy to quit talking like him?

All of a sudden out of the blue Aunt Lucy who hadn't made a peep since we got inside shouted: "Eggs from chickens that are still clucking!"

Man, that restaurant got like the sound just broke on a movie. And every table had people looking at Aunt Lucy, mostly men, truck drivers.

"Still clucking!" I said real quick. "Cluck, cluck, cluck. You know, the sound a chicken makes?" I believe people with false teeth sometimes make c's sound like f's. I thought about flapping my arms but decided better of it. They'd get one of those strait jackets for me. Now I had this guy with a bunch of missing teeth and one with a patch over one eye laughing at me like I was nuttier than Aunt Lucy. Sue Faye lifted a eyebrow at me before she turned with a loud laugh and wound towards the little window to the kitchen.

Aunt Lucy sat there not talking, holding up the placemat and reading it like it was a newspaper. I was believing that Sue Faye kind of liked me. Probably made all the guys feel good just to get a big tip. Sure would like to take her to a movie or something. She might think she's too grownup for me. Probably more than twenty-one. I wasn't used to having Aunt Lucy around when I was checking out girls.

While we waited for our food, me watching Sue Faye's nice bottom going between the tables, I felt Aunt Lucy start looking hard at me. When Sue Faye brought her coffee and said to her: "Put your mat down, sweetie," I knew I was in for trouble.

"I ain't your sweetie. Quit telling me what to do," Aunt Lucy piped up. Then soon as she sipped the coffee, "Stuff's so weak it needs help getting up out of the pot." Lucky for me Sue Faye didn't hear that or decided not to pay any attention to her if she did.

"Aunt Lucy, you keep your mouth shut about your coffee. Sue Faye's not Mother, you know. She might decide to smack you."

"Benny. Did you know a ostrich's eye is bigger than his brain?" Aunt Lucy had her finger on the paper placemat.

"No Ma'am, I didn't."

"Do you think my eye is bigger than my brain?" she asked.

"I sure hope not. You're pretty beady-eyed."

"Benny?"

"Yes ma'am."

"Me and you got nowhere to go but up."

"Yes ma'am." Right then I felt like I had so much on top of me, I wasn't sure I could stand up, much less go up. When my eggs got there, my "no runny whites" looked like I'd run over them with my truck, but I was so hungry, I ate them and half of Aunt Lucy's. Sue Faye probably thought I thought they were real good, but that's OK.

"Can you think of a animal we eat before it's born and after it's dead?" Aunt Lucy asked.

"What?" My mouth was full of toast with three of the jelly things smeared on it.

"The answer is the chicken, you moron. That was the easy one."

"That placemat is for a little kid."

"How old am I, Benny?"

"Eighty-four, I think Mother said."

"Quit talking about her so much. Eighty-four years it took me to get to set down to eat in a restaurant."

That hit me harder than anything she had said in a while. "You never ate in a restaurant before?"

"Never got to set down inside one. Eat out of the trash behind a few. The honest truth, Benny, I ain't been missing much. Don't cook a sight better than Mona."

I thought a minute. It was the first time I'd gone to the trouble to take her inside a restaurant. Even McDonald's. Daddy just took her to church, the bank and the graveyard and once to Duke Gardens in Durham. Aunt Lucy spread out her napkin and stacked her toast and one sausage patty in the center, putting the red apple washer on the top. Then she folded the whole mess up in her placemat and stuck it in her purse.

"I do hair," Sue Faye said from right beside me. I almost jumped out of my skin when she picked up my long hair with both hands. "You got nice hair but you let it get too long. See, it touches on your face and makes your skin all oily." She put the check beside my plate with a greasy paper bag on top of it. "It's for your dog in the truck. A big old hambone."

"Why thank you." I could barely talk. Now I was getting a damn hard-on and here I'm out in public. I pulled out my shirttail.

"I got a dog too. Half fighting bull. Woman's best friend. I give your dog some water. It's getting hot out there today."

"I sure do thank you. I was meaning to ask for a bone."

"He's a sweet dog. You oughta treat him better."

"You want him?" Aunt Lucy asked.

"Aunt Lucy! Shut up, please." I was way too loud. Made this prissy looking lady near the cash register clear her throat. I ought to give her Aunt Lucy. I can't believe Aunt Lucy was trying to give my dog away. I jerked her up from her chair, not sure which way she would go if she decided to fall. All I needed now was her to say something about the bottom of my t-shirt poking out.

"I got to pee."

"Shut up, Aunt Lucy, please." Boy, was I getting mad at her.

"I got to go water the lily," she said, even louder. That was Aunt Lucy's idea of good manners. I looked at Sue Faye who pointed towards a door behind the cash register. I heard Snaggle Teeth and One Eye laughing their heads off at Aunt Lucy.

"Maybe number two. You rushed me out before…"

"Aunt Lucy, stop it," I said straight in her face. "You're telling the world your private business. Get in there." I shoved her through the door that said LADIES, maybe a little too hard, but I couldn't help myself. I couldn't even look at Sue Faye, just at the change she put in my hand.

"It's all there," Sue Faye said. "Count it."

I hope she didn't think I thought she was cheating me. The dollar ninety-nine breakfast was up to two ninety-nine plus extra for Aunt Lucy's coffee but those signs were pretty old. I just couldn't look at Sue Faye right then. I put all the change and a dollar on the counter for her tip then stood outside the Ladies room. I didn't know what I would say if I had to send Sue Faye in after Aunt Lucy. I would of had time to go three times if I needed to. I couldn't pee now if my eyes turned yellow.

"I couldn't find the flusher," Aunt Lucy hollered when she finally came out, loud enough for Sue Faye to hear way over at the cash register.

"I'll take care of it, Sonny," Sue Faye said to me as she went in the ladies room.

Sonny. Sonny, like I'm a little kid. Man, that Sonny went through me like a pitchfork. At least my hard-on was going away. I heard the toilet flushing. I felt like kicking Aunt Lucy in the behind as she headed towards the door. Before I could reach around her to open the screen, she swung her foot back and kicked it herself like she used to nail the screen on her own house. The door swung around and slammed against the outside wall so hard the OPEN sign fell off.

I couldn't look back when we were going to the truck. Nice as Sue Faye was to me and Polar and then the old biddy damn near kicks the door off her restaurant. I threw the hambone in the back and let Polar tear open his own bag. I couldn't get out of there fast enough. No sooner than I got rolling, Aunt Lucy said: "It runs in your family to get messed up with women."

"Messed up?"

"What you doing making eyes at a woman like that, Benny Foushee?"

"Because she's pretty as a picture, I guess. And real nice."

"Humph," she grunted. "Don't you know that woman's door knob will burn your hand?"

"I don't know what you're talking about, Aunt Lucy. Talk real English. If the guys at the Exxon saw Sue Faye, they'd be flipping out over her."

"What I mean, Benny, is that judging from the way she dresses and carries on, that sorry woman is selling more than bacon and eggs. That enough English for you?"

That sure made my face get hot. I don't know why somebody like Aunt Lucy wouldn't come right out and say it: "Do you mean you think she's a whore, Aunt Lucy?"

Aunt Lucy cleared her throat: "Most probably."

"You mean she's not a lady like you are, Aunt Lucy?"

She chuckled a little and stuck out her tongue like a little kid. I hate it when she turned mean on me. I wasn't used to that. She was mean to Mother and Uncle Tendall but she was usually real nice to me. Early morning and I felt as tired as I did after a day in the garden plus the night shift at the Exxon. And we weren't even out of North Carolina yet.

I could see Polar in the rear view mirror, chewing on his giant bone. Aunt Lucy wasn't nice to Polar either who never even bit anybody to my knowledge and minded real good. The greasy bag he tore off was dancing around in the air behind the cab instead of blowing out. Not a few times in my life I'd rather be a dog.

Aunt Lucy said Sue Faye was like my daddy's mother Gertie, sorry, her word. I thought that meant she was real bad. Sue Faye couldn't have been real bad at all. Look how good she was to Polar. Neither is my mother real bad who Aunt Lucy fusses about all the time. And maybe Grandma Gertie wasn't real bad either. I'm not so sure she knows as much as she thinks she does about people.

Sue Faye was gone from my life, just like that, and I really liked her a lot. I wished I had covered up my worse zits with that skin colored medicine Mother bought me. I forgot to bring it. Aunt Lucy couldn't keep me from thinking about Sue Faye so I planned to do a lot of that to entertain myself on this trip. If me and Sue Faye got by ourselves, I wouldn't mind one bit confessing that I hadn't really done it yet.

You know what I'm guessing now? Maybe Uncle Tendall couldn't wait to get off that farm, even if he had to go to war and get shot at. Maybe Grandpa liked Lucy better than Tendall. Gave her presents...and she never let Uncle Tendall forget it. Like Daddy told me, when he was growing up and wanted to do something with Uncle Tendall, it was Aunt Lucy's way or the highway. Maybe I'm learning what he meant. And the truth was Benny Foushee had a lot of highway between him and that big cactus. And he was stuck with Aunt Lucy going with him.

It was a whole lot scarier now than it was before I left.

3

"Bucksnort. What kind of stupid name is that?" Aunt Lucy asked, reading a road sign in Tennessee.

I kind of liked that name. Sounded like a mad deer. Good name for a boy dog. Here Bucksnort.

I got in the shower last night, our first night on the road in a motel in Canton, North Carolina, which was the worse smelling place I ever slept in. Aunt Lucy asked me three times if I broke wind. I didn't know the Smoky Mountains got their smoke from a paper factory. I scrubbed my hair real good after what Sue Faye said about it being oily. What she really meant was it gave me pimples. If I didn't have Aunt Lucy along, I would turn around and go back and get her to cut my hair. I went to sleep thinking about that and I got to admit I imagined her doing more than cutting my hair.

Everything started out pretty much gray looking in the morning: the sky and the road and most everything in between. My mood was gray too, I guess. My truck was bumping and shimmying when we left the motel, which made me nervous. I guess the tires got square at night sitting on the cold pavement. They got OK after they warmed up.

"Look at all the pretty white flowers," Aunt Lucy said. "Wonder who tends them?"

We drove past this guy mowing the shoulder, going right over all the trash and spitting it out in "pretty white flowers."

"Look at that fool, mowing down the flowers. I'd fire his ass," she added. Somehow I kept my mouth shut and didn't mention that the pretty white flowers were behind the mower not in front. You don't win arguments with Aunt Lucy.

Things didn't get much better. Our third morning on the road along side the highway outside of Memphis, the engine started missing so bad my truck couldn't get out of its own way.

"We ought to be going a different way than them big trucks, Benny. They're trying to suck us off the road."

I had to spend about an hour out in the rain in this god-awful traffic that made my truck rock, taking out the gas filter. Siphoned some gas out to Aunt Lucy's spit cup to clean the filter. Goes three months at home without getting trash in the gas then does it right off on our trip. At least I remembered the siphon hose. Daddy would be proud of me there. If he wasn't too mad at me about leaving without discussing it.

Daddy didn't get mad much. He said Mother could get mad enough for both of them, that that's what you get when you marry a girl twenty some years younger than you. If I did that, the girl I'm going to marry isn't even born yet. I never thought of Mother as a girl. I wonder if they thought about coming after us. I bet Daddy figured I'd come back before sundown with Aunt Lucy driving me nuts. I'm nuts for sure.

Everything we bought, I had to wait while Aunt Lucy counted out the money. I still had my last pay from the Exxon but I was keeping it in a different pocket in case I saw something I wanted. Maybe we don't have enough money to do this trip. She was still really mad about the dollar tip I gave Sue Faye for being so nice. And for being pretty too, I guess. I'd hate to have to go to work at a Exxon in Tennessee just to get enough to make it back home.

"Mousetail Landing. Hope you ain't planning to land there, Benny. What nitwit thought that was a name?"

Hi, I thought, I'm Benny Foushee. Live over by Mousetail Landing, Tennessee. Now if that didn't make a pretty girl smile and ask me where in the world that name came from, I don't know what would. I was starting to realize that Aunt Lucy wasn't after an answer anyway. She could just as easy been talking to the post that name was on.

The next day after Memphis when the road got flatter in Arkansas, my truck got happier and a lot quieter. Not much of anything to see since we got past Memphis, not even a sign to tell you how far it was to the next big place. That would be Little Rock, according to the map I swiped when I was vacuuming a car at the Exxon.

I let Polar come inside the cab between us because it was kind of drizzly. He was behaving real good. Lot better than Aunt Lucy. She and Polar turned their heads together following this huge swarm of black birds. Two different sets of eyes looking at birds: Polar wishing he was running after them even if he didn't catch a one and Aunt Lucy's got something going through her head about it being another kind of sign, most likely a sign of somebody dying. She doesn't see much up lifting in things.

"Duck River," she read. "That duck took the river of no return." There was a dead mallard beside the road, webbed feet pointing up.

She hadn't said anything ugly yet about sharing the seat with Polar, but she squirmed over so close to the door, I pushed up the handle to lock it. Didn't miss a beat with her talking though. I'll admit listening to her babble all the time was easier than trying to play cow poker with a old woman who couldn't tell a Charolais bull from a propane tank. And then argued about it.

I tried to occupy my mind with things outside. These newer cars can go a lot faster than us. Kind of depressing. There were tall skinny white birds out there, drilling for something in the dead fields. They were shaped like the pink ones people had in their yards at home. I didn't know if birds ate the same grubs in Arkansas they do in North Carolina, probably those horseshoe shaped white worms that turn into June bugs if nothing eats them. It was well past June.

"Truckers Prayer. We ain't stopping there, Benny. Your mama would like that too much. I'd tell her that trucker was praying his brakes would work at the bottom of a hill and that he'd get him a sweet piece of ass in the Finger Licking Good truck stop." She punched me hard like I didn't get it.

Nothing was growing out there that people plant. Hailstones just bust holes in signs in Arkansas instead of tobacco like they do in North Carolina. Nothing on the radio but preachers and it's not even Sunday. Just as soon Aunt Lucy not see this one sign not busted up out there: "If you die today, where will you spend eternity?" Over and over, the same sign. I think Benny Foushee is going to spend eternity trying to get between Memphis and Little Rock, if you want the truth.

"Stop picking that scab, Aunt Lucy. You're going to make it bleed again," which was a dumb thing to say because she had already made it bleed again which was why I noticed it. It was where she went flying out of her rocker in the dirt. She was sure slow to heal up. She dabbed at the blood on her knee with her sweater sleeve which was so dark it didn't show.

"Even when the big cactus is scorched and scabbed," she said, "it keeps its heat inside." The magazine was open as always but it was hard to tell anymore if she was reading or just saying what she memorized.

"You've got the scab but you look about as much like that cactus as a lizard, Aunt Lucy. Look out for a motel."

"I ain't looking out for a rest home."

"I said a motel. A place to stop for the night."

"Even a dead cactus is a home for lizards and snakes and scorpions."

"Guess I have to drive and look too. Did you trick me into this trip, Aunt Lucy? You just wanted to stay out of a rest home and used the big cactus as a excuse?" She didn't answer me and I couldn't afford to take my eyes off the road to see her expression.

At sunset the gray that was everywhere turned pink, then got black pretty fast. Except for one worrisome gray thing. Rabbits. How come they kept zigzagging down the road? It's like they were trying to commit suicide or something. One makes it clean across the road, I go whew! and there it comes back again. Polar whimpered when this one rabbit kept going back and forth like something you shoot at in the penny arcade. Damn it, rabbit. Go right and stay right.

"You got to speak up, Benny, if you expect me to hear you."

"I'm talking to these damn Arkansas cottontails, Aunt Lucy." I think Polar was too, but I wasn't going to mention that.

"Yeah. I think I'm going to Hell too," she answered a question I didn't ask, then added, "since you ask me. I reckon that's where I'm going to spend eternity, if you ask Mona. Jesus Christ! Look at all the rabbits!"

"That's what I been trying to tell you, Aunt Lucy. Rabbits. Everywhere." So she did see the eternity signs.

"On curves ahead, Remember Sonny, That rabbit's foot, Didn't save the bunny."

"I'm not Sonny. I'm Benny. I hate that Sonny business. I'm not a little kid." I guess I was still more than a little pissed about Aunt Lucy messing it up with Sue Faye.

"Benny and kid ain't a rhyme. Try skinny. Or penny. I'm not Sonny. I'm Benny. And I'm not a skinny penny. They'll never hire you to write signs. Wont talking about you anyway. That's a Burma Shave. Took it out of my mind."

"Do something useful, Aunt Lucy, while you're running your mouth. Try telling me a story to keep me awake till I find us a motel. These rabbits are getting like counting sheep."

"Stories used to put you to sleep. You always liked the one about Reddy Fox and the buffalo. You laughed and laughed when the fox built a fire with buffalo shit."

"Tell me what happened to Grandpa, Aunt Lucy. If I'm old enough to drive you to Arizona, I'm old enough to hear Grandpa's story."

"That one will keep you awake." She sounded serious. "For the rest of your life. Papa got kilt."

"What killed him, Aunt Lucy?"

"It was sorry and had four legs."

"A horse, a cow, a pig? Dodged a rabbit and hit a tree?"

"Naw, none of them." Aunt Lucy's voice cracked. "I lost Papa in the most terrible way imaginable." She shoved Polar so hard he fell over in my lap.

When I thought her telling had stopped like it always did, she started up again, her voice shrill like it was blowing through a whistle: "Me and Papa, and Tendall too, was in the back field, picking the last of the cotton."

I couldn't believe it. She was going to tell me about Grandpa.

"Up come this big old dog. 'Hey Rascal' Papa said, just as matter of fact as me speaking at you. Papa went over, meaning to pet this big spotted dog, 'Hey Rascal. What you doing out of your pen?' It was Rascal belonged to Flonny Glover down the road. Papa knowed their dog from hunting. All of a sudden, Papa lifted up his cotton bag, and throwed it hard between Rascal and Tendall." Aunt Lucy kept moving with short rocks, working her juice up to keep talking. "Rascal shook his head. Foam slinging out of his mouth like dish soap. Making this growling sound, r-r-r-rugg, down deep, like some demon was trying to climb out. Nicest old pet dog you ever seen and he'd went mad.

"Papa let out a screech and Rascal took off with his tail drawn up under his belly like he'd been beat. Papa shoved on me and Tendall to get in the wagon. He slapped the mule hard and we all lickedy split home. Papa got his gun. Tendall wanted to go with him, but Papa told him to stay put, which didn't sit well with Tendall who wanted to act like a man, which he wasn't.

"Papa found Rascal. As he told it - I wasn't witness to this part - Rascal was laying down whimpering, wagging his tail, licking at a sore place on his leg. Papa figured a bat had bit him. Rascal was always running inside the cave over on the Shippe's place. Papa picked up that big old hound dog, toting him clean up to the wagon. When he was settling him down gentle on some burlap bags, the madness come back. That dog sank his teeth in Papa's hand. Papa's soft spot for animals was what done him in." Her story was making me shiver and sweat at the same time. Polar sat still as a stuffed dog.

"Papa blowed Rascal's head off. When they come to take the head to Raleigh, wont enough brain left to use. This skinny little government man asked Papa why he had to go blow its head clean off. Papa went after that little weasel like he done gone mad. But he wont mad, not yet." Aunt Lucy kept sniffing. "Tendall knows I'd bust his head if he told this story wrong. He'd tell it different. He'd tell what a big brave fellow he was. I never told Rupert. I was going to carry it off with me to the grave, Benny, where it ought to have gone."

I couldn't say anything. It was my fault. I just kept driving and dodging rabbits, feeling sick in my stomach when she started again.

"Papa scrubbed hisself good with lye soap and turpentine. We all got our hopes up. That dog bite healed up so good. Papa took to having nightmares about killing poor old Rascal. He buried that headless dog in the woods by the road before Flonny seen it. "'Kilt that poor old dog over a little old bite that healed up good, Lucy,' he told me when he was picking off the scabs. 'Rascal must of eat something bad made his mouth soap,' he was reasoning. 'He bit when I hit a sore spot.'

"Papa grieved day in and day out over Rascal. Went clean through the summer into the fall, ducking when Flonny come by. Then one night in October, Papa had trouble swallowing his supper. The noise he started making wont words. Foam come bubbling up out of his mouth like a beer running over a glass. Fell off on his shirt front in big blobs of spit."

I tried to make hearing her go away. Tears were coming out of my own eyes and I didn't even know Grandpa. I just knew the funny stories about him, like the one about him getting drunk and painting a yellow stripe down the watch dog's back at the licker store.

"Papa's eyes not carrying sadness no more, not like when he was grieving over shooting poor old Rascal. His eyes stared across the table like he was in a room of strangers. Rupert was a tiny baby. That sorry girl Gertie who Papa made fresh with little Rupert, who never had two words to say to me, was still there. Tendall was in the chair that didn't sit solid unless a grown man was in it, and I could hear that short leg, thumping like a dog tail beating the floor. Me and Tendall was so scared, we didn't know what to do. And there set little baby Rupert, laughing at Papa's antics like he was doing it on purpose."

I couldn't tell Aunt Lucy to stop now. All I could think of was my friend Buddy who told about his grandpa who died of a heart attack at the supper table, and fell over on his birthday cake when he was blowing out the candles. Didn't make sense to think of that, but that is what I was trying to think of.

"Papa's madness done just like that old dog, Benny. It'd go away and he'd be feeling just fine. Then out of the blue, he'd feel a fit coming on. We thought to tie him to the walnut tree out front but he didn't want us to see his fits. He'd make me lock him up real fast in the closet under the steps. And swear to him I wouldn't let him out. We'd hear him beating his head on the walls, begging us to open the door, screaming the most awful bloody murder you ever heard. Then he would go quiet, and I would crack the door and he would be Papa again. Only his face would be bleeding and his knuckles ripped off and he'd act shamefaced over how he got that way. Papa hugged me tight every time I let him out. He patted me on the back and I shut my eyes to make everything stop right then. But it didn't. He kept on saying he was sorry he let us down.

"Gertie moved on, scared to death of Papa. Left your daddy behind in a bushel basket. Took with her his little cradle Papa made. Papa kept trying to tell me he was dying and asking forgiveness. Said he didn't use the good sense of a man with two children and a baby depending on him.

That's the kind of man Papa was, a good man. I couldn't make myself believe he was going.

"Five days and nights that went on, locking Papa up and letting him out. I washed his face and hands and rubbed in pine tar and lard which was all the medicine we had. Me and Tendall tried to sleep with baby Rupert wrapped up between us with Papa yelling out the awfulest things. 'My brains have fallen on the floor. My insides is tangled together. My hair is choking me and my fingernails is slashing my throat like a hog at killing time. I'm running out on the ground. Help me. Help me.' Sometimes I cried, all the time Tendall did. We didn't know what in the world to do. Tendall kept on saying he would have kilt that dog first thing. Tendall's always got the right answer after everybody knows it."

Aunt Lucy was beating her fists in her lap. This was why my mother said there were things better left unsaid.

"Tendall hollered at me how Papa tried to bite him the last time I let him out. Don't let him out. Tendall wanted to take Papa's shotgun and kill him. I hid that gun good under a floor plank. Tendall took a quilt and Rupert and went out to sleep in the smoke house. I was all by myself when I cracked the door, after Papa got quiet, believing the fit to be over. I'd boil him some water to clean where he messed on himself. He'd be Papa again like before and give me my big hug.

"Not to be. Papa was drawed up in a ball, his eyes and mouth wide open. Me and Tendall tried to straighten him out. Tendall put rocks on his eyes but they popped back open. That's how he died, rolled up in a ball, like a grub worm. Papa didn't weigh hardly nothing by then. We carried him out in a old wheel barrow and made him a hole. Took turns digging. Not a hole like you think for a grave. A round hole to fit him. Didn't go as deep as you're supposed to, we was so weak and so hungry. Tendall kept throwing dirt in Papa's face, covering those eyes staring at him he said. He don't want to help me find the place we put Papa. Pines growed over it. Tendall's still mad at him for dying."

Aunt Lucy stopped talking. I glanced at her face, shining when headlights went past us. She was making a funny noise, a crying sound like she was hurting on the outside, but I knew it was the inside. Poor old soul. Carried that all these years. What did I think? That somebody dying was going to be a nice story? Like watching a movie except it was my own kin? I didn't think it further than that before she told it.

I was imagining the inside of that closet under the stairs. It's in the house I live in. I didn't see any bare walls to beat a head on. I saw all the rows of canning in jars, sitting on the shelves that me and Daddy put up. Red and green and yellow jars, pretty colors that Mother is so proud of. Finally I made myself say something to Aunt Lucy.

"Grandpa died in the closet where Mother keeps her canning."

"Don't tell her. She'd throw out a season's worth of string beans and tomatoes." Aunt Lucy's regular voice came back, not her storytelling one. "Don't you tell her if your life depends on it, Benny Foushee. I'll wring your neck."

"I won't tell her or anybody, Aunt Lucy. When you tell me not to tell something, I don't. Just like you'd do for me. Besides, she's a long way off for me to tell." It felt funny to say that.

Aunt Lucy kept rocking hard like she was in her chair, like she was warming up to get mad now instead of sad. I didn't know if she was still thinking about her Papa dying or just getting mad at my mother. Most women I know, meaning my mother, my sister and Valinda, got in a certain mood and stayed mad till it thundered. Or maybe it was a snapping turtle didn't let go till it thundered. I'm so mixed up. I think I had really messed up now and we hadn't even been gone but three days. Lucy and Tendall, two kids like me and Ethel, digging a round hole to bury their daddy. I couldn't make my tall daddy roll up like that in my mind, which was good I believe. The reason she didn't tell me before was because it hurt too bad to remember about it. What she told me made my hands feel clammy. It was getting hard for me to steer without them slipping.

"I'd appreciate it, Benny, if you'd put that dog back in the back," Aunt Lucy said finally.

I pulled over and did as I was told, asking Polar to get back in the truck bed. "It's a nice cool night out so the fresh air will do you good," I lied to him. He didn't understand so I added, "Now don't you jump out after any of these rabbits, Polar. They aren't ours," I said, feeling a long way from home.

When I started driving again, I looked for Polar in the rear view mirror. I never saw another rabbit after we started going up hills again. I had to turn on the heat in the summer. I felt bad for Polar out in the cold. I saw his white fur catching a headlight like he was a ghost. He set there right through that whole awful story and didn't make a peep. Because he didn't understand what was being said. I don't know why I have to make out like that dog understands everything that's being said, like he's a person. Then I go and lie to him why I'm making him get in the back. Like I'm lying to a person. I hated to treat him so bad.

His head was hanging over the side with his tongue blowing out like a flag. Just looking at him, my mouth went dry as a bone.

"Thought you wont never coming back, Benny," she told me when I walked in with the food. She grabbed it like a starving animal.

That night in the Ozark Mountains, we set in our two beds, me and Aunt Lucy, eating burgers and fries. I couldn't make myself drag her in another restaurant right then. I felt tired as a old man, hurting in my back and legs. The sign out front that said "Color TV with every room" had a lot better color than the black and white snowstorm flickering at the foot of our beds. Aunt Lucy didn't seem to care.

"This here food's a sight better than that runny egg breakfast you got us this morning. What did it set me back? Meat's a little cold but this place is a lot nicer than the county home I'm figuring." I reckon that was

Aunt Lucy's way of being appreciative.

"Went to McDonald's to get you some fries, Aunt Lucy, but it was closed. Had to go clean over to the other side of town to find somewhere open. Started out warm."

I could hear Polar out in the back of the truck, still thumping the big ham bone Sue Faye gave him back in North Carolina. When I filled up his water, he slobbered it down happy as a bug. Wish I was. This trip has been a couple of firsts already, I guess: Aunt Lucy in a restaurant and me in a motel. I never slept anywhere but my own bed except on the church retreat. And I hadn't been sleeping too good. Aunt Lucy leaned back, hit her head hard on the wall behind the bed, and turned on her talk button: "Obediah's ship broke in two in the cold water."

"Whose ship broke?" Obediah was her husband who died before I was born. She was falling asleep because her breathing sounded like snoring. "I thought Uncle Obie died on the manure spreader. What ship broke in two?"

"Papa promised me when his ship come in, he'd take me to see the big cactus, but he never had two nickels to rub together."

One minute it's Obie, then it's Grandpa. I thought she went to the shipyards with Uncle Tendall. When she stopped talking, I could hear my stomach growling.

"Was Uncle Tendall riveting the big boats too?" After I said I wouldn't ask for any more stories, I kept trying to keep her going. "It's not fair to start something and not finish it, Aunt Lucy."

"Papa's story got me thinking on dying," she said real clear. "They say dying's like cutting off the light. Lucy means light. Cut off old Lucy." I sure hated making her think on dying. "Cut off the light, Benny. You still got on your shoes."

"My shoes aren't on." I got out of bed to cut off the useless TV and the light, stepping on Aunt Lucy's rocker leg in the dark on the way back, mashing my other foot. Then I tripped over the black plastic bag I packed our stuff in.

Her snoring stopped. It was the first quiet I heard all day. I rushed to turn the light back on fast. Aunt Lucy had the sheet pulled up to her chin. Her face looked a whole lot whiter. Nothing moved. Not those albino lashes. Not her buttonhole mouth. She was still as the photo of Aunt Agnes in her casket.

"Aunt Lucy!" When I grabbed her skinny shoulder through the sheet, her eyes popped open, throwing her white lashes to the side like fringe.

"Thought I was dead, did you?"

I sat back down on my bed, my knees going weak.

"It's real mean to tease me like that, Aunt Lucy."

"I'll get on about the ship that broke in two on another day. Give me something to live for. Something to go along with getting to the big cactus. Cut off that damn light. Just because you ain't paying the bill."

"Yes, Ma'am."

"Benny. I promise not to tease you anymore. Next time I won't be teasing."

"Yes, Ma'am."

"Benny, you're more like Papa than Tendall and Rupert put together."

I cut the light off again and laid in bed for a while, listening to her snoring. Now she gave me something else to fret about. I sure didn't think things out like I ought to before I left. What in the world would I do if she died? Can't just go out and dig a hole in a strange woods. They would all blame me for sure, for taking a old woman on such a long trip. I was in a big mess. And I sure didn't want to be like Grandpa, be like a man who got bit by a mad dog and beat his head on the wall till he died. Aunt Lucy was sure right about one thing; that mad dog story could keep me awake the rest of my life.

The fan in the heater and her snoring made more noise than my truck. I put my shoes back on and slipped out of the room. When Polar heard me coming, he thumped his tail on the truck side and whimpered real quiet like he knew not to wake up people.

"Polar buddy, I got it figured why that old women wont so much as give you a pat on the head," I whispered the truth to him. "She's got it out for dogs. And total by accident, I end up setting her right beside a dog to go thousands of miles. She should of told me before we left." I climbed up in the truck bed. "I didn't mean to do the wrong thing again Polar, taking you with me. I thought you'd like going and it'd hurt your feelings if I left you. Something else. I know you think I'm going nuts, Polar, but could I get you to sleep in the cab tonight? I'm pretty sure I saw bats circling that Sleepy Time light."

I shut up because this man went by the back of my truck and looked at me. I started to explain I was talking to my dog but thought better of it. None of his concern. "I want you to know, Polar," I kept on after the man went in his room, "that when you hear a story like Aunt Lucy told me, you get silly as a woman. I know you don't understand what the heck I'm talking about, but I couldn't stand it if something happened to you. Especially if it was my fault."

He whimpered again real soft, I guess to tell me the motel light was out now except for a big red "No". When I made a little hiss, Polar jumped down to run around to hop in the cab. After I cracked the window so little a bat couldn't squeeze in, he looked out at me like I'd fooled him into thinking we were going for a ride. Not nice to fool him. There I go again, expecting too much of a dog. Aunt Lucy told me when I was talking to Polar, I was talking to both sides of my own head. Well, that was the nice part of what she said.

Now I was getting like Mother, "Doing it for your own good, Polar." One minute, it's Mother. Next minute, it's Daddy. Or Aunt Lucy. Ethel calls me a dumb idiot. I guess I don't know who Benny Foushee sounds like any more. Or maybe Benny Foushee is just a dumb idiot who couldn't help egging a old lady on to find out what people don't see fit to tell him about. Something my own daddy doesn't know and he ought to.

I can't see why he wasn't curious enough to find out. When I asked him once, he said, "People didn't use to live long as they do now, especially men." That wasn't a good enough answer for me.

Mother calls her parents my proper grandparents, whatever that means. I guess it means the not proper grandparents were on my daddy's side: a girl named Gertie who'd be a old lady now, who Aunt Lucy calls sorry, who we don't even have a picture of, who left my daddy in a bushel basket; and a man who left all three of his children by themselves after he went crazy from a mad dog bite. That thought made me shiver like it was wintertime.

Couldn't be like my daddy and just say: "Papa died", and leave it alone. Me, I've got to see him, bashing his face bloody inside the closet where Mother sends me almost every day for the oldest jar of tomatoes. I remember in my mind's eye, that one real picture we got of Grandpa, drunk and sticking his face over a cardboard cowboy's body. Only now I see blood all over his face. I might just have learned what leaving well enough alone means, Mother.

About all I know for sure about Benny Foushee right now is he's got one real good dog and a pretty good old truck. And a cranky old woman depending on him, who had her heart broke in two more than once. I do feel real bad for how she had to dig a grave for her own daddy and see her husband after he got chopped up by a manure spreader. I don't think I could have stood it unless I had to.

Just as I was leaning against my truck, fretting that Benny Foushee was nowhere near as far away from home as he was from that big cactus, I heard my name, loud enough to wake the dead for a mile. I ran towards our room and pushed the old lady who stood in the doorway in her nightshirt back inside.

"Aunt Lucy," I whispered. "Other folks here are sleeping."

"I thought you done took off and left me. Just like Tendall did. Went back for that waitress woman." Her fingers were digging in my arm like chicken claws.

"I'm right here, Aunt Lucy. Now you get back in bed." I turned her towards her bed and gave her a little shove.

"You were fixing to leave me. How come you were doing that? I didn't mean no harm by what I said to you. I won't make fun of you no more. I was just making talk to pass the time. I never meant to be so much trouble. I used to could take care of myself just fine."

"Hush, Aunt Lucy. Quit fretting. I wasn't leaving." I pushed her down to a sitting position. "Why would I do that?" She didn't answer so I tried a funny. "I'm not leaving you. You've got all the money." I heard a little chuckle before she laid back. She snored right off, her big black purse propping her head up from under her pillow.

I tried sleeping but I couldn't stop dreaming crazy things. In one dream I was trying to tell Aunt Lucy that Grandpa ate Lux flakes which was why he was foaming at the mouth. That he didn't really die. She got the maddest at me I'd ever seen her because she knew the truth and I was pretending I didn't. When she woke me up, I didn't know if I was glad it was a dream or not.

Aunt Lucy woke me up that night more times than I can count to see if I was still there. I don't know why in her mind I had to be awake to still be there.

4

Arizona Highways stayed in Aunt Lucy's lap, always open to the big cactus. Hadn't even seen a small cactus in Oklahoma. All I saw was plants that look like pine trees that didn't get enough water, like the farmers were hoping for it to rain but their stuff died already. She was telling me again how much rainwater the big cactus has inside: eighty pounds a foot. Sure looks like that big cactus on the front is giving Benny Foushee the bird, if you ask me.

I sure know more than I ever wanted to learn about the big cactus. And probably as much as I needed to learn about Grandpa. I'm even tired of hamburgers and fries, to tell the truth. But, if I'm figuring right, we are better than half way to that big cactus. I'm not making Polar ride outside anymore and get sunburnt and sand in his eyes to boot. Every time he stands up and wags his tail, Aunt Lucy shoves him away. He sets back down up close to me. I wish she'd try a little harder to like him.

I imagined there was a really big blue sky out west, like in the cowboy movies. Got the sky all right but not a single cowboy. Maybe it was the movie music that made things more exciting. My radio quit working. I could do with a little music. Between busted trees in flat fields, they got signs hollering about Southern food at the next exit. And I got Aunt Lucy hollering about what every one of them says: "'Git yer down home Southern cooking right chere.' I don't say 'chere.' I say here. Don't like getting made fun of by no damn Yankee."

I'm not going to tell her it wasn't a damn Yankee wrote that. But they're not going to fool me with that Southern cooking mess again either. A blop of greens come out of a can and no chow-chow on them. And barbecue made out of a cow. I ordered me a ground steak last night and really got my hopes up. This lady who looked like dead Aunt Agnes brought this meat so covered up with white gravy, it looked like it got snowed on. Trying to cover up how small the meat I dug out was.

I got to admit right now I wouldn't mind standing with the refrigerator door open, deciding whether to get out the sweet gherkins for my ham sandwich or eat it plain. I miss that old refrigerator more than Mother or Daddy or even my own bed, if I told the truth. Well, it's a different kind of missing something. I couldn't help but keep looking in the rear view mirror to see if I saw Daddy's truck with Mother in there making him come after me. Wouldn't mind seeing Mother coming with a dish of candied sweet potatoes in her lap with melted marshmallows burned a little. Never hear the last of me wanting that from Aunt Lucy.

Mother would say stuff was tacky that had big signs. Like this filling station restaurant where we were eating with a yard full of cement dinosaurs that called itself the Terrible Jurassic Lizard History Museum.

Aunt Lucy ate about half her hamburger and said: "Redskins ate every last one of them. Ought to be ashamed."

"Ate every last one of what, Aunt Lucy?"

"Them big lizards. That's why they're all gone."

"Maybe this fancy dinosaur museum ought to hire you to tell folks what really happened."

"Don't get so smart before you think about it, young man. Supposing you're the redskins on this side of the hill and you're eating on a dinosaur for supper, same as the redskins on the other side. Every time you eat up one, you think there's going to be another one on the other side of the hill. Then one day, you can't find one to kill so you go over the hill and lo and behold, the other redskins are sucking on their last bones too…never mind. You're too thick to get it. That's how things get extinct. Did I ever tell you, Benny, about the time I was sucking on a chicken leg that Mona turned into a burnt stick, and got my teeth stuck and had to crawl under the table and take my teeth out…"

I nodded yes to Aunt Lucy, that I had heard the prying her false teeth off Mother's chicken leg like pulling open an animal trap story. Aunt Lucy had gotten into repeating stories almost as bad as Uncle Tendall.

She lifted up her half hamburger lid, the meat as red inside as catsup. "Get this one over to the cow doctor, Benny. I think we can save it."

I felt my face heat up when the waitress passed us. "I wish you'd said something sooner, Aunt Lucy. You can't send back a half eat-up hamburger."

"Humph. The half I eat wont bleeding to death."

"Be a little quieter, please," I begged. The waitress girl looked towards Aunt Lucy with these big sad eyes. I only flirted with her a little because I felt sorry for her. Her hair was pulled back in a droopy ponytail, not really what Ethel or Valinda would call a hairdo. It looked like the "Before" in a shampoo ad on TV, but her eyes were like the starving children from Africa pictures at the church, round water holes about to run over the sides. When she went back in the kitchen, I saw that her behind fell in like a rotting cantaloupe beneath the bow of her apron. I wished I hadn't watched her backside, but I can't seem to help doing that. Not many Sue Fayes in the world. I shouldn't even look at girls that aren't pretty.

"You give her enough tip to buy another meal," Aunt Lucy fussed after we got out to the truck.

"She looked hungry," I said. "Besides I used my own money."

"People who work in kitchens don't go hungry, if it's food they want."

Every restaurant we went in, Aunt Lucy reached across to my plate, picked up the dill pickle, which I never have liked and won't eat unless I'm still awful hungry, and that clump of green stuff centered with the red apple washer I never knew if you were supposed to eat or not. She wrapped the mess with her leftovers in her placemat that she always read me even though I got one just like it, folding the ends like a package she was getting ready to drop in the mail. Then the package got stuffed in her purse which was starting to smell like the trash can that Mother told me to take out five times.

"What's that green stuff you're eating out of your purse?" I asked her later, forgetting what I watched her do every day.

"Dun know," she replied between munches. "Not bad though. Could have used a little mayonnaise. It's a good thing we're traveling in a truck, Benny. That girl back there in that restaurant, that scrawny one?"

There were times I wished my life with Aunt Lucy could be more like a flat rock skipping across the water. With her the rock always falls through. Ploop. That skinny girl bobbed back up to the top like a cork. I didn't intend to ever think about her again, about what she might spend about four hours of my work at the filling station on. And there went those floor mats with the checkered flags I wanted to buy.

Aunt Lucy kept on, "If you'd been walking, that scrawny girl would be trotting along behind you like a cat you shouldn't have fed."

I hate to admit it, but there've been more than a few times since this trip started, I wouldn't even mind having Valinda to talk to for a little while. Or asked Mother if she thought giving the waitress a big tip was the Christian thing to do. Or asked Daddy about the gas filters that kept plugging up. Well, at least I hadn't missed Ethel yet.

"Don't worry, Aunt Lucy. I won't be filling my truck bed up with stray cats and skinny girls. In fact I might put a scrawny old lady back there if she don't stop bugging me…"

"Doesn't stop bugging me. Don't talk so ignorant. You got to try harder. Don't you ever want to learn nothing and stay stupid like your kin the rest of your life? Want to grow up like Tendall and be a lost ball in a weed path?"

"I haven't seen you be nice to one person this whole trip, Aunt Lucy. Not even me about half the time. But you're right. Look what a mess I got me in when I gave a stray old lady a *Arizona Highways* to amuse herself."

She began to cackle, then pulled a red apple washer from her purse and popped the whole thing in her mouth at once. She began to blow red bubbles, the bubbles not on purpose.

"Wipe that red mess off your chin, Aunt Lucy. You look like I popped you in the mouth."

She pulled out a holey Kleenex and dabbed at her face, looking at the red that soaked in the tissue then back at me. Uh oh. That look said I really had popped her in the mouth. I never got so mad I hit anybody. Well, nobody but Ethel who asked for it. And not since she got so big. I'd die before I'd hurt Aunt Lucy.

"You hit me so hard," Aunt Lucy said, "you made me bleed."

I dropped a wheel off the pavement, making rocks rattle under the truck like I set off a string of firecrackers. I better pay attention to my driving and not have a wreck. And be careful what I say. Now she has put it somewhere in her head that I hit her and people have to know whether to believe me or her if she tells it. Get stuck with somebody in the cab of a GMC pickup for a few weeks if you want to find out what they're really like. And keep it straight which one of you is nuts.

I saw the backside of a woman beside the road. No rotten cantaloupe for a behind on this one. No barn door either. She made me drive so slow, I had to shift to low to keep her in front of me. She had on jeans with both hands stuck in her back pockets. Under those hands was a butt that filled her jeans with a perfect shape that could have been bouncing up and down on a horse or peeking out from a short white skirt on a tennis count. That kind of a nice butt. Like a rich girl butt from the big houses in Durham. Not one bit fluffy, real athletic. But she wasn't sitting in a saddle or playing tennis. She was staring at the back of a little car, her hands, I guess, not of much use to her when it came to cars.

I put the clutch in and coasted with the brake on. At first I thought she was looking in the trunk, maybe to change a tire. When I almost stopped beside her, I saw a engine in the trunk. I didn't spend a second deciding what to do. Or think either. I pulled to the side of the road in front of the little silver car and got out before Aunt Lucy could tell me not to.

"Hi, need any help," I called so I wouldn't scare her. She was out in the middle of nowhere for sure.

"The red light came on," she started talking, like she had known me since first grade. "Maybe the green one is the bad one, the oil one." She wrinkled her nose and squinted. She was blond with long hair with curls that went all the right directions naturally. "At least I think that's what my father told me to remember. Yeah. Red is bad. Green is good. No, maybe green is worse. I stopped the engine as soon as I saw the red light. Oh, I'm so frustrated. Silly little lights, telling me what to do."

I saw the light, yes Lord, I saw the light went ripping through my brain, luckily not out loud. I couldn't make a peep out loud right then.

"I probably should get the book out," she added, but didn't move. I wanted to keep looking at her, but I looked at the engine because that was what a man was supposed to be interested in. I tried looking from one side to the other so she wouldn't guess I was the dumb redneck that I was.

There was writing on everything on the engine in some foreign language. I hadn't taken Spanish at school yet. It was one weird looking engine with carburetors on both sides. Then I got a lucky break, like seeing a piece of green paper rolling down the pavement turn into a twenty. I saw pieces of shredded black stuff.

"Appears to be the fan belt," I said, like a man with his name in a oval on his shirt. I hadn't gotten good enough for a "Benny" shirt at the Exxon yet. "Shouldn't be hard to fix."

"Oh, that's wonderful," she said and began clapping like I'd scored a run or something. "I am so lucky that you stopped."

I almost did a double thumbs-up until I realized she was looking at me, my brain still working well enough to keep me from making a ass of myself. At least I was wearing my last clean t-shirt.

"Problem will be finding a belt to fit it out here in the sticks," Benny-in-the-pretend-oval-on-his-shirt explained. I looked at what held the fan belt to the fan. Biggest damn nut I'd ever seen, except maybe the guy who was wondering if they even made a wrench that big.

"There are tools and stuff in the front," she offered with a look that was the combination of grateful and impressed along with the prettiest smile I'd ever seen. "Do you want me to open the trunk for you?" she asked. Meaning I guessed, are you going to fix it for me?

"Sure," I nodded. "I'll be glad to take a look." So far I don't even think Mother would have fussed at me. Now don't mess up, Benny.

"Oh boy, I'm so glad you stopped." She reached under the dash and pulled something that popped the nose up a couple of inches. "If you fix it, I'll buy you lunch, I promise. Is that your mother in the truck?"

"Aunt," I replied. "She's eighty-four." So having old Aunt Lucy along meant safe was written all over me.

"Is she OK in there by herself? It's awfully hot."

"Oh yeah. She's fine. She lives by herself." I don't know why I felt the need to lie in the first five minutes of my new relationship. Just a guy thing I guess. Now I had a lie I had to remember with Aunt Lucy's words echoing in my mind: if you start out telling the truth, you don't need a good memory.

The girl reached under the nose of her car, lifting the lid up like somebody who'd done it a hundred times. She had been in there a lot because it was packed with plastic shopping bags that she started piling on the ground outside the car. Definitely been on a major shopping trip and we weren't even near a town. I couldn't help but think there ought to be a engine under all those bags. I started to tell her to put her stuff inside where it would be safe, but when I looked in the passenger part of the car, that was filled with bags too. She left just enough room to get in there and drive the thing.

I checked out the real trunk of the car after she emptied it, trying not to appear shocked because the spare tire was where the engine should have been. I took out a tiny tool kit, tied with two black bows. Those guys at the Exxon would be howling over that. But when I undid the bows, there it was: a fresh new fan belt stuck in a little pocket made just for it

"Ah, there's a new fan belt," I said brightly, thinking if only the bozo standing here had the foggiest idea of how to put it on. "Glad we don't have to look all over Oklahoma to find one of these." I held up the stiff black oval.

She clapped her hands again, this time like a little kid who saw her birthday cake coming to the table with the candles burning. "Typical Germans," she said. She looked so young. She didn't look old enough for a driver's license much less to know the difference between a typical German and a typical North Carolinian. But she sure was pretty as a picture.

"Right on," I replied, not remembering what movie I got that from. I think it might have been English, not German. The movie, that is. There was a sign at the Summit Exxon that said we wouldn't even change the oil in a foreign car. Our tools don't fit them the boss said.

"Uh, maybe I could trouble you to go keep old Aunt Lucy company while I do this little job. That is, if you don't mind dogs?" I asked, thinking so you won't see me smashing my knuckles and cussing your fancy car.

"Sure. Oh, look at the big white dog with the cap on! I just love dogs. I have two of them," she smiled. "Tracey and Lacey."

I think this may have been the first time in my life any girl: mother, sister or girlfriend, said "sure" to me in a nice way. Maybe that's why I couldn't stop lying, I was so afraid she was going to change and be mean.

"If he smells too bad, tell him to get in the back of the truck. Haven't had time to bathe him since we've been traveling."

Haven't bathed him in his life. That was only a half lie actually. Polar didn't have a bar of soap when I threw him in the pond after he rolled in something unmentionable. The truth is Aunt Lucy needed a bath worse than Polar.

"Thank you again," she said. Another first. Then she added: "I'd rather die than let my father find out this happened."

Mine too, I thought, and luckily didn't say it. He would be laughing at me, old Benny-going-nowhere-fast, he called me. Daddy would figure out how to fix it in about two minutes. I watched the girl crawl in beside Aunt Lucy, as obedient as Polar who hopped out, then back in the cab beside her. When I saw the door slam, I had the fast thought that I might watch all three of them drive away and leave me. Aunt Lucy might think it was a funny little joke to tell this girl I was just released from prison and was kidnapping her for all her money.

The truck didn't move. I was starting to feel the sun myself, cutting through the hair on top my head. Polar could have given me my Durham Bulls hat back since I was the one in the sun now. More than a few times already, I'd rather be him than me. Please Aunt Lucy, don't be mean to her.

I walked to the back, glancing at the engine lid to see if it was a Volkswagen. Porsche was written in gold. Fancy. Fancy or not, you're broken, little car. And you are so likely to break; you have a tool kit with a pocket custom made for a new fan belt. I hate foreign cars.

I spread the tool kit open on the ground. OK, you little Nazi. That's what my history teacher would call you. Think you're so smart giving me a fan belt. Where's your fan belt tool? And there it was. A big, silver hex wrench with a bunch of stuff stamped on it that looked like @$a0#^&! in the comic books.

I picked the shredded rubber that was still hot as black spaghetti from around the fan on the little motor. I had a clear view from the top of the big nut that the wrench with the big nut hole would fit. Things were looking up for Benny Foushee. That is if Aunt Lucy wasn't in there telling this pretty little girl I had knocked up my girlfriend Valinda and was leaving town. She'd do something like that to me in a minute. I know her.

I patted the engine. Still warm, but not too hot to work on. Maybe it thought I was being affectionate. I pat my truck in different places now and then because I really believe I should show it I care. I didn't know if I could fool this little motor being we didn't even talk the same language. I slipped the wrench with the big hole over the big nut. Upside down. Looked over my shoulder. She wasn't there, of course. I turned over the wrench.

I could hear the buzz of female voices from my truck cab. Be nice, Aunt Lucy, please. I put some pressure on the wrench and said a prayer to somebody that I didn't turn to very often. Come off, Jesus Christ. Don't say it, Mother. Don't fall apart in a little pile on the ground. Don't let some German SOB string me up on a church steeple for stupidity and shoot a hole in my butt. The nut snapped loose with a quiet crack. Almost a sound of respect.

I felt a sudden rush of affection for the little hurt motor. I'll fix you, little buddy. I'm sorry about all those Nazi thoughts. That's my old history teacher, the football coach's fault. I'll save the damsel in distress. Like Popeye, with Olive Oil crying help as she floated towards the waterfall. Then I saw the bloody flap of skin lifting up on my knuckle. Could have given me a little more working room. I thought Germans were supposed to be big.

Hadn't even felt it, but twenty minutes later with more flaps of bleeding skin on three of my knuckles and a few more prayers, this time to my old auto shop teacher, Mr. Melvin, who told me to stick a screw driver in to hold it while I was tightening it up, the belt was in place on the fan. No radiator. Air-cooled. I hear you, Mr. Melvin. Do I dare to start the motor? Sir?

With a stinging fingertip sliced on some unknown part of the Nazi mobile - there I go again, I'm sorry, little car - I pressed the belt. The tension seemed OK. What could happen? Mistakes only burst into flames in the movies. In real life they farted and broke again.

I got in the little car and saw she had left the key in the switch. Holding a nice round shift knob that fit my hand perfect, I put in the clutch and took it out of gear. Boy, I'd like to put that shifter in my truck. When I started it up, it ran like it ought to have a mower blade sticking out the side. I watched the tachometer go up and down when I gave it gas. Like sitting in a little silver bathtub with a motor. No red or green lights came on. I shut it off before I had to admit I liked it.

Polar's face popped in the back window of my truck, making nose daisies from the inside out this time, my cap with the bill turned up against the glass like a punk kid. He heard me coming. When I stuck my face in the window of my truck, as I left the sunshine, black dots danced in front of my eyes. There were three white faces with black polka dots in there, my baseball cap on the one in the middle. That damn Polar had wiggled between Aunt Lucy and the girl who had her arm around him.

"Well, are we glad we come across Tennessee?" Aunt Lucy said with one of her nastier chuckles. I heard the girl start giggling. Maybe Aunt Lucy had been decent.

"We came across Tennessee near about a week ago," I said and both women busted up laughing. I got a embarrassed feeling that conniving had been going on behind my back.

"Meet Tennessee Gentry," Aunt Lucy said. "Benny Fousheè."

The brown-eyed girl stuck her tiny hand up for a shake. I felt pains shoot up my arm, afraid I had left splotches of my blood on her cool skin. Tennessee. Girls from Summit might be named Ruby Jane or Sarah

Jean, or even Valinda Sue. but Tennessee? Only parents with a lot of money would have the nerve to name their daughter Tennessee. Now I'd have to ask Aunt Lucy a million questions to know what those two girls talked about while I fixed that car. And that damn Polar just sitting there in the shade, smiling and drooling dark spots on Tennessee's jeans. He had died and gone to heaven, as they say.

"It's fixed," I managed to say. I looked right at those little hands so I could see them clap. I tingled all over.

"I drove into this gas station in Oklahoma," Tennessee's voice was sweet and high pitched, more like a tree full of birds than a girl. "Nobody came out and the pump wasn't self serve."

I wondered but didn't ask why she was in Oklahoma, since her car was pointed the other direction. Her license tag said New Mexico; maybe on the way home. We were eating lunch in this fancy Indian Trading Post and Café, my pay for fixing her car. When I got Aunt Lucy through the door and headed towards a table, I prayed that she wouldn't do or say something so bad I'd wish the floor would open up and swallow us.

"I saw this guy wearing bib overalls," Tennessee went on, "come sneaking around the corner of the station, really slowly, as if he were hiding from me or something. And you know what he said?"

I couldn't even guess. I know what I would have said: "Where have you been all my life?" I shook my head without speaking.

"He said 'Is you from Mars?'"

She began to giggle. Aunt Lucy didn't say anything, which surprised me. She was trying to get her silverware out of this rolled up napkin and was probably pissed because this place didn't have a placemat to read.

"Is you from Mars?" Tennessee repeated, "and I thought Mars, Oklahoma, and then it hit me. I mean Oklahoma is really full of hicks. We call them Okies. This Okie thought the Porsche was a space ship."

"Are you from Mars," Aunt Lucy piped up as her knife and fork clattered out on the table. "Bib overalls is dangerous," she added. Tennessee wrinkled her nose instead of saying "huh?" which is what most people would do around Aunt Lucy. I knew Aunt Lucy meant her husband Uncle Obie got his overall strap caught in the manure spreader, which wasn't something I wanted to try to explain. Maybe Tennessee had already figured out that Aunt Lucy was nuts.

"Don't your feet hurt, Mrs. Williams?" she asked.

"Wearing what skirt?" Aunt Lucy answered.

"Your shoes might be on the wrong feet, I think," she added real timid but louder at the same time. Damn. I forgot to check Aunt Lucy out before we left this morning. I looked under the table: she had them messed up again. At least they had to be the same color. Maybe she's done it wrong so much her feet feel better bent the wrong way.

"Naw, never been to Chinquapin," Aunt Lucy said. "Been through there. Didn't get out."

Tennessee looked at me. I imagined two little x's for her eyes under those blond curls on her forehead. So pretty.

"Some things she hears," I explained. "Some things she hears something else. Ours is not to reason why," I added. That ought to impress her. I remember something like that from Miss Briggs' English class.

"Theirs but to do and die: Into the valley of Death," Tennessee recited with glee, doing a cute silent clap with her hands.

Thank you, Miss Briggs, I thought. Ninth grade English.

"Twenty-third Psalm," Aunt Lucy piped up.

"No, it wasn't, Aunt Lucy."

"OK, so I cut church that Sunday. Hotter than Hades in here."

Aunt Lucy was trying to talk nice. I had to be thankful for that. I didn't know she even knew the fancy word for Hell.

"I got to be honest with you," I said for some stupid reason. "I never worked on a Porsche before." I can be so lame. Soon as I meet her, I lie.

Now I get too honest.

"You put a new board where the floor rotted out under my rocker," Aunt Lucy yelled like we were the deaf ones. "Never got around to painting it." The wrinkled nose on Tennessee again.

"Porsche, Aunt Lucy." I said real loud. "Pors - che. Not porch."

"Benny's just like his daddy. He can fix the crack of dawn." Why was Aunt Lucy being nice to me?

"Oh, that makes it ever more impressive," Tennessee exclaimed. "Fixing it just like that and you never worked on one. My father takes his Porsches to this really expensive place in Santa Fe. He is always complaining about them ripping him off."

Porsches. He had more than one.

"Hotter in here than jumper cables at a colored funeral." Aunt Lucy said colored, more fancy talk, or probably because she thought there were enough dark people in there to kill all three of us. Her face was pretty red. Her skin was starting to get wrinkles like mud when it went from too much rain to drought.

"Oh, it was just a fan belt," I said to Tennessee, using all my best false modesty. "Not really engine work."

"Is the light screwed up in here?" The waiter had put Aunt Lucy's food in front of her.

"How's that, Aunt Lucy?"

"Would you look at that? Ain't that pancake blue?"

There went a song again, "Don't it Make My Brown Eyes Blue". I think I even sang it out loud. I'm not sure. I'm an idiot. Tennessee had eyes as clear and shiny as a buckeye. She giggled again. She seemed to like idiots.

"I ordered the pancake for you, Mrs. Williams, a surprise to go with your hamburger," Tennessee said. I felt a big relief. Finally somebody else to answer Aunt Lucy. "Thought you might like to try an Indian pancake."

"Didn't know them redskins was so damn colorful," Aunt Lucy

answered, a little too loud considering where we were.

"Aunt Lucy. Remember. Indian corn. It's colored," I offered.

"It ain't that color. And it ain't edible."

Tennessee began to laugh. She really seemed to get a kick out of Aunt Lucy. I had to admit, as Mother would say, my kicks were getting fewer and further between.

"The corn is blue, Mrs. Williams."

Aunt Lucy grunted and poured syrup on her pancake. If I had ordered it, she would have asked if Mona had slipped in the kitchen and spilt ink in her batter. Aunt Lucy forked a blue bite in her mouth. I had to admit it was a little weird to see somebody eat something blue.

"Blue corn don't taste near as good as yellow corn," she smacked. The real Aunt Lucy was starting to come back.

"Then put more syrup on it, Aunt Lucy," I told her.

"I don't see them redskins eating blue pancakes."

I looked across the restaurant and she was right. Tennessee clapped her little hands again in that cute way she has. Maybe it would get old after a while, but I sure loved it. A big Indian family sat at a table in the middle of the restaurant, a circle of square people with faces like hubcaps and bodies like tractors. They were sticking long yellow catsup dipped French fries in their mouths and every plate had a double cheeseburger.

"Guess they just make blue pancakes to poison the tourists, Aunt Lucy."

"Caterpillar eats poison plants so birds don't like him." She didn't read that one off the placemat because there wasn't one. "I'm like a pigeon."

"The old bird's a pigeon?"

"Smart ass." Aunt Lucy talked between chewing. "Heared a story once, about this feller, lost in the woods, didn't know, which stuff to eat, saw this pigeon, eating berries, thought he was being smart, et them, they kilt him." She swallowed real loud, more like a pill than a pancake.

"And who lived to tell that story, Aunt Lucy?"

"The pigeon."

"Come on."

"Preacher told it. God told him."

"That's too easy a answer."

"I forget the moral of the story. God works in mysterious ways, that'll do. I seen Him get mysterious. He even got mysterious with the preacher. Dumped him off a ladder when he was changing a light bulb. In this tacky cross he put on the front of the church."

"Like the one we seen in Arkansas, Aunt Lucy."

"Saw in Arkansas," she corrected my grammar. "Probably bought that cross off the same traveling salesman that come through North Carolina. Preacher come to church on his knees, preaching that God meant for him to stay on his knees before him. That's a preacher for you. Clumsy bastard falls off a ladder. He has to come up with that God had a good reason for doing it. Then he started getting pissed, if you know what I mean. Not God, the preacher got pissed. I think God is pissed about half the time too. He lets us know it enough."

Welcome back, Aunt Lucy. We can only hope that Tennessee isn't religious like Mother. She was listening to Aunt Lucy like nobody else was in the world.

"Anyhow, when the preacher had a long way to go, he got hisself pulled along in a red wagon which would have been fun, ifin he was a little feller. See, he didn't mind being on his knees in front of God and Jesus and the rest of the holy bunch, but he was getting pretty ticked off having to crawl around in front of the likes of us. Especially jackasses like Tendall."

"Tendall's her brother," I put in.

"I know," Tennessee said. "You two are so funny," she laughed. I had to talk to Aunt Lucy when Tennessee wasn't around and find out how much she told her about our family.

"Preacher come over to Obie and had him weld him up a chair with wheels. Obie made it out of two girl's bicycles. Preacher was damn near tall as Tendall and Obie, just sitting in that chair. Obie didn't have nothing to go by, but I seen a picture of Roosevelt in a chair not far off that one Obie made. After Roosevelt passed on, the picture of his rolling chair come out in *Look* magazine. He didn't want to let on to us he couldn't walk. God got pissed and give him polio," she cackled.

"Aunt Lucy is really into history, Tennessee. Actually Aunt Lucy is so old she is history." She was starting to make me feel like Uncle Tendall by ignoring me. Gets pretty full of herself with a new audience that listens to every word she says.

"That sorry son of the preacher who took over after the old cripple croaked ought to get down on his knees like his daddy. So I could kick him in the butt. Couldn't work up a ounce of excitement at a hanging, if you ask me. And he likes Mona's fried chicken which really means something's wrong with him."

"Mona?" Tennessee asked.

"My mother."

"I bet Mona is a better cook than I am," Tennessee said with a handclap. "I blew up a boiled egg last week and stuck it to the ceiling. Juanita got a big laugh. She cleaned the ceiling before my father got home. I bet even you're a better cook than I am, Benny, and you probably can't even cook. Who's Obie?"

Tennessee had started to talk louder when she wanted Aunt Lucy to hear and soft when she was talking to me. Aunt Lucy was working on the last of her blue pancake. She could talk a blue streak and eat everything on her plate at the same time. Except the green stuff with the red apple washer. I hated to see that mess sitting there because now Tennessee was going to see it go in Aunt Lucy's purse. And she doesn't have a new placemat. And the napkin is made out of cloth so we're not supposed to take them. I started eating my red apple washer, which I never do, but that was the only way to keep Aunt Lucy from reaching across for it. Not too bad. Better try to eat hers too.

"Obie's her dead husband," I explained to Tennessee. "And Rupert is her brother, my daddy."

"She told me about Rupert. Tendall and Rupert. Her brothers."

"Oh no," I laughed and so did Tennessee. She was a good sport, as Daddy would say.

"She told me you were taking her to see the big cactus. The saguaro."

I nodded. Kind of hard to talk about it even though I hadn't had to try yet. Tennessee was the first person we'd told, except in my letter.

"I think you are a really nice person to drive her all the way from North Carolina in that old truck," she said so soft Aunt Lucy couldn't possibly hear her. "You must really love her."

I could have died and fallen out of my chair easier than kept my face from turning red. I don't think there is another person in the world that I know who would say I did the right thing to leave town with Aunt Lucy. From day one, to tell the truth, I've felt like Benny the Kid, some kind of criminal who got too big a head start for them to catch me.

"Wash your food down with some water," Aunt Lucy said to me. "Look like you're choking to death."

"I know where they are," Tennessee told me, ignoring Aunt Lucy. "The big saguaro cactus."

"You do?" I said stupidly. "And where are you going?"

"I'm running away from home."

Tennessee didn't laugh this time. She didn't clap her hands either. Aunt Lucy looked up with a frown while she was stuffing her red apple washer in an old placemat that had already seeped through inside her purse.

"Me too," Aunt Lucy shouted, but before she spoke my heart had already fluttered out of my chest, like a scared sparrow out of the bushes.

5

"Hot enough to fry spit in this truck."

"Are you sitting on my map, Aunt Lucy?"

"Can't you tell chicken poop from putty without a map? Just go west, young man."

"Lift your scrawny butt up off my map." I reached between Polar's legs to jerk the map out from under Aunt Lucy. More than a few times on this trip she made me want to scream like a cat with my tail under her rocker.

"What's the matter, Benny Boy? The butter done slipped off your biscuit?" Aunt Lucy wouldn't quit making fun of me. "Don't we talk sweet after our little fairy princess has run away in her silver pumpkin and left us?"

My mind hadn't been on much else but seeing her again since lunch. She was acting like she was trying to run away so fast, nobody could catch her. She told me we could meet to have dinner where the two big highways cross in Amarillo. I can't keep track of the numbers. It was pretty depressing. My old truck couldn't go fast as she could in that sports car. I bet there wasn't a guy in Summit with a car that would go that fast. I was trying hard not to miss the roads.

When I pushed my truck hard, it drank gasoline like it was iced tea. And getting money for gas from Aunt Lucy was like trying to pull a bone out of Polar's mouth. I don't know how she thought we could get to the big cactus without burning gas. I got off the big road in Texas on empty, which put me on some of old Route 66. First station was shut down. Had a bunch of black birds sitting in the busted Texaco sign like it belonged to them. Kind of sad that all those motels and filling stations couldn't just grow legs and walk up beside the new road. I sure knew what it felt like not being able to keep up. I hadn't seen Tennessee's Porsche in a long time. Got a tank full at the first open station and out came the screaming nickels from Aunt Lucy as Daddy would say. Slower than cold molasses as she would say.

I got to get my mind on something else. Try the signs by the road. Out here in Texas, signs are all for the biggest something. Biggest rattlesnake, biggest buffalo, biggest steak. Aunt Lucy reads them all out loud like she's the only one who knows how to read. She said Grandpa couldn't read but I sure can. If you want to know biggest, Texas is the biggest nothing I've seen so far.

"World's biggest cross," Aunt Lucy read then added her own comment: "His trip ended here."

From a distance, the world's biggest cross got all mixed up with telephone poles and to tell the truth, I don't even think somebody real religious like Mother would get out of the truck to go see it. Especially if you had to pay. I sure hope the big cactus isn't as big a letdown as the big cross.

The mountains in the distance looked like hills that had their tops loped off, like stumps of a bunch of dead mountains. They're a lot further off than you think they are. You drive and drive and don't get there. And the wind makes you rock like you're stuck out in the middle of water instead of on land.

I'd try and eat the world's biggest steak - 72 ounces - that was free if you ate it all. But I was a little scared I couldn't finish it and then I'd have to pay for it. Aunt Lucy would have it in her purse before you could say Jack Robinson. That big steak was near Amarillo, Texas, where I was supposed to see a row of Cadillacs stuck in the ground, if you were to believe Buddy at the Exxon, engine end first. I forgot to ask him which side of the road. I'd like to pull one of those Caddies up and drive it off.

The sky is all the way around you out here. Not getting her off your mind, Benny. I couldn't stand to just lose her. I spotted the big roads that she told me about. I turned off the interstate so fast, Polar fell over on Aunt Lucy like a chopped down tree.

"Sorry, buddy." I said.

"Don't mention it," Aunt Lucy answered.

When I saw Tennessee's little silver car in the parking lot of the Wild West Steakhouse, I have to admit I felt like jumping out and running and hugging it. She had the top down with a flat canvas cover made to fit over the seats. There were lumps under the cover not supposed to be there where she had stuffed all the new things that she bought at the Indian trading post.

"I need to start buying smaller things," she had laughed. One thing she bought was collars for her dogs, Lacey and Tracey, with enough blue stones stuck on them to be a girl's bracelet. They were about big enough to be bracelets for Polar, if he was inclined to wear something dumb like that, so I figured those two dogs must be pretty small. Piss dogs, Aunt Lucy would call them. My daddy, the comedian, calls little dogs bedroom shoes.

As we headed in the restaurant, I felt like I was walking with a broken leg, pushing on Aunt Lucy's backside every time she stopped. "Go butt a stump, Benny."

"You can walk faster than that, Aunt Lucy, if you want to, because I seen you do it."

"Saw you do it. Watch your mouth."

"Get the lead out and quit correcting everything I say."

"Early bird gets the worm, but the second mouse gets the cheese."

If I screamed every time she said one of those sayings, people would think I was a crazy man. I shoved Aunt Lucy through the door of the Ladies room and waited for her for what seemed like a year and a Sunday.

I tried to spot Tennessee but it was too dark. Restaurants out in the West pretend to be the Wild West, which it isn't any more as far as I can tell. The West's bigger and flatter and dryer than anywhere I've ever been before, which is North Carolina and South Carolina, but the filling stations look just like the Exxon where I work only they are a little newer. Probably didn't used to be a Esso first, which a lot of old people still call it. Waiting on Aunt Lucy was getting harder and harder.

Anyhow, these restaurant people put a bunch of wagon wheels inside where people eat, hung them down from the ceiling, and put light bulbs on them. Looks like it would be easier to just hang down the light bulbs. I mean what's a wheel doing on the ceiling? It's too dark for my taste. If there's a hair or a bug in my food, I want to be able to see it to get it out.

I was starting to wonder if Aunt Lucy fell in their commode like she did once at our house when Uncle Tendall left the seat up. She crawled up on Mother's little vanity another time and peed in the sink, thinking she was back in the outhouse she used to have. No telling what Aunt Lucy might do on her own and I sure couldn't go in the Ladies room to find out.

The truth was I was about to go crazy to see Tennessee. She had to come out this way, even if she gave up on waiting on us and meant to leave. All kinds of stuff tacked on the wall that you use to hook up mules and wagons, the kind of stuff the Foushee family nails on the wall in the barn because we don't know how to throw stuff away. Tendall's old Junebug mule just eats and sleeps and breaks wind and works on the record for being the world's oldest mule. You could hang all these fancy harnesses on Junebug and he'd probably fall down. I bet half the people in here don't know that thing over there by the Men's restroom door is a singletree. Don't think I'd impress Tennessee with that. I couldn't keep busying my mind waiting on Aunt Lucy any longer. I went in the main part. Tennessee was sitting by herself in the dark. I almost ran to her booth.

"Where's Mrs. Williams?" she asked first thing. "Oh, I bet the Ladies room." She answered her own question. "I'll go make sure she's OK." She didn't even brush my arm when she left. I was hoping to touch her by accident. I'll admit it made me proud as a red rooster to go up to her and have her act glad to see me. I felt a little disappointed though when I sat down by myself. And mad at Aunt Lucy for being so slow. Until I saw Tennessee's little purse that she left on the table. That kind of got me for some reason.

What made the talk get going after Tennessee came back with Aunt Lucy wasn't one of those horse hitch things on the wall. It was this picture behind the cash register of these two little buck naked boys sitting under a wolf with big tits hanging down, the kind of picture Mother would say was too risqué to be on a wall where children could see it.

"Romulus and Remus," I heard Aunt Lucy shout before bee lining to the booth, knocking over two chairs I had to get up and set back up. She was going faster than I thought she could move, except going towards the bathroom. Must be hungry, not that she does anything but run her mouth to work up a appetite.

"Who's Romulus and Remus?" I asked Aunt Lucy then realized my mistake, looking stupid in front of Tennessee. All I could think of was this story about Uncle Remus and a rabbit jumping in a briar patch. At least I didn't say that.

"People babies raised by a wolf," Aunt Lucy answered as she wiggled across the booth seat to the window, a inch at the time. "Mean, rotten SOB king throwed them in the river and the mama wolf pulled them out and for some reason decided not to eat them. I forget that part. Her wolf babies died and she was getting milk fever. She wont hungry. I don't know. I sure am. Hungry enough to eat a baby and a wolf."

Tennessee was already giggling at Aunt Lucy. Not tired of her yet like I am. "How did you know that about the wolf?" I couldn't help but ask Aunt Lucy.

"Sunday school. I already told you a lot more than I know."

"You are right about the wolf," Tennessee put in as she slid in the booth beside Aunt Lucy. "They were brothers and the founders of Rome."

"Guess you went to the same Sunday School," Aunt Lucy said.

"I don't go to Sunday School," she corrected. "I go to Saint Catherine's Prep. I did a paper for school on Kamala and Amala. They were two little girls in India raised by a wolf pack. People think they're so great." Her voice changed and her pretty little face screwed up. Uh oh, I thought, and I was right. She was getting upset by what she was thinking.

"You know what happened?" Tennessee went on. "People saw the children with the wolf pack so they killed the mother wolf and took the children away. The littlest one died really soon. The other one got a people disease, typhoid, and then it died too. The little girls never talked to the people who thought they rescued them. They made animal noises and understood each other. They walked on all fours. They could see in the dark. They were doing perfectly OK without people." Her bottom lip went out when she added: "I wish I was raised by wolves."

Right then I saw a Tennessee I hadn't seen yet. It worried me a little. Maybe we were getting to why she was running away from home. She definitely wasn't raised by a wolf. I waited for Aunt Lucy to say something while I watched Tennessee's perfect pink fingernails ripping up her napkin. She had on a ring with a silver butterfly that opened and closed its wings. Her arm jingled from all the stuff on her bracelet. I got to admit I'd rather see those smooth little hands clapping. I kept my hands in my lap because I couldn't wash the fancy Porsche crud off of them.

Aunt Lucy held her menu at an angle, catching the sunset through the window and ignoring both of us. Tennessee kept going on about the wolf children, almost as bad as Aunt Lucy about the big cactus. I couldn't come up with anything to talk about except something totally dumb about a wolf not owning a little silver car for her to run away in. Or that maybe it was better not to learn about things in school if they made you so sad. Lucky for me, I kept quiet. I wanted real bad for her to keep liking me and something told me that saying those thoughts right then wouldn't do the job.

"Damn wagon wheels are one sorry excuse for light," Aunt Lucy finally spoke. "Dark as two black cats in a coal pile in here. They got any fried chicken?"

Tennessee looked at her menu. I couldn't do anything right then but look at her. She was pretty enough with that blond curly hair to be in a ad for shampoo as the "After" girl. Tennessee made a big sniff and said: "I think they have chicken fried chicken, Mrs. Williams. Or maybe it's chicken fried steak. I don't know the difference between chicken fried and fried chicken."

I did. Finally something I knew, but I decided being a redneck wasn't a good subject to try to impress her with so I didn't say it. Tennessee's eyes got glassier. I wasn't sure how she could see through the water in her eyes to read. I felt a hurt inside seeing her so sad and not knowing how to help anything.

"How about a buffalo steak, Aunt Lucy?" I offered to break the silence. "Haven't seen a lot of chickens out here."

"And how many lobsters and shrimp you seen dancing round out there? See. Seafood!" she shouted and pointed at the menu. "Blue pancakes are enough weird crap for one day."

Boy, she was bitchy. As Daddy would say, better feed her soon before she bites somebody. Truth was, I could barely pay attention to Aunt Lucy now that tears were rolling down Tennessee's cheeks and falling off on her white shirt that looked like it just came off a ironing board. Aunt Lucy wasn't even noticing it. Tennessee was breaking her own heart, thinking about those little dead wolf girls that she didn't even know. I didn't think I said anything to hurt her feelings, not on purpose, but I couldn't think of anything to unhurt them either.

I wanted to hug her so bad. "We could just go to McDonald's," I offered, "or take our food outside..." The waitress, who was older than Mother, got between us before I got it said, and asked if we wanted anything to drink. Tennessee looked up when the waitress listed: "Coke, Sprite, Root beer," without being asked. Then the waitress turned to me and said, "Got Miller's on tap." Tennessee was wiping her eyes on a little piece left from her napkin, getting something black she had on her eyes smeared on her face. I hadn't asked her how old she was, but I think the waitress was telling us Tennessee wasn't old enough to drink and she thought I was. Tennessee was driving a car; she must be every bit as old as I was.

"Give me a beer," Aunt Lucy said. "Couple of Co-Colas for my kids. You want to check my license?" After the waitress left, I said "Very funny," to Aunt Lucy, but it must have been a little funny because Tennessee was smiling again.

"Beer's good with Sweet Peach," Aunt Lucy piped in.

"You hold off on the Sweet Peach till we're in our room tonight, OK, Sweet Peach?"

"I could of said Co-Colas for my two daughters," she snapped.

"You could of just said Benny needs a haircut, for the umteenth time."

"Benny needs a haircut for the umteenth time."

Tennessee was looking at her watch, not paying any attention to me needing a haircut or Aunt Lucy fussing at me, which I was glad of. I better get a haircut soon as I can.

"Guess where I'm supposed to be right now?" Tennessee offered, a little cheerier all of a sudden.

"Wednesday night prayer meeting," Aunt Lucy answered.

"No. New York."

"New York," I exclaimed. "You're a long way from there for sure. You weren't even going the right way. Why were you going to New

York?"

"On my way to Europe. I was supposed to go to Europe with this group of girls from school. I've got all my traveler's checks and my passport in my purse. But I decided to steal one of my father's cars instead. I picked one of his favorites so it would really upset him."

"Good idea," Aunt Lucy said. "But you might of picked one that run a little better," she added. I didn't know what to say.

"Did you leave him a note so he wouldn't worry," I asked and as soon as I said it, wished I'd kept my mouth shut, which seems to be the thing I wish the most often.

"Of course not."

"Reason I asked is we left a note, at least I did so they wouldn't call the police or wonder what happened to us."

"I want him to wonder what happened to me."

"How about your mother?" I couldn't stop asking stuff.

"She's on a trip. A cruise. She won't even know I'm gone. He won't have the nerve to tell her. She'll blame him. Serves him right."

Something funny was happening to Tennessee. I believed every word she told me about little girls who walked on four feet and had calluses on their palms and growled at people. But I wouldn't know a thing right about her parents until they got asked to Sunday dinner and had to pretend to like my Mother's peach cobbler. I wasn't getting a clear picture in my mind of her mother and daddy, just people out of those TV shows that Ethel and Valinda watch about rich people.

"I left when he was asleep," Tennessee went on. "I let the car roll down the hill from the garage. I didn't start it until I was on the other side of the street at the end of the driveway. I popped the clutch to start it, just the way he showed me to. I bet he is wishing he never taught me to drive a stick."

"Where were you going?" I asked. "I mean you weren't really going to see the big cactus too, were you?"

"I don't know where I'm going." She looked at me with eyes that had dried up, but looked like they'd been punched. "That should make it extra double hard for him to find me."

Tennessee stayed in the Holiday Inn on the other side of the interchange from the Econosleep where we were. I told her that I better follow her for a while the next day, just to make sure the repair was OK. I was trying to come up with something not to lose her. That seemed fine with her. I didn't know where she was running away to, but since she didn't know either, I told her she could go to the big cactus with us. She didn't say she would, but she smiled when I asked her. If she had said no to that, I didn't know what I was going to come up with to keep her from leaving. Even Aunt Lucy admitted she was "cute as a speckled puppy in a red wagon." She's the cutest thing I've ever seen.

When we got in our room, I braved up and asked Aunt Lucy to please take a bath, which she hadn't since we left. She went grumbling in the bathroom and the next thing I heard was her screaming bloody murder. She was using the Lord's name in vain, as Mother would say as well as a few more cuss words. The lady from the office came to the door and told us to leave, that she wouldn't have people who used such foul language in her motel. I had to beg her to let us stay. That really scared me because there wasn't another cheap motel near where Tennessee was staying.

After the woman left, Aunt Lucy walked out in her wet night gown that she wore under her dress, the skin on her top half red as a ripe watermelon. I didn't stop to think she wouldn't know how to use a shower.

"I guess you got to have permission around here for hollering."

"Might be what you decided to holler, Aunt Lucy."

"I didn't decide, smart ass. That's just what come out. That woman acts a damn sight too much like your mama for my tastes." Aunt Lucy spotted the Bible open on the pillow. "I got no use for her telling me what to read before I go to sleep either. She don't even know me."

"Well, she does now. Kinda."

Aunt Lucy picked the Bible up and threw it at the wall. With all my upbringing, I had to admit that gave me a twinge, like sticking a bobby pin in a socket. Or maybe more like running with a sucker in my mouth. Not only were you doing something you were told not to do, there might have been a good reason for it. I picked the Bible up, straightened out the pages and stuck it in the drawer by the bed.

Sometimes Aunt Lucy seemed like a grownup who broke rules that didn't even need breaking. It was hard to put together what I meant. Like she was mad at people for no good reason. It wasn't that religious woman's fault Aunt Lucy didn't know how to use a shower. And she didn't seem a bit like Mother to me, but I didn't disagree with Aunt Lucy. I guess in a way I was tired of arguing with her. Aunt Lucy got so argumentative sometimes, you didn't say what you felt, just to keep down a row.

I did have to admit I didn't think for a minute that the motel lady believed me when I said that Polar would rather sleep in the back of my truck than in her motel room. But this room was a little nicer than the places we usually stayed. Had Kleenex and shampoo they gave you. Cost fifteen bucks more. Had a nice swimming pool I wasn't even going to get to use. Didn't think to bring my swimsuit anyway. Maybe I ought to throw Aunt Lucy in the pool with the bar of deodorant soap in the shower. Just kidding.

When I was trying to get her up off the commode in the morning, like picking up a puppet when you can't figure where the strings are all hooked up; it was getting pretty clear to me that she was getting harder to take care of. She had dressed herself, which meant putting her dress back on over her now half wet nightgown, but she got two sleeves on over one arm. Trying to get it back like it ought to be was worse than changing that damn fan belt with my hands hurting like I'd been beating on them with a rock. At least the car didn't wiggle around on me and cuss and call me stupid. Made me want to smack her behind, like you would a little kid, but I'd never hear the end of that. I had to wait for her to put all the pins and rubber bands in place to make her dress stay on her like anybody would care if it fell off. Tonight I'll run her a tub full of warm water and make her use it. For my money, Polar smelled a sight better than she did.

"How is old Aunt Agnes been getting along?" Aunt Lucy asked me as we finally drove out of the Econosleep parking lot. I considered ignoring her until her brain started working for the day, but that would just get me punched. I was sure hoping Tennessee hadn't left already.

"Aunt Agnes died about three years ago, Aunt Lucy."

"Humph, she did? Wondered why the old coot hadn't been by to see me."

"Where do you think you are, Aunt Lucy?"

"Riding in my nephew Benny's truck in the middle of nowhere with his smelly dog sitting beside me because he's too good to ride in the back where he belongs."

"OK."

"And why did my nitwit nephew ask me that question?"

"Forget it."

The day had just started and already I felt tired. Truth was I was already missing Tennessee real bad since I hadn't seen her since the night before at dinner. She was so sad and I had been trying to think of something to make her laugh or clap her hands again. Couldn't buy her anything because there was hardly room in that car for her. To tell the whole truth, I was imagining how nice it would be if Aunt Lucy wasn't with me. I guess I ought to be ashamed of myself for thinking that.

Lucky for me, Tennessee was just leaving. I could see her car from the McDonald's drive-through where I got breakfast for me and Aunt Lucy. She tooted and waved as she headed back up to the highway. That

Porsche went around that curve like the roller coaster at Myrtle Beach. I think my truck would have laid over on its side like Polar just did in Aunt Lucy's lap again, if I tried to go fast enough to catch her. I need me one of those NASCAR trucks for that.

"I wanted fries with that, not this wood chip," Aunt Lucy complained but kept eating the hash brown.

The little silver car disappeared in the heat waves over the pavement, just like that. Gone. Gone like a airplane in a bright sky.

"'Don't lose your head, To gain a minute, You need your head, 'cause your brains, Are in it.'"

"What, Aunt Lucy?"

"'Burma Shave.'" Another Burma Shave. Aunt Lucy must of remembered every one that was ever written on a post. "You're going to burn this old truck up trying to keep up with that little pixie," she added.

"That doesn't rhyme," I threw back what she said to me once.

"That's not a Burma Shave, Benny. That's a fact of life."

I let off the gas when Aunt Lucy said that, feeling like I just smacked a wall. She could see clean through me as usual. But the truth is, if being around her a lot wore off on me, before this trip is over, I ought to be able to see right through a tree trunk. Every time I start thinking she's nuts, I realize I can't hide a thing from her. I was glad Polar was between us on the seat so she maybe she couldn't see my face.

"Yeah. She'll have to wait for us at the big cactus," I answered, trying to sound like I didn't care. "That little piss car is pretty fast."

"She's rich as two feet up a bull's ass, you know, Benny."

"Yeah, probably."

"Probably? Not probably rich. Rich. All that stuff she bought at that Indian place. She didn't even look at the price tag. Did you see what she paid for lunch and dinner with?"

"No. Money, I suppose."

"You need to learn to pay attention, Benny. She used this little green and purple piece of paper the size of real money that all she had to do was sign it and they give her change. She pulled out a whole book of them. It wont real money. Ain't got no president on it."

"It was real money if it paid for lunch."

"And rich as she is," Aunt Lucy went on, "don't you reckon she ought to have a pair of britches to her name that ain't so raggedy?"

"That's the style, Aunt Lucy. Don't go thinking you know everything there is to know. They even got them at Belks in Summit. Raggedy jeans like that cost more than good ones."

Aunt Lucy began to cackle. "Benny baby, you're heading up the slippery side of Fool's Hill."

Soon I saw the pages of her *Arizona Highways* turning. I'd look next time I saw Tennessee pay for something. I never even wrote a check myself but I seen Mother write them. Saw Mother write them. I got to be careful in front of Tennessee not to sound like one of those Okies she threw off on. I know what Aunt Lucy was telling me. She could tell I was getting a crush on somebody who wouldn't give me the time of day if her car hadn't broken.

It was getting even hotter and dryer outside. That little silver car was long gone again, much closer to the big cactus than we were. Part of me worried she wouldn't wait for us at the big cactus, I got to admit, but part of me said she really liked me. I didn't know what there was to like about me, but I would take really good care of her. She was so young and trusting. Bad things could happen. Running away and letting some bad man pick her up. What if it hadn't been me? I almost couldn't stand to think about that. What a bad man might do to her. Maybe it would be nice to be Polar right now and not have the slightest idea of what to hope for except a new ham bone.

Aunt Lucy licked the tips of her white fingers with each flip of the pages of her *Arizona Highways*. That magazine looked like something Mother would throw away now without batting an eyelash. Over Aunt

Lucy's dead body, I can tell you that. "Just thought of something pretty cool, Aunt Lucy," I offered. "You're looking at *Arizona Highways* and I'm going to be driving down Arizona highways real soon. Cool huh?"

She ignored what I said, if she heard it.

"Damn Benny, we're too late to see the big cactus flowers. They bloom in May. Has red fruit that is good for jelly and wine, says here. Can't you just see Mona now? Have some of my cactus jelly, Mona. Good, ain't it? Don't taste like that grape crap you waste the wax on could be used to fix cracks in the highway. Or maybe I'll make me some cactus wine and tear Tendall a new butt hole."

"I don't think you'll be allowed to take any of the cactus away, Aunt Lucy."

"Did you know it takes seventy-five years to grow a sidearm?" I didn't feel like asking her what she meant because I'd find out anyway. "On the big cactus," she said in her you-are-so-stupid voice. "Took me eighty-three years to grow my side arm and I can't hit a lick at a snake with it no more."

"Eighty-four," I corrected.

"Eighty-four what?"

"Never mind."

I always got a funny feeling about stuff a lot older than me that was living. Like the walnut tree in front of our house, that grew there long before the mad dog bite. Aunt Lucy said they talked about tying her Papa to the tree like a yard dog. Except a walnut tree doesn't have a big mouth like Aunt Lucy. "Can live to be two hundred," she read on.

"That's it, Aunt Lucy. That's why you want to see that big cactus so bad. Get some tips on making it to two hundred."

"Have lots of thorns and stick every sonavabitch you can. It's probably going to stay alive till I get there. Now I got to stay alive till I get there. Don't do no good to make it to two hundred, if you feel like crap warmed over. You don't get to two hundred still feeling like you do now, Benny. Remember that. All these folks who want to live forever forget about that part of it. Like Aunt Agnes' fat daughter, Inez."

"Inez isn't as old as you, Aunt Lucy."

"Listen to me, Benny. You and me ain't on the same road now. Pay attention. Every time I told Inez she was getting too fat, she said, 'I don't care if I get a little fat. It becomes me.' A ton of lard in a molasses can don't get to call theirselves a little fat. A little fat and a little old and a little bit pregnant. Now Inez' big as a barn and I'm as old as dirt. Older than the rocks the dirt got made from. Inez' first cousin Rupert told her if he asked her to haul ass, she'd have to make two trips. That Rupert's a mess, ain't he?"

She flipped another page in the magazine. I guess for people who don't know her ways, talking to Aunt Lucy makes about as much sense as talking to a walnut tree. "Wouldn't mind making it to eighty-four though," she added.

"You already did, Aunt Lucy."

"Already dead? I hurt too bad to be dead."

"Do you really think she's going there too, Aunt Lucy, like she promised?" I couldn't believe I asked that. Maybe she didn't hear me and I wouldn't have to sound like such a fool.

"She'll be there. She's sweet on you too." She heard me a lot of times when I wished she didn't and that was one of them. Then she began to make her witch stirring her brew noise.

"A rich girl like Tennessee wouldn't give me the time of day if I hadn't fixed her car," I went on, just asking for trouble.

"Benny Foushee. Knight in shining armor."

"Stop making fun of me. You want me to dump you out beside the road? I'm your knight in shining armor. You couldn't have got out of Summit if it hadn't been for me." For some reason Polar barked real loud, right out of the blue.

"Who asked you your opinion, fleabag," Aunt Lucy snapped. "Don't bother your master with your problems. He's in love."

"Uh Oh."

I saw the little car. Just like before. Engine open. Girl looking at the engine with her hands in her back pockets. Only this time my heart fell down in my stomach.

"Keep driving, Benny. Let somebody else stop to help her. Let somebody who knows what he's doing try to fix it this time."

6

"It's so crowded in here, I need to get out to change my mind," Aunt Lucy shouted, loud enough to hear it herself.

I cut off the main road west in New Mexico, near as I could tell picking the way the crow would fly to the big cactus. When I pulled the air vent open trying to cool us off a little, dog hair blew all over the truck like somebody had busted a thistle. We were pretty stuffed in, I had to admit.

I slipped and hit this big pothole. The rusted metal on the front fender rubbed together, sounding like a dog scratching. Polar was leaning up against the door on my side, not doing any scratching. That old dog could sleep anywhere.

"What's four times zero?" Tennessee asked with a giggle.

"Zero. Zero. Zero and Zero," Aunt Lucy grumbled then added: "Tighter than a rat's butt hole over a Mason jar in here."

Can't make her stop saying that dirty stuff no matter where she is. And I don't know why Aunt Lucy had to keep harping on how tight it was. I can't help that's how Mother would put it - harping was her word - but Aunt Lucy was trying to make Tennessee feel bad for crowding us. It wasn't Tennessee's fault that car broke again. On one side of me, I'm feeling real bad about that. I did think I had it fixed right. If I could just be as good as Daddy. He'd say did you hear click-click or click-click-clank or clunk-clink. Then he'd go and fix it, just like that. I don't think I'll ever be that good.

But I got to admit, the other side of me is just tickled to death it broke and I got her here in my truck and don't have to try to catch that fast little car anymore. But there is no getting away from the fact I got Aunt Lucy in here too. And we left that fancy little car just sitting out there by itself. That's kind of confusing my thinking right now.

I was trying hard to think on Tennessee's silly riddle about the zeros but keep part of my mind on everything else I got to worry about. I think a arithmetic teacher gave us that question in school. It was a trick question. "I believe it might just be one zero," I said out loud, just waiting for Aunt Lucy to call me an idiot. Tennessee clapped her hands, but didn't tell me if I answered her question right.

"Far as I can tell," Aunt Lucy snorted, "there's four zeroes sitting in this truck. And there'd be a lot more room if there was one zero."

Now, that made me mad. I couldn't help it. "And how good is the one zero who come up with that brilliant answer at driving this truck, huh? That scrawny old zero can't even reach the pedals much less drive." All I got for an answer to that was a growl that was so real sounding Polar let out a yap. She really pisses me off when she bitches about something I can't fix.

"I feel like we're riding in a space ship," Tennessee said real cheery. "Like E.T. buzzing down the road to Earth."

Now, that was nice. "Pretty nice thing to say to my old truck," I said, giving the dash a pat, "since you left your Porsche space ship sitting in the desert." The glove box fell open. Tennessee ignored what I said about her daddy's car and started catching all the tools and junk falling out of the glove box. Leaving that car was really bothering me. A bunch of bad guys could just pick it up and throw it on a flatbed.

"I love the sound this truck makes. It sounds like it's really powerful." All I could hear was the hole in the muffler getting bigger. She sure acted like she was in a good mood.

"Hey," Tennessee offered, "I want to take all of us somewhere really, really neat. A place I went once on a school trip. Don't worry. It's on the way to the saguaros. Here's your first hint. It's about North Carolina."

I was looking out, thinking this was about as much like North Carolina as the moon. Not enough cows out there to even play cow poker, or dead car poker, which I sure did better at than her silly riddles. But Tennessee never fussed at me. That was good for something.

"Here's the second hint," Tennessee added. "We're going to see two graves."

I couldn't help but shiver at that. I thought about that round grave with Grandpa in it that Aunt Lucy can't find. Some famous person must have died of thirst out here, like this pretty little girl might have done if I hadn't picked her up.

"Cat walked over your grave," Aunt Lucy said to my shiver. She decided to shout like we were the ones who were deaf: "I ain't ready to jump in mine yet," meaning her grave, I guess.

"Hint number three," Tennessee went on. "Neither one of the graves are people graves."

"Oh brother," I said out loud. "We got some of those on our farm. One's got Uncle Tendall's shotgun that me and Aunt Lucy buried for meanness after he shot my pet dog. And one's got a headless mad dog. And there was Great Uncle Fab who buried his mules and let the buzzards eat his daddy. Or maybe old man Glover down the road who shot his broke down tractor and went and bought another one to bury the old busted one with."

Tennessee was laughing and bouncing up and down like a singing sparrow at all my graves without people. Man, if my truck was back there by the road catching tumbleweeds like that silver car, I wouldn't be able to laugh at anything. I'd be near about crying by now.

"You're getting warm," she squealed. "They used bulldozers to cover up one of the graves. And you missed a big hint. E. T. That's your hint. E. T. OK, that's all the hints you get." She crossed her arms like she'd made up her mind.

"E. T. is buried out here? I didn't think E. T. was a real person. I thought he was just a movie character."

"Now you're being silly, Benny," she said.

Not silly, I didn't say out loud. Stupid. "I give up," I answered.

"I'm not telling," Tennessee said with a clap. "Doesn't work to just give up."

Boy, I'm glad I never got those bucket seats I always wanted or I'd be in real trouble getting four across. Tennessee put her little leather suitcase behind my seat after I raked out all the bottles and burger wrappers. Her suitcase had a "T.B." in gold on it. "B" must be her middle name since her last name is a "G"—Gentry like in gentlemen. I even pulled out Valinda's bent umbrella that got left after the prom. I said it was Ethel's, just so I could keep on being a perfect liar, like she'd care if I already have a girlfriend. Had.

The truck bed was full up too with all those bags of stuff Tennessee had bought. I put the rocker on top of them real careful, hoping none of them would go blowing out or get busted inside. Now I had to look backwards as much as forwards, waiting for all that stuff to go rolling down the highway. I sure didn't expect to see Mother and Daddy come riding up on me back there anymore. My home seems like the inside of my truck right now.

Never saw anybody who did that much shopping. There's no way to lock a crook out of those little Porsche cars. Tennessee seemed a lot more worried about not leaving behind any of the things she bought than she did about her daddy's fancy car. Maybe because the car was his, not hers. Boy, I'm the other way around there.

Another thing was kind of embarrassing. Tennessee had to have noticed Aunt Lucy by now, being how tight it was in the cab. Maybe Polar was getting blamed, but I don't see it as a dog smell. I just hope Aunt Lucy keeps her shoes on. Her feet smell like flowers that got left in a pot too long and I tell you the truth, her breath smells like she's been chewing on her socks.

The way Polar was setting next to my window, he was near about behind the wheel. This guy going the other way looked at us funny, I bet because he thought a dog was driving. I'll admit I'd rather have Tennessee in Polar's spot or Aunt Lucy's, instead of over by the other door. No offense to Polar, but I did need something on one side didn't have people legs, and on the other had real short legs, so I could get to the gas pedal and shift the gears without poking anybody in the stomach with my elbow. Made me wish I'd left the shifter up on the column like it come. Came. Most people wouldn't ride to the filling station this stuffed in.

That fan belt must have been old or something. It come apart as bad as the first one, came apart, and them know-it-all Germans didn't see fit to put in but one extra. Those. Not as smart as they think they are, if you ask me. I don't care how fast they go through curves. Give me my good old American truck any day of the year.

We were coming up on a town, Wonita, New Mexico, it said on the sign. I noticed right off the Christmas decorations were still up in Wonita and it was the middle of the summer. Daddy would say something cute to the first person he saw like "Got your decorations up early this year, huh? Finished your shopping too?" Boy, Tennessee could say "yes sirree" to that one. She's done enough shopping for ten Christmases and more friends and relatives than I've got for sure.

Didn't look like Wonita would be the place to find a Porsche mechanic. About like Summit, kind of hicky looking. I didn't know what to say to Tennessee about the Porsche, to ask if she was sure she didn't want to get a tow truck. Or get another new fan belt and try again. If I'd had a chain or a real strong rope, I'd have tried to pull it along. She was quiet as a mouse about leaving that car.

After a while Aunt Lucy got quiet too, for a change. Probably asleep. I can't believe Tennessee just jumped up in my truck beside Aunt Lucy when I pulled over. She said to me: "I'm sorry. I broke it again. Did I drive too fast?" I didn't answer "yes". I just said: "That's all right," knowing damn good and well driving too fast wasn't the reason it broke. Pretty dishonest of me I guess. But to tell the truth, I didn't know why it broke again. Couldn't impress her anymore as Benny Foushee, ace mechanic, that's for sure.

To tell the rest of the truth, I didn't know what I was going to do to impress her. I sure couldn't answer her riddle about E.T. I just lucked out on that zero business. The amazing thing, at least to me it was amazing, she wasn't even mad at me for screwing up her car. She just jumped in my truck the way Polar did the night of the prom and didn't fuss about anything. That was nice. I never knew a girl like that.

I like to think Polar picked me to be his master that night in the rain when me and Valinda were all dressed up and I let him jump up in the truck out by the highway. Boy, Valinda sure unpicked me after that when he put his wet paws on her pink dress. But I got me a good dog. I'd do it again the same. And Tennessee seems to like me better than any girl I've ever known. And she likes my dog too.

While I was staring at a bird nest inside a busted plastic Christmas bell, waiting at what seemed to be the only stoplight in Wonita, New Mexico, as well as the longest one in the world with nobody going in either direction but me; I saw a barber pole. I pulled in the parking lot, just a reflex; my brain sure wasn't working. Polar and Aunt Lucy went over like dead trees in a windstorm; Polar right square in my lap and Aunt Lucy in Tennessee's. I sure hope my shotgun door doesn't pop open one of these times I turn too fast, and dump Tennessee out. Something else for me to worry about. I'm getting like my mother.

I guess the reason the barber pole caught my eye was I was bad in need of a haircut. If you listened to my mother, I needed to get my hair cut a week before we left. Then Aunt Lucy got cute and called me her niece in front of Tennessee. Even Sue Faye had something to say about my hair not looking good, nice as she was, everybody on my case except Tennessee who hadn't mentioned it one way or the other. If she even noticed. The hair down the back of my neck was sticking to my skin. No cool air in this truck at all. Sweating like a whore in church, Buddy at the filling station would say. I just kept it long at home to piss Mother and Daddy off, to tell the truth.

Wait, if you want the rest of the real truth, I turned off more than anything because I was getting confused about what to do next. That's it. I wasn't used to being the one who had to do all the deciding. I had to figure out what to do about that car we left outside of town before it got too far behind us. It's a stolen car really. But I don't want to report it and have them come looking for Tennessee. And I kind of wanted to look a little nicer for her. Hard to tell if she was noticing how I look which I guess isn't much like a movie star like my daddy looks.

"Can you amuse Aunt Lucy while I go get my hair cut?"

"Aunt Lucy can amuse herself," Aunt Lucy snapped.

"Yeah, and everybody in the truck but Polar. It's just an expression, Aunt Lucy. You're the one who keeps making the looking like a girl comment to me."

"What predicament?"

"Come on with me, Mrs. Williams. We'll find something to do while Benny gets a haircut." Tennessee talked right in her ear then opened her door and jumped to the ground.

"Don't pee on my head and tell me it's raining."

"Get out, Aunt Lucy and quit talking ugly. It's too hot to set in the truck."

"What come unglued? So hot out here my shadow done set down to rest."

"Out, motor mouth."

I went around and pulled Aunt Lucy to the ground and got her balanced. She's like a cat you finally get in a cage then you can't shake it back out. Tennessee still hadn't mentioned finding a mechanic or a tow truck. It's like she just forgot she ever had a car once she got all her stuff put in my truck. I reached over in the bed and mashed the bags with my hand like I knew what I was doing. Well, I guess my truck does hold more. Wonder if that made me look kind of manly to her, mashing the bags I mean. Sort of in charge of things.

Tennessee tugged on Aunt Lucy's arm till she got her headed towards this store with a OPEN sign on the door. I sure appreciated her helping me with Aunt Lucy, taking her to the bathroom and everything. She acted just like she was already a member of my family or something. I just stood there watching her go across the lot with Aunt Lucy and it made my heart start fluttering. I sure wasn't thinking she was like my sister. Now that perfect little behind in those ragged jeans had dog hair stuck all over it. I'd like to run up and brush it off. Probably get smacked.

When the seat got empty, Polar spread out on his belly and groaned. I left his door open so he could take his time getting out. I think he might be tired of riding. Maybe tired of people. Nutty people. And speaking of nutty people, I was about to meet a real one I wasn't even kin to.

When I went in the barbershop, there was this guy sitting in the barber chair that I thought was next. But Pete the barber just laughed when I asked what about him and told me to sit down in the barber chair, that Ferrell Graywolf was like a piece of furniture.

"Ferrell, get your rear end out of that barber chair. Might have another customer come look in the window and think I'm busy. Get back over there by the TV." Pete didn't say it in a mean way.

Ferrell grinned, a sideways grin like Robert Duval in *Lonesome Dove.* His cowboy hat was tipped a little, his skin so tan it didn't look like he spent five minutes of his life inside. He hopped in the customer chair across from me. I was glad Tennessee didn't see him. He made me feel a little jealous. A real cowboy, first one I'd seen.

Ferrell watched Pete drape a white cloth around my neck, looking ready to kill bad guys, the whites of his eyes a little yellow. His clothes were like mine, straight out of the washer with no ironing. I rolled my eyes down to check out his feet. He was wearing sneakers instead of cowboy boots. That didn't seem right to me.

"I was the king of the cowboys, wont I, Pete?"

Pete hesitated for a split second from pinning the cloth over my shoulders.

"Yes sir, Ferrell, you were the king."

Ferrell's smile got wider, but he lost that part in *Lonesome Dove* real quick. His teeth were almost all gone except for a couple of rusty looking stobs on the bottom that didn't sit straight.

"When I get up to them Pearly Gates, Pete, I'm gonna tell them I knew Roy Rogers, and they're gonna let me right in. Ain't that so, Pete?"

"Yeah, and you tell Saint Peter I knew him too, Ferrell," Pete answered.

"Knew who?"

Just as I was thinking that maybe Aunt Lucy would like to meet Ferrell, that they seemed to have a lot in common, the door to the barbershop came flying open and crashed against the wall.

"Can I help you, Ma Barker, or is this a holdup?" Pete asked Aunt Lucy.

"Ain't got room for my rocker in that truck no more," Aunt Lucy shouted in my face. "You planning on dumping me out in the middle of Hell and running off with that woman?"

"Granny, you done made my customer's ears turn blood red. Are you related?" Pete started snipping my hair that was falling in my lap and on the white cloth.

"Benny Foushee, I'm aggravated as a cold fly on a hot dropping. That girl near about bought out that store before I could turn around." Then Aunt Lucy squinted at me and added: "Well, at least I can see his ears now. Look a little burnt."

Ferrell got so tickled, for God knows what, that he got choked and started beating on his knees. Aunt Lucy was staring at him now. Jesus, please close her mouth for me, just this once, please Jesus. I could see Pete in the mirror as he started cutting around the back of my head.

"Get up, Ferrell," Pete ordered, "and give the nice old lady your seat." Ferrell jumped up like he set on a hot stove. Aunt Lucy looked at the seat like it might burn her butt too.

"Have a seat, Granny," Pete said, "while I tell the story Ferrell come in to hear. You might get a kick out of it too."

To my surprise, Aunt Lucy set down. I never saw her mind anybody. She was looking at Ferrell like she liked him. I hope not too much, because I sure didn't have room in the truck for him too. Ferrell tipped his head sideways and narrowed his eyes like he was trying to read backwards the name of the barbershop on the window. s'eteP.

"s'eteP," I said out loud. I can be as big a idiot as a real idiot.

"Huh?" Pete said.

"Uh, said up in the mountains, we might hit some snow, even this early," I fumbled.

"Yes sir, you might," Pete answered. "I seen butterflies on the snow in them mountains. Monarchs."

"I saw butterflies," Aunt Lucy corrected.

"There is a lot a deer up there, ain't there, Pete," Ferrell started up again. "And some elk. There is a lot a elk up there." I don't believe Ferrell could read the name of the barbershop front-wards.

"Isn't, not ain't," Aunt Lucy said.

"Lot a deer, Ferrell. And a lot a elk."

"He dropped his bombs, right out there in the desert, Pete."

"Yes sir, he did. Now here comes your favorite story, Ferrell. Here's the true story. It was 1944. Before my time. My grandpappy told me about it. A B-29 bomber landed right here in Wonita. Engine broke so he dumped all his bombs out in the desert because he was afraid he was going to crash and blow hisself to kingdom come. He come barreling in and slid clean off the end of the little dirt runway outside of town, rolling hisself up in cactus…"

"He bombed the cactus!" Aunt Lucy shouted.

"He dumped his bombs," Ferrell repeated with a pretty un-cowboy like giggle. At least he heard things better than Aunt Lucy even if he didn't have a lick of sense.

"Did anything important blow up?" I asked, thinking of all the movies I saw.

"Naw, not here in Wonita, it didn't. Military guys went out to the desert in a bunch of army trucks and hauled out the bombs under covers. The bombs weren't live, so we was told. Then Grandpappy said a bunch of government guys come in here, stripped everything out of that B-29, trying to get it so light it could take back off without a real runway. According to Grandpappy, they didn't want no local help fixing it. Secret stuff. Then one day, he seen that big plane go. Took it forever to get up in the sky. Used up a mile of desert past the end of the dirt runway before it was gone. Nothing left behind but a story."

"He saw, not seen, that big plane go," Aunt Lucy corrected.

"Did you seen him fly off to the sky, Pete?" Ferrell asked.

"Naw, don't forget I wasn't born yet, Ferrell. I just heard about it. It's about the only thing that ever happened in Wonita, New Mexico. When they set that big bomb off on purpose before we bombed the Japs, must have been over fifty miles from here, Grandpappy said it shook the pictures off the walls. It turned the sunrise into a rainbow."

"Shook the pictures off the walls," Ferrell repeated Pete and stood up, swiveling his hips like Elvis.

"Whole lot of shaking going on, Ferrell."

"Got to go, Pete."

"See you later, Ferrell."

"I'm going to get on my bicycle and come out shooting."

"You be careful shooting, Ferrell."

"Yes sir, Pete. I'll be careful because you told me to."

Ferrell got up and walked to the door, as bowlegged as a real cowboy. He went around the corner then I saw him ride across the lot on a bicycle.

"Cutting off that long hair, boy," Pete told me, "makes a redneck a white neck. Be careful out in the sunshine."

"Yes sir. What's wrong with Ferrell?" I asked Pete.

Aunt Lucy butted in. "He's missing so many buttons, his britches going to fall down."

Pete got tickled. He seemed to kind of like Aunt Lucy and just ignored her when she corrected his grammar. I thought his B-29 was another World War II bedtime story for her, but she was wide awake.

"Lot of people got their heads messed up by what happened over near Alamogordo, Granny. Some people like to tell it that Ferrell's mama had him passed out drunk on cactus wine, that he was blue as the sky when they found him. Indians are bad to drink. Holding up the buildings all over this town for sure. But my Grandpappy told it come about because Ferrell's squaw mama lived over near the test grounds, in this little mud house that nobody knew was there. And being she was pregnant, she was inside, and she was the only one in the family didn't get burnt up. Ferrell comes in here, watches my TV and makes me tell him that B-29 story about twice a week. But I say to myself, there but for the grace of the good Lord go I. Lord Almighty, look at the pretty thing talking to him now. Ferrell just died and went to them Pearly Gates for real."

When Pete took the white cloth off my shoulders, I leaned forward to see outside. I felt the hair go down my shirt like a bunch of little knives. Ferrell was stopped on the sidewalk, straddling his bike, talking to Tennessee. Made my heart start beating fast seeing him do that. I reached in my wallet, but when I looked out again after I gave Pete his money, Tennessee was gone. Ferrell was riding away by himself on his bicycle. I pulled Aunt Lucy up and pointed her out the door, closing it real careful behind me.

"Did you catch on to that story?" Aunt Lucy asked me when we got outside. "I generally favor a good story."

"I think so, pretty good," I answered. I didn't get the point of it, I was ashamed to say.

"All the things I lost, I miss my mind the most. Are you going to leave me here with that crazy fellow, Benny?"

"He don't want you, Aunt Lucy."

"He doesn't want me," she corrected.

"Maybe I ought to throw out your rocker and throw in his bicycle." She punched my arm, but she didn't give me one of her cackles. When we got back to the truck, Tennessee and Polar were already inside. Boy, was I relieved to see her in my truck. She jumped down to the ground to let Aunt Lucy in.

"What did that guy on the bicycle say to you?" I asked Tennessee after I pulled Aunt Lucy away from looking at her rocker in its black bag, sitting on top of a bunch more new bags. Tennessee was twisting her curly blond hair like a rope and stuffing it under a new straw hat. She had put on dark glasses.

"He said he saw me on television. I'm afraid he's going to tell someone he saw me, Benny. Maybe he went to get the police."

I looked down the road where I could still see Ferrell, wobbling on the bicycle, his shape wiggling in the heat coming up from the pavement.

"He's retarded," I told her. "Don't worry. Nobody would listen to him. Maybe your daddy would but he isn't going to find your daddy out there in the desert." I tried to see Tennessee's eyes through the dark glasses. She looked even smaller with her hair gone. Now we could pass as Aunt Lucy's two sons if she didn't have on red lipstick and glasses that were shaped liked two pink hearts.

"My father is trying to find me, Benny. I just know he is. I got a speeding ticket last week. The patrolman asked for the registration. He knew it was my father's car." Tennessee was starting to sound like a little kid. "Don't make me go back home," she whimpered.

I told her not to worry; I promised never to tell on her to her daddy. How could she think that I would make her go back home? I hadn't even asked Pete about getting the Porsche picked up for fear he'd ask too many questions. "You can hide out with me until the end of time," I added. She got a funny look when I said that. I hope I didn't get too forward.

"My father put my photo on TV."

"Safe and sound with Ma Williams and Benny the Kid and their trusty dog, Iceberg," Aunt Lucy piped in with a chuckle. Should have known she'd be hearing what I didn't want her to hear. Where did that come from in her old brain? Like we were outlaws or something. I thought of the trip like taking a vacation, or I was trying to. But that was the nicest thing she ever said about Polar - trusty.

All of a sudden, Tennessee put her arms around my middle and hugged me. She didn't let go, like if she did, she would drown. I knew I had Aunt Lucy's eyes on me right then that were worst than my fourth grade teacher when she caught me scratching my initials in the water fountain. I didn't know what to do with my arms. I never wanted privacy so much in my life, I can tell you that, and there was Aunt Lucy.

I would like to be Harrison Ford right then, wearing my pilot's cap and taking that B-29 down that runway, bowling down every damn cactus in my way and heading right up in the sky with one hand on the controls and the other arm around Tennessee's shoulders, watching Aunt Lucy turn to a speck on the ground underneath us. But I can tell you that your imagination doesn't work worth a hoot when Aunt Lucy won't take her eyes off you.

"If you don't see fit to feed me soon, Benny, I'm going to swallow whole the first edible critter that walks by."

Boy, that's a picture that will make that B-29 take a nosedive and slide on its belly and spit me out like a owl ball. Aunt Lucy eating something alive. Tennessee let go of me and went dancing off like a butterfly I had let out of my hand. I felt my heart break and fall in a pile of pieces in my stomach, I really did. I didn't ever want to eat again.

I took Aunt Lucy and Tennessee to a lunch place down at the end of Main Street in Wonita, the opposite way that Ferrell went peddling. Tennessee held on to the big black purse while I loaded Aunt Lucy back out of the truck, expecting her to hit me any minute. Hard to tell what Aunt Lucy really felt about Tennessee. She seemed to have gotten over her mean fit about all the stuff Tennessee bought for now, leaning on her as she made her way to the picnic table. I didn't see how anybody couldn't care for Tennessee, but I was about to quit trying to figure out Aunt Lucy's feelings about people. I think she might have married Ferrell if he'd propose to her.

One more thing for me to do before I left town that's driving me crazy. Crazier than the hair Pete got down my back. Me and Polar walked back to the filling station across from the barbershop. Whether Tennessee cared or not, I couldn't stand leaving the Porsche like that. I didn't want the filling station guy to see my truck and charge me for the tow in. And to tell the truth, see Tennessee was with us.

I tried to explain to this guy who was changing the oil on a new Chevy pickup, that I would appreciate it if he would get the Porsche towed in to the station, that I was giving the owner's daughter a ride home. The guy looked at me like I was talking pig Latin. He pulled out the loosened oil pan plug and the oil started pouring down, missing his drip pan by about a foot. Maybe this guy's mother drank some of that cactus juice and watched the bomb go off too. He seemed about as smart as this guy who used to work at the Summit Exxon named me, I guess. I don't think nobody, anybody in this town has got a lick of sense, except maybe Pete the barber. I just get around a filling station, as Mother would say, and my grammar goes to pot.

"I'm sure the person who owns the Porsche will pay for the tow," I went on, though he was cussing pretty loud, looking at the mess he'd made of his shoes. "It's a nice car to some people, but I wouldn't have one." Then I added before I walked away, "Tell the owner that his daughter is OK. That she is with friends." I had to force myself to walk back to the eating place because my legs wanted to take off running like Polar. I felt like such a stupid ass. That guy might not have paid attention to one word I said.

Back at the lunch place, Tennessee got out another one of the purple and green checks without the president's picture to pay for our hamburgers. This Indian looking guy behind the counter squinted at it, grunted, then gave her change. I don't think he liked it very much.

When the burgers got ready, I carried them over to this picnic table where Aunt Lucy and Tennessee were beside each other. Aunt Lucy was already talking a mile a minute, but I did like Uncle Tendall does and cut her noise off before my ears. One minute she was jealous of Tennessee; next minute she was making me jealous with Tennessee listening to every word she said. But when Aunt Lucy saw the food, we might as well have been invisible.

Our table was under a plastic shelter that creaked from the heat. Polar ran around, peeing on all the signposts at the intersection. He went behind some bushes and I saw dirt flying out when he was finished. Dogs sure don't have to watch their manners. I wished Tennessee would take off that silly hat and glasses, at least in the shade, so I could look at her better. First thing she took her burger back to the Indian and had him open it back up to put a pickle on it. I never have the nerve to ask for anything special. She's pretty brave in that way.

I got all tingly seeing what it said on those signposts. For sure we were a long way from home. I saw signs to Utah and even to Las Vegas. "Utah

Beach," I said out loud. "Uncle Tendall said Utah Beach was where the Americans landed. Only I don't think Salt Lake Utah is the same thing." What happened next made me wish I'd kept my big mouth shut.

Tennessee was poking holes in her hamburger bun with her finger so it looked like cheese in a cartoon. "I went there. To Utah Beach," she said. "It's in France. I went to the very same place that Mrs. Williams' brother Tendall landed in World War II. Utah and Omaha were the code names. It was my second trip to France when we went from school for a month."

"Aunt Lucy told you Uncle Tendall's boring story? She slept through it herself most of the times he told it."

"It wasn't boring. Not to me. All my grandmother says to me is wash your hands, every time I pet an animal. I can't remember her sharing a single story. Mrs. Williams believes the Germans shot him while he was swinging like a pendulum and he didn't get a one of them."

Tennessee giggled like Aunt Lucy had told about a pin the tail on a donkey game.

I couldn't believe that Aunt Lucy told her about Uncle Tendall and the church steeple. "That wasn't quite how Uncle Tendall told it," I added. "Of course, he was the only one of us there." I glanced at Aunt Lucy, but her eyes were shut.

Tennessee began telling about a town in France: Sainte-Mere-Eglise. The Virgin Mary was in a stained glass window in the church with parachutes falling behind her. They hang a dummy of the man who got caught on the steeple and have a celebration.

"Was the dummy named Tendall Foushee?" Aunt Lucy shouted and made us both jump. I guess she wasn't asleep.

Tennessee wrinkled her nose so cute when she was thinking. "I don't think so. I don't remember. John Something. He was in a film and Red Buttons played him. Is this a riddle?"

"You mean we don't get to go to Saint Mare Egg List," Aunt Lucy asked, "to celebrate Tendall Foushee Day?"

Tennessee laughed, almost like the bark of a little dog. "Maybe poor Tendall got caught on a different steeple, Mrs. Williams. France has lots of cathedrals." She described tall cliffs near Utah Beach that the American soldiers had to climb. "My Outward Bound teacher was the chaperone. He kept talking about the cliffs and the Rangers. He said to us, three points, you have to have three points: two hands, and one foot or the other way around. As if the most important thing in the whole wide world is climbing. Because that's what he knows how to do. No one cares about climbing when they're getting shot." Then she said something I couldn't have imagined, that she was so disgusted with the chaperone that she imagined she was the bad guy, hiding in the bunkers. She was the German and she was shooting all these Americans coming up the side and he was one of them. I couldn't say anything to that. I couldn't even pretend to kill Americans.

"Did you see the pasture where Uncle Tendall's cows were?" I asked just as Aunt Lucy's head fell forward and she started to snore. She couldn't stay interested in anybody's story but her own. Tennessee looked confused by my question.

"There were lots of pastures," she answered. "They were full of holes where the bombs dropped. The holes were supposed to have been on the beach for the Allied soldiers to hide in, but the planes missed with the bombs. They leave the holes there. That's the way they do it in Europe. They leave it like it was and let the grass and flowers grow over it. It looks like a big, deep wound with daisies in it. Stuff grows back with a funny color like hair on a head wound. You know what I mean?"

"Sure, a big funny colored wound with daisies in it." I had no idea what she meant.

"But the ground doesn't grow back. The craters will always be there. And all the crosses. Crosses as far as you can see, all alike except a few have a Star of David for the Jewish men who died. All the dates on the crosses are almost the same. They died within minutes of each other. Somebody kept really good records of dead people. I don't know who did that. Maybe they made it up."

Tennessee could get real talkative. She had sure done a lot of things I'll never get to do, taking trips and all. But right now she was supposed to be on another trip to Europe with a bunch of her rich girl friends and here she was in my truck with my dog and my crazy old aunt. I'd sure like to be the fly on the wall when she tells her friends about this trip someday.

"Tendall's hiney has a belly button," Aunt Lucy piped in. She may of just woke up, but her mouth didn't take long to start moving. "That's where he got his Purple Heart. Right in the butt. But I promised not to tell Rupert."

"We already know about the Purple Heart, Aunt Lucy. What about the cows that needed milking? Do you think he made that up too? Why didn't you tell Daddy?"

"You know, Benny. I'm thinking that might be another man's story. I bet you sure as I'm sitting here, that the real hero died. Tendall swiped a story off a dead man."

"My grandfather took a sword off a dead Jap," Tennessee put in, not catching what Aunt Lucy meant. "He has a picture with another soldier and they have a Jap between them, but the Jap's dead. My father calls him a Jap too. We have a girl at school, but we call her Japanese or we get in trouble. My father has the sword in his office."

There goes Tennessee's bottom lip out again and it's not over that dead Jap. Every time she mentions her daddy she gets upset but she keeps bringing him up for some reason. My daddy says some funny, corny things, but I guess he's not that interesting. I do catch myself thinking of how he'd put things. I didn't know that until this trip. If he saw that bracelet of Tennessee's, he'd say something un-cute like: "Emptied the whole jewelry box on your arm, huh? Got room on there for the kitchen sink? Need a plumber to hook it up for you, Ma'am? T. R. Plumbing, at your service, Ma'am."

I'm not good as him with corny stuff, but I'm kind of glad of it. I saw him mess up once. Buddy and Joe the boss were playing checkers at the filling station and Daddy said: "Led any good rooks lately?" Even I'm smart enough to tell the difference between checkers and chess because I saw that Russian guy on TV. They looked at Daddy like he was a loony tune. Sometimes I just think things and don't say them and most of the time, I'm glad.

"Your grandpa stole a sword and Tendall stole a story," Aunt Lucy put in. "Or two or three," she added. "Can't trust a thing he tells."

Well, he did get shot somewhere by somebody I wanted to say but didn't. Aunt Lucy was talking to herself, mostly saying "uh-huh, yep, uh-huh," ever since she figured Uncle Tendall swiped his church steeple story from a dead man. She jabbed my arm with her sharp old finger, warming up one of her meanest looks.

"Benny, I'm putting this together. Now I'm thinking that church steeple was as much bull crap as the cow pasture. Name was John, not Tendall. Wait'll I get back and tell that lying Tendall what Tennessee told me. The real man was so famous they made a picture show about him. Put him in the church window like he was Jesus Christ. Tendall Foushee, naw, he's the one over there, hanging up in that tree with a bull's eye on his fat butt. They rolled him off to the hospital in a wheel barrow."

Aunt Lucy started laughing her most hateful laugh. I have to admit I felt bad for Uncle Tendall and he wasn't even there. "How come you won't let Uncle Tendall be a little bit of a hero?" I asked. "Seems like getting shot is pretty bad no matter where the bullet hit. Don't you think a bullet in the butt hurts bad as one in the shoulder?" I couldn't stop now.

"Hurts worse if you set on it all the time. Rupert acts like Tendall's his daddy. Tendall wouldn't give either one of us air in a jug. I was the one raised Rupert."

"I mean he did get a Purple Heart, Aunt Lucy," I kept on though my brain was telling my mouth it shouldn't. "He jumped out of a airplane right where the enemy was."

"Tree limb stuck in his butt. Called it a bullet hole. Purple heart and a yellow soul. A lot of things in this life hurt worse than a bullet hole in your butt. All you got to do is bleed in a war to get a Purple Heart." Aunt Lucy was getting so mad at me for talking back to her that her white face was turning red and she was getting red splotches all over her arms. "That sonavabitch don't know what hurting means, Benny. Takes a woman to know how to hurt."

Aunt Lucy was so loud I wanted to hold my hands over my own ears. I really wanted to cover Tennessee's. Aunt Lucy sure couldn't take anybody disagreeing with her. I guess I didn't usually. I sure didn't know when I said that about Uncle Tendall being a little bit of a hero, what I was setting off. She never give Uncle Tendall credit for nothing. Anything. Gave. Well, I sure lit the fuse on the Aunt Lucy bomb that didn't bounce dead in the desert.

"Talks me into leaving Rupert with Aunt Agnes when it like to have broke my heart, telling me that sweet boy was better off without me trying to be a mother to him. Telling me I was past the age for any man live to marry me. Then no sooner than we get to Wilmington, Tendall takes off in his fliver. I got no money, nowhere to sleep and go to the toilet. Dropped me in a parking lot at a eating place. Said go find us some food. Drove off with my spare dress and sweater. Made like he was coming back for me. I didn't see him for two years.

"Come to find out later he took off with these two men he come upon in a drinking place. On their way to join the Air Force. Me, I was scratching through the garbage cans trying to come up with something for both of us to eat. Watching the people inside at the tables till I got shooed off like a vermin. Found these two hard rolls and picked off the green spots so Tendall wouldn't see them."

Aunt Lucy's voice got softer, the shrillness gone. Tennessee looked at her like she didn't want to miss a word.

"All these little sparrows hopping around me, eating them green spots like they tasted good. I was thinking, God knows every sparrow that falls. That's the bullshit they taught me in Sunday School. I thought that for the first three hours. Three hours in the rain took care of all the church bullshit I had drummed in me. Then I figured God didn't care one tweet about me or them sparrows, neither one."

She finally stopped talking and was breathing hard like she'd been running. "I think the way the Sunday School lesson goes, Aunt Lucy, is the sparrow has to fall out of the sky if God is going to notice it." There goes stupid Benny again and here comes Aunt Lucy. Just like throwing a stick for Polar.

"Well, you can have your God, Benny, and your Uncle Tendall too. They can both rot in Hell. I'm the one got a purple heart, right here inside me. I slept in the bushes with it raining like a mule pissing on a flat rock. Clothes all stuck to me. Stinking and burning from bug bites. Tendall always getting to go places. New Jersey. Fort Bragg. France. Just because he got born with two balls and a dingaling. Aunt Agnes acting like it was OK too and her a woman. He was just doing what boys do naturally, Lucy, so that was just fine. When I get back home from this trip, he'll make like he already saw the big cactus first. Lying sonavabitch. Well, he didn't see it. If Obediah hadn't come along and took me in, I'd of starved to death for all Tendall cared. And he never saw a big cactus."

I never saw Aunt Lucy this mad in my whole life. She never told me this part of her story before. "I thought you met Uncle Obie when he was your welding teacher," I put in.

"I told you the truth. I told you most of the truth. Obie seen me sleeping in the park three days before he took me to his room. I had to take up with somebody." Her face was still glowing red. "Worked my skinny little behind off, making them big boats. All they said to us was faster, faster. We make them, they sink them."

Tennessee shivered and it was as hot a day as I ever felt. Then she spoke out about what made her tremble: "That must have been awful, Mrs. Williams. Not having any money at all. No money for food and clothes and nice things and to pay for a place to sleep out of the rain. And having to move in with a strange man because you didn't have a house to go to. At least he was kind to you. I'm really sorry you got treated like that by Tendall. I could never love my brother, if I had one, if he treated me like that."

Aunt Lucy stared at Tennessee. It didn't seem there was anything to break that stare. I don't think I could have asked another thing about what happened to Aunt Lucy if you paid me money for it. For sure, that wasn't like me. Bad as I needed money of my own right then. And I wasn't sure by that look she was giving Tennessee, if she wanted to shake her or hug her. I sure know what I wanted to do.

"Tendall is three eggs short of a omelet," Aunt Lucy sputtered. I saw three-egg omelet on the menu at a place where we ate. She meant that Uncle Tendall wasn't even one egg. He was nothing. She always has to dress up what she feels with sayings. She ought to just say she hates Uncle Tendall. For good reason. But how come she wants to beat Uncle Tendall with storytelling so bad?

I learned one thing; I never want to make her really mad at me. I hate to admit I even thought about driving off and leaving her in a parking lot, just to be funny, when she was really being pokey. I planned to turn around and come right back. There must be a God somewhere that kept me from doing that.

After Aunt Lucy finally stayed quiet, her chin stuck out so far she looked like she was pointing across the street. I was looking at the sides of both their faces: Aunt Lucy like a sparrow and Tennessee pretty as the caramel-colored lady on Mother's church necklace. Neither of them looked at me.

Aunt Lucy reached in her big black purse, scratched around, then opened her white palm out to Tennessee. There were two clear shiny stones there. "When Tendall come back from the war, he brung these shiny things to me, trying to get back in my good graces. He didn't have no woman to cook for him at home was why."

"Those are really pretty, Mrs. Williams. What are they?"

"Cape May Diamonds. You can have one of them. I don't want them no more."

"I don't believe they are real diamonds," Tennessee said softly, "but they are very pretty."

"They're rocks out of the Cape May River, is what they are. That sorry brother of mine wouldn't buy me a real rhinestone. He thought he was fooling me. I didn't cook for him but forty years after that."

Tennessee picked up the shiny rock from Aunt Lucy's hand, putting it inside a little purse that was inside the little bit bigger purse she carried over her shoulder, where the purple and green checks were. I still couldn't believe what I was seeing. Daddy always said Aunt Lucy never gave anybody anything but a hard time. She gave me a lot of chocolate covered cherries he didn't know about. But nothing like that shiny rock.

"Thank you very much. Are you certain you wish to give one away, Mrs. Williams? We haven't known each other very long."

Aunt Lucy nodded. "I'll be checking out soon and I want it in good hands. I'll will the other one to Ethel. Benny'd just shoot it in a pea shooter."

"I'm very flattered, Mrs. Williams. I'll get it put on my charm bracelet where I keep my special things." Tennessee held up her fist and shook her bracelet. In the bunch of dangling things: I saw a gold jumping horse and a blue glass hummingbird before she dropped her arm.

Her special things. I guess Benny Foushee better get going thinking of something to hang on that bracelet. Boy, she sure was young to have already collected that many special things. And I don't believe they come from the likes of Burt Crawling Rock's Combination Trading Post & Hot Dog Stand where we were setting.

"Why'd you stick that pretty yellow hair up under that hat?" Aunt Lucy asked Tennessee. "That hair's the prettiest part about you."

"Because I'm not interested in being pretty."

"Me neither," Aunt Lucy answered with a shrug.

All of a sudden, Tennessee put her face in Aunt Lucy's lap and started crying her heart out. I don't think I could have moved when she did that if the tree we were under was falling over. This was the saddest little girl I'd ever seen in my life and I didn't know why. I watched Aunt Lucy pat her on the back. For some reason, Aunt Lucy's story must of broke her heart.

Polar came running to me and jumped up with both feet in my lap like he read my mind. I reached over for what was left of Tennessee's hamburger, which was most of it as usual and Polar swallowed it, pickle and all, the pickle she went back and made the Indian who sold it put on it and she didn't even want it. Polar got mustard on his nose. I got to admit that right then, for a just a split second, it felt good to be with a guy for a change.

Tennessee kept sobbing away and Aunt Lucy kept patting. And I still couldn't come up with an answer to that riddle of Tennessee's about E. T. That's how lame I am. Or figure out what she had to cry about. Or why Aunt Lucy stayed so mad at Uncle Tendall after all this time. She got a husband out of that trip that I never heard anybody speak ill of which is saying a lot in our family. I thought shooting my dog Bear was about as bad a thing as Uncle Tendall ever did. And Tennessee leaving that little car out there by the road without even a thought about what might happen to it. I guess women see things different. I was real confused.

Right then, as Daddy would say, I felt like a bucket under a bull.

7

We left behind Wonita, New Mexico without a peep from Tennessee about her daddy's Porsche. The wrecker that had been parked by the side of the station was gone somewhere. I sure hope that guy went after it. The truth is I'm a lot better at dumping oil on my feet like he did than I am at acting like a customer. After Tennessee put all the stuff she'd bought in the back of my truck, that Porsche was no more than a Co-Cola can she threw out the window. She didn't even bother to put the top back up, not even that canvas cover after she got her shopping bags out. I didn't want to sound like her daddy, but that car was filling up with flying stuff like a big old washtub. Got to remember the town name—Wonita, because that's where to find that car.

While I was driving along, thinking we had enough World War II for one day when I wasn't even in school, we came up on this place called Alamogordo. Tennessee said turn off quick because she wanted to show us something. You know how when you're a little kid and you start walking in a zigzag when you don't want to get somewhere? Tennessee acted like that about getting to the big cactus. But I didn't feel too much rush anymore either unless the big cactus had a place where I could park Aunt Lucy for a while and go off by myself with Tennessee. Tennessee had two black eyes from all her crying.

"There," she said with one of her claps when we got out in front of a big building. She pointed at these two little tombstones. "I thought I remembered it said North Carolina. See, Benny. Ham, the Astrochimp, died in the zoo in North Carolina."

"My birthday," I said without thinking as I read the tombstone. "That monkey died on my birthday. January 19."

"Naw. He come back to be another monkey," Aunt Lucy put in.

"Ham the monkey was only twenty-seven," I did the arithmetic. "Hope I live longer than that. How long are monkeys supposed to live?"

"I don't know," Tennessee said, wrinkling her nose. "His girlfriend lived to be forty-one, see. Minnie. I guess Ham died young. They were mean to him. They shocked his feet when they were training him and tried to make it all right by giving him a banana pellet. He bruised his nose when the space ship landed. Chimpanzees don't have any fun being famous. After he landed, he reached out to hold a man's hand. He was scared. That made me so sad. He knew they used him in case something went wrong. They didn't want to risk letting a real man die."

There she went, getting all worked up again as Daddy would say. And I thought I was bad, talking to Polar like he understood every word I said. Tennessee thought that monkey was smart as a astronaut.

"Take it from me," Aunt Lucy grumbled, "Women live longer than men." She added: "That monkey is a lot bigger hero than your Uncle Tendall, Benny, who's outlived two good men." Aunt Lucy started fussing about Uncle Tendall again. I wish she would quit it. Tennessee was already getting used to being confused by her, I guess. I don't know, for some reason, and it wasn't just because Tennessee was so cute, I wanted to give her a hug right then. She wanted me to see the monkey grave because he died in North Carolina where I was from, and she didn't even know it was on my birthday. But I didn't hug her. I'm so chicken I hate myself.

Before we get back home, I got to make me up a good story to tell about that monkey. I'll get made fun of since it was a monkey, I bet. Maybe I better keep this story for the front porch, not down at the Exxon. When I get the chance and Aunt Lucy isn't around, maybe I'll tell Tennessee about the lost round grave on our farm. I know I promised not to tell it, but Aunt Lucy will never know. I could make a good story out of it if I tell it right. But I can't let Aunt Lucy hear me tell it. Tennessee likes stories with people dying in them.

While we were riding back through pretty much nothing outside again, Tennessee studied the things on her jingly bracelet, resting her feet on the dash and her head on Aunt Lucy's shoulder. At least her eyes weren't teary anymore and she had washed off the black in the Ladies room at the monkey grave store. She also added a gold circle with a green glass center to her bracelet that took five of those purple and green checks. Glad I didn't offer to buy it and have to borrow that much from Aunt Lucy. Tennessee said the green center represented the hole the atomic bomb made when it blew up in the desert and melted the sand.

Aunt Lucy had a leather bag of colored rocks that Tennessee bought her dumped out in her lap. She started reading us stuff out of this pamphlet that a weird looking guy with a beard gave her outside the bomb place where they wouldn't let us in. *What they don't want you to know* was the name of it. Tennessee told us you could only see the bomb place twice a year: "My teacher says it's not healthy in there even now."

That pamphlet is the only thing Aunt Lucy's read since we left except her *Arizona Highways* and her place mats. Well, damn near every sign between here and North Carolina. Never even picks up a newspaper, which she studies front to back at home every time I bring her one. She read to me and Tennessee from the pamphlet, just like she used to read about Reddie Fox when I was a little kid: "'The Atari Burial grounds holds five million video games, buried under a concrete slab. And you think corporate America isn't trying to hide something toxic?'"

"Oh no! That's cheating," Tennessee exclaimed. "You read the answer to my riddle about the second grave without a person in it."

"Why did they bury video games?" I asked, hoping it wasn't a stupid question. So that was the other grave that doesn't have a person in it.

"Because all the game could do was make E.T. walk in a circle. Dumb and boring. You kept E.T. from falling in holes. My father knew the rich guy who got poor after he designed it. At least that was what my father said caused the burial…"

Her bottom lip went out and I don't think it was because she was thinking about poor little E.T. falling in holes. She's got some kind of big time problem with her daddy she calls father. Even I can tell that.

"Oh, I see," I said, not seeing much of anything.

"'The toxic games,'" Aunt Lucy read on, "'were discovered to contain enough plutonium to kill every man, woman and child in America on Christmas morning. But a national tragedy was averted.' And they didn't even have Tendall Foushee in their army."

"You didn't read that last part, Aunt Lucy. You stuck that in yourself."

Tennessee balled up and put her head in Aunt Lucy's lap, her bottom lip still sticking out when she fell asleep. Because she brought up her daddy by accident, I'm figuring. To tell the truth, I wasn't that eager to see a grave for five million video games. I'm eager to get a shower soon because I'm itching like crazy down my back from my haircut. I'd like to know what Tennessee's daddy did to her that was so bad she'd steal his car and run away. He's sure not stingy with money. But I don't see how I could just come right out and ask her. Not yet anyway.

Me and Polar are just looking out the windshield wishing we were somewhere else anyway. I'm crazy about this old dog. Guess that's the difference between us guys and girls. We don't need a book to read out of or a bunch of shiny stuff to be happy. We can just use our imaginations. I sure wish Tennessee's head was in my lap instead of in Aunt Lucy's, that's my imagination. And it's pretty darn good to think about. I don't know what Polar's imagining. Maybe a new bone. Or a girl dog. To be really truthful, I would spend my last dime to put something on that jingly bracelet that said Benny Foushee was in her life. Couldn't be that honest out loud. Except to Polar.

"Says the desert sky lit up around here from red to purple to white." Aunt Lucy went on talking, looking up from the pamphlet and pointing out the windshield. "Looks like it turned brown on the ground to me. They don't let on about that in that *Arizona Highways*, but I'm seeing it with my own eyes. What if they done that to the big cactus, Benny? Turned it to a shadow like them Japs, after we come all this way."

Tennessee's head wiggled like Aunt Lucy had a yellow cat in her lap. The straw hat and sunglasses had fallen off to the floorboard. I wasn't paying much attention to Aunt Lucy. I was trying to get back to the main road without waking up Tennessee so I wouldn't have to go to that other grave.

"I believe you took a wrong turn, Benny."

"How can that be, Aunt Lucy? I watched the signs real good when I turned off."

"I believe you done took a wrong turn into Hell. They meant to test that big bomb out here, but they slipped and blew up everything."

Aunt Lucy started nodding like one of the plastic dogs that sit in people's back windows. At least that's where they sit in Summit, North Carolina, which was starting to look real good in my mind right now. Aunt Lucy was right about stuff being burnt up. Saw what used to be a nice old '46 Chevy pickup out there, burnt up so bad part of it made a metal puddle on the ground. I hated seeing that. They don't make them anymore.

Just as I was wondering if there were bones in the burnt houses, I saw the bones of a poor old horse, got locked up and couldn't get out when his barn got hit. Guess he wouldn't have anywhere to run even if he could of got out. Or maybe he ran inside thinking he was getting away from it. Poor old horse, like Ferrell Graywolf's mother. Going down a gopher hole wouldn't have got away from this. I'm real glad Tennessee didn't see the horse bones. She probably would of cried some more.

I stopped my truck and backed up, trying to find a way around the rocks in the road. There was too much stuff to dodge. Just when I was thinking there wasn't a bit of color left in the whole world, I saw bright blue fly up over us, the brightest blue I've ever seen. It flew out across the burnt stumps like Technicolor got mixed up with black and white. The noise it was making was nothing but pissed off mad.

The blue bird circled over and around my truck, not far from the roof. It dived toward Polar behind the glass and he snapped into the empty air. Polar was stomping all over me, trying to get to the bird through the window. The bird kept fussing, louder and louder, until I opened the door and let Polar out. He ran in circles barking. Then all of a sudden, he came back to my door, scratching it like a mountain lion was after him. When I opened it, he squirmed in my lap between me and the steering wheel and started whimpering. The noise that the bird made was so loud, I could hear it over the wind with the window shut. I never saw Polar so scared.

"Polar, it is just a big blue bird."

"He thinks you done it," Aunt Lucy said.

"Done what?"

"Devil told him, you the one blew up the world. That bird's a evil omen. He's got a black head, telling you he got burnt. Blue jays ain't got black heads. He's too big to be a real blue jay. And that ain't a blue jay noise he's making. You stole this little blond girl. You could go to jail for that, Benny Foushee. You better take her back where she belongs."

"Stop that crazy talking, Aunt Lucy. I didn't mean to steal her. I couldn't just leave her beside the road. She's as trusting as a grasshopper in a chicken house."

"Tell it to the judge."

"You stop teasing me. I didn't mean to do anything bad. We're in a predicament here and it's on me to get us out of it. And then you got to start picking on me when it's all I can do to drive through this shit in the road…."

"And where would she be if she looked like me or your sister Ethel?"

"Standing beside the road waiting for the tow truck, OK? Now shut up. I got to get this figured out." I backed up and tried picking my way around the burnt stuff. It was slow going, a lot of crunching and thumping and banging underneath.

"Might as well go back home, Benny."

"How come, Aunt Lucy? We're near about there."

"Listen to me! Because somebody done dropped that big bomb and burned up the big cactus."

"Naw, Aunt Lucy. Something like that couldn't have happened. Not in America. That was a long time ago. I'm not giving up now with us this close."

"There's nothing left, Benny. This *Arizona Highways* was wrote a long time ago. The book that man give me I been reading is a lot newer. I ain't seen one living thing in a long time, except that loud mouth devil bird." Polar began to whimper from my lap. "We come a long way for nothing, ain't we, old fellow?" Aunt Lucy said.

Out of the corner of my eye, I saw her petting Polar's rump with one hand and Tennessee's blond head with the other. She hadn't petted Polar this whole trip. There was white in his left eye as he rolled it up towards me. He didn't know what she was up to. I thought I saw Tennessee open and shut her eyes.

I couldn't quit, not now, after going this far. Just when my head was starting to hurt from trying to think out of this, a brand new pickup came up on us fast, coming from the other direction. It slowed down when it got into the stuff in the road that we were in, but then it went right on over it, whump, whump, whump. He's got 4-wheel drive in that new truck I bet.

"This is the Big Lick fire," a soft voice said. "It burned out almost a month ago." It was Tennessee. She sat up from Aunt Lucy's lap and yawned out loud. "I hadn't seen how bad it was before. First they said it was lightning. Then they said it was a campfire or arson. People set it probably." Tennessee had to be pretending to sleep, as much noise as we were making.

I dropped my truck in the granny gear and drove on the shoulder, around this big rock. I had to make it over the hill where the new truck came from. What do you know? That ugly, brown west started turning into the sweetest, greenest green I think I ever seen. I'm not kidding. I felt like that guy in that movie *Paris, Texas*, the guy that couldn't talk after he walked out of the desert. That green stuff out there gave me the biggest relief of my life so far, I can say that. Like getting that last report card and not failing nothing. Anything. For sure the fire didn't get all the way to the big cactus. But I was different from that man coming out of the desert. I wanted to talk now, to give Aunt Lucy a piece of my mind for lying to me.

"It wasn't a bomb, Aunt Lucy. Look outside now. You listen to Tennessee. You got to learn to listen to people who know more than you do sometimes. It was a plain old forest fire, burned without even having a forest. You were telling me a story about things blowing up. And a devil bird. It was just a old bird whose nest got burnt up. Telling me a fib. That's not like you to do that, Aunt Lucy."

"Naw, I wont. I was storytelling to pass the time."

"You had me believing I was seeing what a bomb blew up, Aunt Lucy. You're supposed to tell me the truth."

"You thought it was from a bomb?" Tennessee said, real loud. "A bomb?"

"That's the answer," Aunt Lucy said. "The A-Bomb. You're the one needs to pay attention, Benny Foushee. See? Even that moron cowboy got it right."

That made Tennessee giggle for some reason so old Polar wiggled all the way out of my lap and across Aunt Lucy to lick her in the face. He didn't have the nerve to lick Aunt Lucy. Or want to, I guess. Polar stayed in Tennessee's lap and he looked bigger than she was. I saw her suntanned arm around his white back. I sure knew where my old dog was coming from.

I can just hear Mother now, clear as a bell: "Benny, what in the world were you believing her for?" As wrong as my mother can be about almost everything, she would have said to me: "Benny. Please. Be a grownup. Lucy has slipped beyond repair and we all know it. Imagining a forest fire was the atomic bomb? In the United States? And it's not been on TV? Come now, Benny."

I better not forget that again. Lucy has slipped beyond repair and we all know it but Aunt Lucy. But I don't intend to tell her that. Arguing with Aunt Lucy is dangerous. I looked at Tennessee and she gave me the cutest wink I've ever seen. Our little secret about Aunt Lucy and her A-Bomb. That made me feel so good, you'd think she'd kissed me or something. But my good feeling had some bad feeling behind it. The feeling that Aunt Lucy was getting too crazy. And boy, am I glad we're getting close to that big cactus. I just saw the sign. Only two hundred more miles.

Late in the afternoon, we crossed this line called the Continental Divide. Tennessee told me it meant the water on the east side of the line ended up in the Atlantic Ocean and on the west side in the Pacific. I asked her what water, but she was already nodding back out again. That girl must never sleep in the bed in those fancy places she stays in. Shame to waste the money. I couldn't sleep that much riding in my truck if you tried to make me.

I kept seeing these yellow road signs with black cows on them. Kind of looked like a bull, but it could have been made to look even more like a bull if the guy who painted it wanted it to, if you know what I mean. I was trying to remember in Drivers Ed what the sign shape was supposed to mean. Had to memorize that to pass the test because the test didn't show the cow. Yellow color. Diamond shape. And then all of a sudden, I didn't have to try anymore to come up with what it meant.

I came up over this rise and there was a whole herd of them, not black on a yellow sign, but dirty white on the gray pavement, standing right square in the middle of the road. Man, if they knew how bad the brakes were on this old truck, they wouldn't have stopped there.

"Jesus Christ," Aunt Lucy screamed, her short legs braced against the dashboard. "You trying to make us enough hamburger for a year." Tennessee rolled off Aunt Lucy's lap down in the floorboard with Polar on top of her.

The cows started moving out of the way so slow you'd think they never saw a truck before, kind of like they were even more retarded than a cow is. But, good thing, I didn't hit me one. That would have been the end of all of us, right there. "You OK, Tennessee?"

Polar was licking her in the face when they both crawled back up on the seat. I hated to admit it but we came really close to a bad accident. I saw a really messed up car once, towed into the station after it hit a deer and those cows are three times as big as a deer. Even the baby one that mooed at my truck and ran to its mother was bigger than a deer.

"Open range is what it's called," Tennessee explained as she looked out the windshield. "Cattle can roam any where to look for grazing land," Tennessee talking just as matter of fact, after I almost killed all of us. I mean she would see one of those mushroom clouds and start telling you how it's the third one she saw.

"Well, I could tell the cowboys in the movies what that cow sign means," I said. "It means the people out here in the West are too damn lazy to put up fences. Ought to spend some of the time they spent putting in that sign building them a decent fence." To tell the truth, I felt pretty mad about it being no big deal for their cows to be out in the middle of the road. Pretty soon I got rid of my shakes enough to start my truck moving again.

One of the cows wasn't going to need any more grass, laying on her side with her legs sticking out, stiff as a turned over table with tits hanging under it. Hope she didn't have a baby. Glad I wasn't the one did it. The others were eating grass around her like she was just a rock that rolled over in their way. That's what I mean about how retarded cows are.

"Could stand her up, throw on a tablecloth and make a piece of furniture out of that one," Aunt Lucy said when she saw it. "Poor old soul. Little one done sucked her tittie the last time." Sometimes when she was thinking the same thing I was thinking, it made me realize, for better or for worse, that we were kin. Glad I wasn't the one said it.

"Hadn't been dead long enough to start stinking or draw buzzards. I always wondered," I added, just making more conversation to calm my nerves I guess: "Why do buzzards fly in circles over something dead? It's not like they're looking for it. They already found it."

It got real quiet in the truck.

"No buzzard experts here, I suppose," I said.

"They're trying to pick the best place to land," Aunt Lucy answered, "so they won't get their claws dirty. Buzzards are real dainty creatures like your mama."

"Thank you, Aunt Lucy."

"I'm not sure you deserved an answer."

"I'm not sure my mother deserved to get picked on either, for something she didn't do, especially when we're talking about buzzards. Wonder what the cows do out here for a drink?" I asked. For some reason I needed to be talked to. To be honest, I was still shaking. I could of killed us all. My parents and Tennessee's parents would read about it in the newspaper and cry their hearts out.

"Looks like all their water decided to run to the Pacific Ocean," I added.

"They bring water in trucks." This time Tennessee answered me.

"Putting it into these big metal tanks. I'll show you one when we pass it. I had a boyfriend who drove a water truck. Just to make my mother mad. I didn't really care for him. He works over where I keep my horse. He would know about the buzzards going in a circle. I'll ask him."

Damn. She could have gone all day and not told me that. Boyfriend. I guess I was just dreaming I'd be her first boyfriend. Another thing I hated, always being the one driving because I couldn't turn and see what expressions were on people's faces when they were talking. That was a big part of knowing what they were talking about, I was starting to learn, the expression on their faces. Having to look at the road was as bad sometimes as talking on the telephone when it come, came to really knowing what a person meant to say. That did give me a hurt, I have to admit it, kind of a mad feeling actually, even if she didn't like him much. Boy, I bet Benny Foushee would really make her fancy mother mad, off on her cruise with her rich friends.

Tennessee kept talking and I kept watching the road, a lot more careful, I might add. I come to find out, came to find out, what had stopped that Big Lick fire completely: a riverbank where the flames turned left and right but didn't go forward anymore. Fires could jump roads, but a river did them in, even if it wasn't wet enough to sink a hook. I'm pretty sure Aunt Lucy still believes it was the A-Bomb that went off out there and probably always will, but that's OK. She might even tell Uncle Tendall about it but she's not going to fool me again. Her favorite and only nephew, probably the dumbest person on earth next to Ferrell Graywolf, has caught on to her now.

When Tennessee pointed out one of the water tanks that had about a million cows around the pond beside it, I got mad all over again about the boyfriend, just seeing that stupid water tank. Never knew I could be such a jealous sonavabitch.

I stopped early at this little motel because I hadn't seen one in a long time and I was rubbing my itchy back on the seat like a cow up against a tree. After I got done showered and combed my new short hair, the three of us set out in front of mine and Aunt Lucy's room, Aunt Lucy rocking in her own rocker that I took out of the plastic bag.

The motel was all one level with the rooms in a row. There wasn't a fancy motel in town for Tennessee so she stayed there too. They gave her a room down at the end, but she came up to set with us outside of ours. She still had on that hat and sunglasses because she believed she was on television. I borrowed a broom from the motel lady to sweep the busted up burnt tumbleweeds off all of Tennessee's plastic bags. While I put them back in straight in the truck bed, Tennessee just set there, playing with the special things on that bracelet.

Pretty much every thing they had planted around the building had died in the heat except the green ends of a few pink petunias or pansies or some such. First time in my life I bet, I couldn't tell you the name of a single tree. None of them looked very good. Kind of twisted up and dusty without many leaves. Looked like they were really suffering. I know I would be if I was a tree and couldn't keep rolling along. Rather be a tumbleweed.

Tennessee explained to us about the big jaybird we saw where the Big Lick fire had burned. It was a different kind of blue jay, I forget the name already, a girl's name: Stella, but I do remember its head was supposed to be black. It wasn't burnt. I got to quit believing anything Aunt Lucy tells me. Telling me that bird was the Devil. Crazy old woman. And the reason the bird scared Polar so bad, Tennessee said, was it was making a noise like a hawk coming after him. That's how it got the place to itself, making scary noises. Not that anything else would want that place.

Tennessee knows a lot about the stuff out here. But I guess I could pretty much impress her driving through North Carolina. I know a lot about tobacco and there isn't a stalk of it out here to tell about.

I was deciding if I could put together some stuff about Tennessee by asking her some questions. I knew she didn't have any brothers and sisters because she already told me. I wasn't going to start by asking about the boyfriend either because I'd just get mad again. I would like to know why she was so mad at her daddy. Then she beat me to the draw with her own question.

"Do you have a steady girlfriend, Benny?" Oh boy, I thought, then Aunt Lucy decided to answer for me.

"Benny called off the wedding."

"Aunt Lucy, I wasn't planning to marry Valinda."

"Benny told me it was because she got fat."

"I did not say that, Aunt Lucy. I told you that Buddy at the station said look at a girl's mother and you'll see if she's going to get fat. And that Valinda's mother is fat as a hog."

"What's your mother like?" Tennessee changed the subject. I waited to make sure Aunt Lucy wasn't going to answer that one for me too. She had her chin on her chest, making a noise that sounded like running water. There was no water anywhere except out of the spigots inside the room so I knew she was really snoozing.

"She's a pretty nice lady," I said, nothing bad coming to my mind. "You wouldn't think that, listening to Aunt Lucy, but Mother means well. Daddy says she married beneath herself."

I kind of liked talking to Tennessee because I was starting to feel like I didn't have to worry about what I said too much. Wasn't like that for me with Valinda. A pretty darn good feeling.

"My mother thinks everybody is beneath her," Tennessee put in quickly. Her voice could even sound like a pout when she started talking about her family. Maybe she asked me about my mother so she could fuss about hers. "Even the mothers of the girls at school are beneath her, and I bet some of them have even more money than she does. And certainly they went to better schools. My mother wasn't academically talented. The beauty queen type."

Funny that "beneath her" meant the same thing in my language as it did to Tennessee. There's just a lot of layers underneath the old bedspread. "What does she do?" I asked.

"Do?"

"I mean work. Or whatever. Oh, I guess you mean she doesn't have to work because she already has so much money," I answered my own stupid question. Me and Tennessee were so different, I didn't even know how to make conversation sometimes so as usual, I kept babbling. But she never tried to make me feel bad about the dumb things I said. "My mother works at home," I kept on, "doing wife things, cleaning and sewing and cooking and stuff. Aunt Lucy is pretty hard on her there."

I had a picture in my mind right then of yellow and brown banana pudding hitting the pig trough and hearing them sniff and snort and eat without a complaint. It wasn't that bad. And I was actually getting a little tired of French fries myself. A little of Mother's macaroni and cheese wouldn't be all bad right now. Especially if it was the first day we had it. Hit it with some ketchup and it's pretty good. Never hear the last of it if I mentioned that to Aunt Lucy.

"My mother mostly plays tennis," Tennessee went on. "Last year it was golf until she got in a fight with my father about the pro calling her too much at home."

"I'll try to picture Mother playing tennis." I closed my eyes. "Naw, can't do it. Never saw her wearing anything you could play tennis in. Now, I could see her swinging a giant fly swatter. Mother can really nail a fly. She probably could hit a ball pretty hard if she ever tried. I came home one day and she was out in front of the house swinging a sledge hammer at this old bath tub that Daddy took out of the house and promised he was going to get rid of for about forever."

Benny the babbler just couldn't shut up. Maybe because Tennessee always smiled so pretty when I was babbling along: "Mother even managed to bust one side out of it by herself. 'There,' she said. She was really tired, actually had sweat on her face, which I hardly ever saw." I made my voice go up high like Mother's: "'At least now he can't drag it out in the pasture to water the cows we don't have any more. At least I ruined it.'" Tennessee clapped her hands. God, I loved that.

"I took the hammer away from Mother and busted that old tub up in a million pieces, pieces light enough to pick up and haul off to the trash pile. In case you're wondering, old-fashioned tubs have iron inside and break up like a big old egg if you hit them hard enough. Mother made me my favorite cake for dinner, white with pineapple between the layers. When nobody was looking, she kissed me on top of my head and whispered 'At least we don't have to advertise right out in the front yard that white trash live here.' Now why in the world did I tell you that story? I say a bunch of things out loud I ought to just think."

Tennessee smiled big when I said that, a nice smile. "I like hearing your stories," she said. "Tells me what a different place you come from." That comment made my heart beat faster, I'm not kidding. I didn't even know I knew how to tell real stories. Just the fib kind.

"My mother always promises to take me to the South," Tennessee went on. "She loves Charleston, South Carolina and the big plantation homes in North Carolina with the azalea and camellia gardens. She's really into architecture." Then she changed the subject. "I can still smell that fire." I don't think she was very happy when she started thinking about her mother or her daddy. Just couldn't help herself. Maybe her mother and daddy are divorced. I don't hear her talking about them doing things with each other.

"Yeah, me too," I sniffed and said. "Not much here to interest a fire. Those cactus out there look like long haired dead old ladies."

"Don't count me out yet," Aunt Lucy hollered and made both of us jump about ten feet. Knew she'd been quiet for too long. She's hard to get away from.

Aunt Lucy reached in her purse, pulled out half a dinner roll and pinched off pieces for the chirpy sparrows that were hopping around in the parking lot. The birds rushed over near her feet, more and more of them coming for the bread. They made a lot of racket, chirping and flapping and pecking each other, but I don't believe Aunt Lucy could hear stuff that little. Don't usually think of sparrows as very colorful, just kind of brown colored, but out here in the sun they looked pretty bright. Everything here looks pretty bright after what we drove through today. Polar had his chin down between his front paws, watching the birds. It was too hot to do much chasing.

"Look at that big bird," Tennessee pointed across the road. "It's just a raven, but watch, when it turns in the light, it becomes silver." The crow lit on a dull black rock, his feathers shimmering like he was wiggling.

"He picked that dull rock so he'd look good," I said. "Kind of like picking a seat by a fat ugly guy."

Tennessee giggled and when she did, the crow dropped a white blob on the black rock. Then I heard a familiar voice say: "Everything black is nasty." Aunt Lucy's white face had hardly a speck of color left. "Crows, tar, starlings, coal, buzzards…" Polar started beating his tail when he heard her voice and all the sparrows went up in a tree, so many of them the tree looked like it had leaves. "Them crows is like rattlesnakes," Aunt Lucy hissed. "Rattlesnakes throw their noise around like the place is crawling with them. Listen at that sorry crow noise, going ever which way. Far as I can tell, there ain't but one."

I looked at the crows across the highway and I bet I counted a dozen in a minute. Tennessee tapped my arm and gave me another big smile. Another little secret.

Aunt Lucy's bread tossing wasn't very good either so most of it bounced off her feet. Didn't stop the sparrows though. I wondered if Tennessee was thinking about Aunt Lucy sharing her moldy bread with the sparrows in Wilmington. I don't believe it crossed Aunt Lucy's mind.

"I think my eyes is getting better," Aunt Lucy went on, "I can see clean across the highway."

"It's the air, Mrs. Williams. There's no pollution out here."

Aunt Lucy pointed at a little brown spot on the back of her hand. "I used to be that color all over before I turned white. Guess I'm turning into a angel."

"Does that mean that Polar is an angel, Aunt Lucy, because he's all white?"

"That dog is about one hair better than one of his turds."

Polar ran up to her when she said that like she had called him Rin Tin Tin and Lassie all rolled up into one. The sparrows shot back in the tree like yoyos. Polar put the stick he had been chewing on at her feet then crouched down, beating his tail in the dust. She rubbed him on the head with her shoe. I had given up; it was on the wrong foot again. Her feet must of got shaped so her shoes felt better on the wrong feet.

"I had me a good dog once named Black Jack. He would steal a fresh egg every morning from Tendall's hens and come put it on my porch. If it started in to roll, he would slobber on it some more so it would stick."

"Go get a egg, Polar," I told him. Polar barked and ran off through the bushes, looking for a egg.

"I don't want no rattlesnake egg neither," Aunt Lucy yelled.

"Baby rattlesnakes are worse than grownups."

"How's that, Tennessee?" I asked.

"They don't know any better so if they bite, they use up all their poison at once."

"Coral snake'll do that," Aunt Lucy grunted. "If red touches yellow, you're a dead fellow."

Tennessee looked at me with x's for eyes again. "I'll tell you sometime. It's a Foushee family story about a story. About Uncle Tendall and a red and yellow snake."

Aunt Lucy had her *Arizona Highways* back in her lap. It was starting to come apart. I don't know where the A-Bomb pamphlet went. I hope she lost it for good. It kind of messed up her mind.

"A ten year old cactus plant can be so short, you might step on it," Aunt Lucy read, "but a full grown one can be taller than a five story building." She looked up. "I recollect Papa saying that he saw one taller than three houses stacked atop each other. I reckon I'm about to find out. Hard to believe." Aunt Lucy had a nice smile for a change.

"I had a story book about a saguaro," Tennessee remembered, "when I was a little girl. The cactus got old and died. It didn't fall over so a lot of creatures came to live in it. It was almost as if the cactus wasn't really dead."

"Like Papa said: a five story apartment building," Aunt Lucy said as she looked across the road again. Papa didn't say that; *Arizona Highways* said that.

Even though the crows were jumping around like giant fleas, Aunt Lucy stared out like a blind person. I could see now why her eyes didn't see better. In the bright light of the sun starting down, her eyes were white washed with color bleeding through in spots, like she needed somebody to scrub her eyeballs. "Sometimes the sun makes me see black spots," she read my mind before she started reading again. "Nasty spots." Her mouth might have shrunk to a buttonhole in her old age, but it sure didn't seem to have any effect on how much came out of it. "When the woodpeckers make holes in the cactus and leave," Aunt Lucy read on like we were her children waiting for our bedtime story, "the elf owls come and live in the holes. The flowers that smell like overripe melons get pollinated by nectar eating bats…"

"Bats!"

"Benny's scared of bats."

"That's your fault, Aunt Lucy."

"These are honey bats not blood bats. Don't be so ignorant."

My face got red; I could feel it. Hope I looked like the sun reflecting on the cliffs. I could be ignorant all by myself. I didn't need Aunt Lucy reminding me and embarrassing me about it. Nobody said anything for a while until Tennessee jumped to her feet and announced: "I'm bored. I'm going to walk into town before dark and see if I can find a throwaway camera." She started walking away.

"Wait. I'll keep you company," I said and got up fast.

To tell the truth, I was real glad for a chance to get away from Aunt Lucy and be by myself with Tennessee. Polar ran down the shoulder in front of us. Him too, I guess, but he would follow me right through the door to Hell then run around in front and lead the way.

"She's OK by herself?" Tennessee asked.

I looked back at Aunt Lucy in the chair. She looked like one of the old lady cactuses we walked past, but she had her own hair pinned up. I never could figure out how she still did that right. I sure hoped she could keep doing it for herself. Truth was, that wasn't the only thing she did by herself that was starting to worry me. I'd die before I'd wipe her bottom.

"She has to be OK," I answered Tennessee. "She can't go anywhere by herself. She'll be in the same spot when we get back."

"I'm not going to get old," Tennessee said.

"Me neither."

I finally braved up and took her hand to hold while we walked. She didn't pull it back, but I was afraid she thought I was trying to be like a daddy and I knew how she felt about him. At least her bottom lip wasn't sticking out. I've been trying to imagine what she felt like when she hugged me, but it was over with so fast.

When we got to town, we started going in and out of the stores. Padford. Padford wasn't any bigger than Wonita. Lot of hick towns out West when you get off the big highways. I followed Tennessee down the aisle of a drug store in a part I never went through before, all the girl stuff. She kept handing things to me: nail polish, a blue hairbrush, little boxes full of colored circles until I had to go back and get a cart to hold it all. A person didn't have to look to find this part of the store, just close your eyes and follow your nose and it was like being in a room full of sweet smelling girls.

"Sure smells good here," I said. She wrinkled her nose like she didn't like it. "I mean I think it smells good."

"I hate the smell of White Shoulders. It smells like a funeral. It's such a cheap smell." She picked up its box and put it back like it burned her hand. "The name brand perfumes are locked in there."

"What's a cheap smell? I mean is it like something that would be on a tacky woman with peroxided hair who missed with her lipstick." I looked around real quick to make sure one wasn't right behind me. "You don't get much for twenty-five bucks," I looked under the White Shoulders box. "Could get a couple cases of oil for that."

Tennessee didn't laugh. "This girl at school. She was half of a twin only her sister was normal and she was cripple. She dumped White Shoulders all over herself and jumped out the window. I mean she couldn't jump. She dragged herself out on the balcony at the dorm and crawled over. The place where she landed smelled like White Shoulders. Even after it rained."

I think Tennessee had been spending too much time with Aunt Lucy. That sounded like a Aunt Lucy story. Actually the perfume smell was starting to make me feel a little sick to my stomach without even thinking about a dead girl. I liked the way the Exxon smelled better. A lady came and unlocked the case and Tennessee started pointing at boxes that were even smaller than the White Shoulders and a lot more than twenty-five dollars. She put five of them in the cart.

"I'm tired of this store," she said. "Let's go across the street."

I followed her like I was Polar only he had stopped outside the store and set down. I wouldn't have minded doing that too but I knew I would do anything to be with Tennessee, even stupid girl things. We heard a siren and while I watched a sheriff car with a big star on the door go by, Tennessee ran into another store. She sure was scared of the police seeing her. I wouldn't think a town this little would need a sheriff.

This store had more interesting stuff, it said made by Indians. And it was a lot more expensive than the drug store. Smelled better too, more like being outside when flowers are blooming than that funeral flower smell. Tennessee bought a lot of bags of stuff, like bird and people statues that they had to wrap in plastic bubbles. One of them was called a dream catcher. I think they were what Mother would call dust catchers.

At the next store, she looked at these things made like two rugs put together with a slit to stick your head through. Ponchos. Clint Eastwood wore one in that old movie: *The Good, the Bad and the Ugly*. Each poncho had a tag that told how many hours it took the Indian to weave it. The sales lady, who probably thought Tennessee was having trouble deciding which one of the three to buy, said: "You look lovely in the blue green one with your blond hair and brown eyes." Tennessee had taken off her hat and glasses to get her head through the slits. She grabbed her hat off the counter and stuffed her hair back under the hat like she had to hide something ugly.

Tennessee picked up the other two ponchos and asked: "Where is your dressing room?" When she finally came back out, her heart glasses back on too, the lady asked real timid: "Did you find one you liked? I have others in the back." I know what the sales lady didn't know.

Tennessee put them on the counter and started signing the purple and green checks. "I'll take all three," she replied. I knew she'd do that.

The lady looked at me and smiled while she folded the ponchos, wrapping each one in tissue paper. I wonder if she thought I had anything to do with all the money Tennessee had. I wondered what I would do right then if I really was a rich man. Would I say: "Dear, I think two will be enough." Or "Yes, go to the back and get a couple more. She can have as many as she wants." All I could really do was shrug and look at my feet. I didn't know how to feel like a rich man. But I was pretty good at being a packhorse.

When we got outside, she said: "Oh, I almost forgot the camera."

She crossed the street, going back in the drug store. I think Polar was wondering why I didn't bring the truck.

I never saw one of those throwaway cameras before. I don't go to the drug store that much to know if we have them in Summit. Tennessee said she forgot her real one. Every time I tried to pay for something, Tennessee took her checks out and handed them to the cashier first. I was starting to feel a little funny about that. It wasn't a good feeling, kind of inferior though I don't think she meant to make me feel that way.

She went down an aisle we hadn't been on before and stacked me up with a bunch of dressed up bears in boxes. She seemed a little old for stuffed animals but I didn't mention it. When Tennessee came to town, it was probably the biggest sale those stores had all summer.

"I want to be ready to get her picture," Tennessee said as we walked back towards the motel, "the first time she sees one of the cactus."

"I'm glad you thought of that camera, Tennessee. Lot better than just talk about where you've been. Like show and tell in school. Now she can prove to Uncle Tendall where she's been."

Going back to the motel was slower, me toting all that stuff. I guess I thought shopping with Tennessee would be more fun than it was. Pretty soon old Polar wasn't going to have room in the back of the truck, even if he wanted to ride back there. He might want to soon if I can't get Aunt Lucy to take a bath. Ought to ask her to get in the back and see if she gets the picture.

The last of the sun was starting to go away. The gray mountains across the road turned bright red. You start thinking they are really that red color they get right before it gets dark and out comes a million more stars than you see in North Carolina. You wake up the next day and those red mountains will be as ugly gray as a rainy day. It's almost as weird as flowers growing out of rocks. I'm pretty sure I'd never want to live here even though Tennessee seems to really like it. Because it's home to her, I guess.

It was going to be completely dark before we got back. It was getting too dark to appreciate how pretty Tennessee was. She still had on that straw hat with no blond hair showing but the sunglasses were off now that it was too dark to wear them. I sure had liked holding her hand and having her walk beside me, but my hands were more than full. I made her walk behind me. I got too worried about somebody running over her on the narrow shoulder. Acting just like Mother again but the cars were going by pretty fast. Polar was being careful, staying off the pavement. I was thinking how nice it was though, just me and Polar and Tennessee and not having to worry about Aunt Lucy piping in after everything I said with her two cents worth.

"Maybe we can take a hike to a uranium mine," Tennessee offered from behind me. She waited for a noisy truck to go past. "I always wanted to do that. Since you don't mind leaving Aunt Lucy alone."

I turned my head and said: "Sure. We can. But I better get her to that big cactus first. Every day a little less of her mind seems to be here." Finally something Tennessee hadn't done already: a uranium mine.

When I turned back around towards the motel, I stopped in my tracks. Tennessee bumped into me. I think my heart stopped beating. There was a red light going around, right at our motel, right in front of our room. I yelled "Tennessee!", but she was gone. Nothing but dark behind me. I dropped all the bags and started running towards the motel, right past Polar who I could hear panting behind me.

"Oh my god. Oh my god." I don't know why I had to say that. I was scared not to be saying anything. In the porch light I could see that Aunt Lucy wasn't in her rocker in front of our room. Her *Arizona Highways* was on the ground where she'd been sitting and the wind was turning the pages. A man and woman stood next to a man in a uniform wearing a star badge. I saw the sheriff's car with the star on the door that went through town with the siren going.

"Excuse me, young man." The sheriff held his hand up in front of my face. "Want to tell me what you're doing here?"

I don't know why. I couldn't say anything. I went to open the door to our room. It was locked so I fumbled in my jeans for my key. Finally I got my key in the lock and opened it. The light wasn't on. "Aunt Lucy! Where are you? Aunt Lucy?" I was loud but I didn't care. I had to be loud enough for her to hear me. If she could hear me. The bathroom door was open. No one was on the toilet. I pulled open the shower curtain. Empty. The wet pink wrapper with a rosebud sat in the soap dish.

"Son."

It was the sheriff, standing in the door to our room. He didn't sound mad at me anymore.

"Son. I think I know where the person you're looking for is. Lucy Lucy Foushee. Social Security Number 238-11-2376," he read off a little card in his hand. That was when I noticed that he was holding Aunt Lucy's big black purse.

8

"Grandpa named you the same name twice?" I said.

"Papa was ready with Floyd James and I come out a girl."

"But he named you Lucy Lucy?"

"Papa never got to use Floyd James. I don't think he meant to name Tendall, Tendall. He was supposed to be Floyd James. But Papa said he had a little too much to drink and didn't hear Mama right. Thinking back, Papa figured, my mama was getting cold. Last thing she said. Kindle the fire. He took it to be Tendall. He was trying to please her with her hurting bad, so he wrote in the name she said as best he could. My mama, May Linda who called herself Melinda, died when Tendall come out."

I had double names coming at me like baseballs out of a batting machine and I was swinging and missing about half of them. "I thought it was Tendall Leroy. And nobody ought to be Lucy Lucy."

"You're not paying attention, Benny. Kindle the fire. Not Tendall Leroy. Papa wanted me to have one name so he put it in both squares. The government don't know no better. I didn't have no say on my name. Something pretty like Sally Jane would have suited me fine."

"I can't believe you went in the wrong room, Aunt Lucy."

"Well, I thought it was where I left it."

"Where you left what?"

"My room, stupid. I don't know one room from the other in these motels, Benny. They all look alike."

"You scared the be-Jesus out of that woman come from California. She thought you were dead in her bed."

"She ought to be happy she wont dead in her bed. Happens all the time."

"I sure didn't know you got named Lucy twice."

"Well, I did. So you can shut up about it, Henny Benny. And don't you think I haven't gotten enough bullshit in my life about it already. And I'm getting a ration of it now."

"I better go see if Tennessee is back in her room yet. This story she isn't going to believe. She must of thought the sheriff was here for her."

"Car theft. She deserves it."

"They weren't after anybody for car theft. I hear they caught a little old lady for breaking and entering."

"They should put her under the jail. A few rotten eggs can give us old folks a bad name."

Sometimes talking with Aunt Lucy can make you forget which way is up. I sure felt relieved when I peeked at Tennessee through a crack in the curtain at her window. I figured she must be hiding. I guess she sneaked around the back of the motel so the sheriff wouldn't see her. She has to be worried to death about what happened to Aunt Lucy.

The wind came up and sucked her curtain in and back out of her cracked window. Inside her room I saw she had finally taken off that hat and sunglasses. What a doll she was. She was watching TV with Polar sitting on the bed beside her. Polar. Inside. I almost couldn't believe that. He never wanted to go inside anywhere. With her leaning against him. I ought to get that old dog to teach me lessons. I just had to get something going with her soon, or as Mother would say, forever hold my peace. Daddy would just say something crude about doing something or getting off the pot that I don't even want to think about when I'm looking at Tennessee. Your parents aren't much help with this.

I was trying to get my nerve up. I better do better than when I made my first pass at Valinda on her doorstep, and she came up on me too fast.

I busted my bottom lip on her hard chin, and stuck a tooth in my own lip so far that it bled. Made me go home a lot faster than I planned to, since I had to hide my bloody lip from her.

Tennessee looked sad. I hope she hadn't seen herself on TV or something. I finally did something. I tapped on the window frame. When she got up and opened the door, I asked first thing: "How in the world did you get Polar to come inside?"

"He wanted to watch *Wild Kingdom*."

She was getting as bad as me about that dog. "Oh. Well, don't let me disturb your show. I didn't know where you disappeared to. But then I knew you must be safe in here. After I heard the TV on a while ago when I was walking up and down. Polar was gone so I knew nothing bad would happen to you."

I wasn't making a lot of sense. I do that when I get scared even after I'm not scared anymore. Both of these women had scared me to death. I tried again: "I just wanted to tell you I went back and picked up all the bags of stuff I dropped, in case you were worried about it, and put it in the truck. Nobody took a single one of them. Folks around here must be pretty honest." She didn't look away from the TV. I wondered why she didn't ask me about Aunt Lucy. I tried something pretty forward I guess: "I just thought you might like some company."

She ignored me. "Why don't you help him? Why don't you keep the hawk from getting him? How can you stand there with a camera taking a picture of something that awful and not help the little animal? Oh no!"

Tennessee was talking to the TV and not paying any attention to me. I was really glad she wasn't talking to me like that, but I almost felt like it because I was the only person there. The only other person I ever saw do that was Aunt Lucy who was always cussing out the people on TV until she'd get so mad, she'd shut it off.

Tennessee started to cry again. "You know, Tennessee, if it makes you sad, I don't think you need to watch *Wild Kingdom* for Polar's sake.

He likes almost anything. You could watch a funny movie with a bunch of car wrecks. Polar gets a kick out of noisy stuff. He comes running when you turn on a machine. I mean pick something you like."

Polar ran by me where I was standing in the doorway. I heard him jump in the back of the truck and crash into all the new bags of stuff he didn't know were there. He was just doing Tennessee a favor being inside keeping her company. He didn't want to be. Boy, I sure did. Wish she'd ask me to stay a while. If I was a dog, I'd be wagging my tail and panting.

Tennessee changed the station and hit the mute button. The quiet made me even more awkward feeling. "Did you know the sheriff came," I offered, "because this lady went in her room and found Aunt Lucy asleep in her bed?"

"Yes. The manager told me when I told him the air conditioner doesn't work in this place and the window doesn't open very wide. It's really uncomfortable in here."

I felt disappointed he told her about Aunt Lucy. Thought I had a new story for Tennessee. I was grabbing in my brain for something to talk about and couldn't find anything. She didn't ask me to sit down. She was really frowning at the TV.

"Benny?"

"Yeah?"

"Could you take a picture of a hawk eating a little gopher?"

"Naw. I'd miss him. I tried taking a picture of a squirrel setting on a wire once with Daddy's old Brownie Hawkeye and all I got was the sky with this little dot in the middle. Dot could of been a pigeon. Or a pair of sneakers thrown over the wire. Or anything. Never thought of it before. That camera was called a hawk eye. That's pretty cool. But if a hawk couldn't see better than that camera, he couldn't tell a hamburger from a cow pie."

"What are you talking about?"

"How hawk eyes are a lot better then ours, I guess." There goes Benny the babbler again only this time I made her mad. I could tell. First time I did that that I know of. Wasn't a good time to be talking about hawk anything with her being so tender hearted about that TV show. Not much chance of her asking me to stay a while now.

"I'm not talking about nothing, I guess. Anything, I mean. I almost had a heart attack because I thought Aunt Lucy had fallen off the side of a mesa or something."

"Do you love Aunt Lucy?"

Uh Oh. Twenty-four thousand dollar question. Don't mess it up, Benny. "Sure. Sure I do. I wouldn't have taken just anybody on this long trip. Like I wouldn't have taken Ethel if she begged me and promised to feed the chickens the rest of my life. Uh, now I don't mean I don't love my sister. You're an only child so you don't know what I mean. It's just different with a sister, especially one like Ethel."

Don't know why I can't give a short answer instead of digging down in a deeper hole, as Daddy would say. "Sure," I decided to try again. "I love old Aunt Lucy." I finally got it out. "But I can't tell her because she would just make fun of me."

"I think you should go tell her right now."

"You're trying to get rid of me. I can tell." I kept talking so she wouldn't agree with me. "I'm not a bad guy really. I mean Mother and Ethel say I'm selfish, but they expect me to read their minds and figure out what they want without telling me. Some girls are like that. You only get points when you read their minds." Tennessee had quit looking at me. She was staring at the TV and she wasn't moving, like she'd turned to rock. Like she'd freeze my hand if I touched her.

"Good night," I made myself say. Somebody other than Benny Foushee was doing my talking right now. "We'll get started early tomorrow. The way I figure our time we should be at the big cactus way before sunset."

"Tell Aunt Lucy you love her."

"I'll try," I lied.

Damn. I better get Polar to teach me a lesson or two. I went back to our room and just like Aunt Lucy, fell asleep with all my clothes on, even my shoes. But at least mine were on the right feet. About all I got right.

ꕥ

"Sorry son, but there's no picnicking allowed here in the saguaro preserve."

The guy was dressed like a highway patrolman only he had on a green suit.

"Who me?"

"You and your family. The old lady here in the wheel chair with the box of McDonald's fries in her lap. If she is handicapped, there is an overlook on the other side for disabled visitors. And that dog has to be on a leash in the park."

"That's not a wheel chair. That's her rocker. Polar's not going anywhere unless I do."

For some reason, the man looked at me like I wasn't making any sense.

"Where are you from?" he asked.

"Summit, North Carolina."

"Then why does the old lady—I assume she is your grandmother—have a rocking chair? And I mean it about that dog."

"Go get in the back of the truck, Polar. She's my aunt. Old enough to be my great aunt, but she isn't great. That didn't come out right."

Polar ran back down the path and with a flying leap, landed in the back of the truck. Then I heard him doing a little dance on the one spot left in the hot bed before he jumped up on Tennessee's bags.

"Truck's burning his feet," I told the officer, "but he always minds me."

"You drove all the way from South Carolina in that?"

"North Carolina."

"Whatever. North Carolina. In that?"

"It's a real good truck. Burns a little too much gas. '65 GMC V6. People are surprised when you tell them it has a V6, but I can show you the motor if you're interested. My daddy used to use it when he did a lot of plumbing before it got so he had to have a license. Used to have T. R. Plumbing on the door until Mother made him take it off. Everybody would ask him what T. R. stood for since it should have been R. F. if he was using his real initials and he said 'Turd Rassling Plumbing.' He was always itching for somebody to say 'How's business?' so he could say 'Full of you-know-what.' I bet I heard him say that a hundred times only he didn't say you-know-what unless it was a woman. Probably wouldn't say it in front of a cop either, like I just didn't. It was just one of those magnet signs so I pulled it off. Wouldn't want somebody to ask me to fix a toilet while I'm on vacation. If you can say taking Aunt Lucy to see the big cactus is a vacation."

The ranger guy walked around and looked at the truck tag. I could see the top of Tennessee's straw hat. She was so scrunched down, she looked like a midget.

"Truck's got a license," I said. "What I meant was Daddy didn't have a plumbing license, not that you care about that way out here. You was asking about the rocker, not the truck. Were asking. I know better, I just slip."

"I know what you mean. I mean yes, the rocker, not the grammar. The grandma, not the grammar, if you understand my English. If she needs a wheelchair, why is she in a rocking chair? I mean it doesn't have wheels under those rockers, does it? Can't tell with the sand."

"Oh, she don't need a wheelchair. Doesn't. Not yet. She gets around. Enough to get into mischief for an eighty-four year old."

"Eighty-two," Aunt Lucy yelled.

"And she hears when she wants to. Eighty-four, Aunt Lucy. My grandmother as you called her, who is my aunt really. Aunt Lucy Lucy, that's what it says on her Social Security card, two Lucy's, she's in her rocker waiting for the sun to set behind the big cactus like she saw in *Arizona Highways.*"

"Well, she can't sit there."

"I'd appreciate it if you would be the one to tell her, sir. The last person that dumped her out of that rocker got snuff spit on her foot. Well actually it was the next to the last time and she dumped herself out, but she sure as stuff spit snuff on my mother's foot. That was hard to say without spitting myself." I laughed a little, but quit when he didn't join me.

"There's laws against spitting in the park."

"Some people would be scared to spit on a policeman's foot, but not Aunt Lucy. I know her that well. I guess you're like a policemen because you have a badge, but you got on a green suit which I guess means you protect green stuff, which there isn't much of out here."

"Benny?"

"Yeah, Aunt Lucy."

"Why don't you shut up and let me wait for the sunset in peace. You're running your mouth like you're trying to sell that man something. He's going to give you a ticket for mouth speeding."

"I'm trying to sell you."

"I'm not buying," the ranger said.

"Can't say as I blame you. I been riding with her for near about two thousand miles and I can't remember her doing anything I asked her to. She's the opposite of Polar. He even minds me when he's after a cat. She might have a little respect for that badge you're wearing. Might not, though. No guarantee from the management, as Daddy would say. He put a sign over the toilet, 'We aim to please, your aim would help.' Boy, did Mother take that sign down fast. My daddy is a real cornball."

The ranger guy's hands went up in the air and he started wiggling like he was doing a rain dance heebie-jeebie, before he turned around and headed back to his car. I expected him to start writing me out a ticket like those cop guys usually do, no matter how hard you try to talk them out of it. But he just put his face in his hands when he got behind the wheel. Probably tired. Long hot day. Wishing it was quitting time and here these fools he doesn't trust are out messing around the cactus he gets paid to watch out for. And I'll admit Aunt Lucy is the type who might hack a hunk out of that cactus to make some jelly, if I didn't keep an eye on her. Sometimes I can even feel for a cop, just doing his job. As soon as he got in his car, Polar took it as his signal to jump out of the truck and run back to me. I tell you, that dog is so smart. The ranger guy drove away fast.

"I talked him out of giving us a ticket, Aunt Lucy Lucy." She ignored me or didn't hear me one. She had her rocker really going now. Little clouds of pink dust were coming out from under it. Amazing how she can do that with her feet nowhere near the ground. Practice, I guess. Oh boy, it was a long time before sunset and I didn't want her to get burnt so I went to the truck and borrowed Tennessee's straw hat and sat it on her head.

"Did you tell that cop to kiss my behind?" Aunt Lucy asked.

"He wants to give you the electric chair, Aunt Lucy, for illegal rocking here in his park."

"Ain't his park. It's my park much as his. I put in rivets so he could be free. OK, maybe not rivets. But I welded war boats. I'm an American."

"You're a pain in the butt. In his book, not mine. I told him you were my sweet little crazy granny."

"How long I got before the sun does its thing?"

"Till sunset."

"Benny?"

"Yes Ma'am."

"I hope I haven't got my hopes up."

"No Ma'am. No way. It'll set. You just wait and see. Just like you dreamed it would." I looked at the giant green plant with skin like a accordion. It had even more wrinkles than Aunt Lucy. But that was the way it ought to be since it was older. She never told me for sure if that was why she wanted to see it so bad.

"If it rains, that cactus can swallow a ton of water," Aunt Lucy went on with her teaching even though her magazine was in the truck. She had it memorized like for a test. "Fill out them pleats. But if it freezes with all that water inside, it'll bust like a beer in the freezer." I don't think that she got that last part out of *Arizona Highways*.

"Well, Aunt Lucy, I hope it knows better. Must know better since it's lived this long."

All of a sudden my eye caught something I'd never seen before. "Aunt Lucy. Look quick! Look at the little tiny owl, sitting up there near the top in that hole, just like Tennessee said it would. I've got to go get Tennessee and tell her. Can you see up that high?"

"Florence Nightingale carried an owl in her pocket."

"Who's she?"

Aunt Lucy gave me her you are too stupid to live wheeze. I guess it was a good thing Tennessee was over throwing up a stick for Polar to catch and taking his picture when he jumped for it, if I had to make a ass of myself again. That girl could sure disappear when there was a cop around anywhere and act normal as anybody after they were gone. She'd make a darn good criminal if she didn't have so much money already, she didn't need any more.

"OK, is Florence Nighthawk famous or somebody I'm kin to?"

"I'm aching too, but I'm old. What's your excuse?"

"Are you talking to me or the cactus, Aunt Lucy?"

"Is a pig's ass pork? I told you that cactus is older than me. And plants don't listen any better than you do."

The wind was whistling through the arms of the big cactus, probably loud enough for Aunt Lucy to hear. At least she hadn't made me so crazy myself that I started talking to the cactus. Looked like an octopus on a big green tree trunk, arms going everywhere but mostly up. It was a pretty big plant, tallest one I'd ever seen, even counting trees. We'd come a long damn way just to look at it if you ask me, but I didn't want to do what Daddy always said, "Rain on her parade." Aunt Lucy had already rocked a couple of deep grooves in the ground looking up at it and we weren't even near sunset.

"Tendall's never seen nothing like this. This here big cactus is nowhere in that France. Or New Jersey. Or Fort Bragg. Just right here in this one place in the good old U.S. of A. The great American West. Two hundred years to get to fifty feet tall. Papa stood right here where I'm setting…"

"Hey Mrs. Williams. Look at me."

Instead she looked at me. "What's that?"

"It's Tennessee wanting to take your picture."

"Don't waste the film. I'll break the camera."

"To show Tendall," I pressed. "Hold still and let her take it. So he'll believe you were here. It's a throwaway camera so it doesn't matter if you break it."

Aunt Lucy spun her rocker around like it was a barber chair. She had a smile on her face like she was already in a picture. Tennessee started clicking the little camera, stooping down, darting sideways with little flashes of light going off in her hands.

"Don't forget to save one for the sunset," I told her.

Tennessee stopped and froze like she was the one ready for a picture, but her bottom lip stuck out. Uh-oh. I started to say something about that expression freezing, like Mother used to warn me when I made a ugly face.

"Oh dammit. I took too many pictures of Polar. I just used up the last one. Damn," she repeated.

That was the first time I ever heard Tennessee cuss.

We left Aunt Lucy in her rocker by the cactus and drove to the filling station outside the park for another camera. I could count on her not going anywhere this time for sure. I put my Durham Bulls cap on Aunt Lucy's white head, because Tennessee asked for her straw-hat disguise back. I didn't think that green cop cared anything about girls that run away. Aunt Lucy didn't make a peep when I changed her hat anyway. I was expecting something about the smelly dog who wore it last. That big cactus had her attention more than anything I'd ever seen.

At the filling station, our trip took another little turn. Actually it was a big turn. Tennessee opened her black book of purple and green checks and both of us saw that this was her last one. She reached around in the purse, but didn't come up with another book. She tore the only one she had left out, really slow like she was trying to make it last longer.

"I'll get this camera if you want me to," I offered. "Aunt Lucy gave me ten bucks for lunch."

"I don't have any more money," she answered. She sounded scared.

"That's OK. You don't have to buy everything, you know. I'll buy the camera. It's pictures you're taking for us anyway."

She started walking back to the truck so bent over you'd think she'd shrunk up a foot. That money thing seemed to bother her a whole lot, a lot worse than leaving that fancy car beside the road. Polar jumped out and back in and leaned against her like he knew she was feeling bad. I paid for the camera and got in the truck beside her.

"I better go back home now," she sniffed.

"What do you mean?" I asked, knowing exactly what she meant.

"I better get you to take me back home. My dad will give you some money when we get there."

I felt like a bus driver with a little kid who jumped on my bus and turned his pockets inside out. Right before he started blubbering and saying he wanted his mommy. And did she say 'dad' instead of that fancy word, 'father'? Boy, did I hit the nail on the head there.

Tennessee started crying, not like a grownup, sobbing like a little kid. Then she fell over, ka-plunk, like she was made out of wood and kept on crying, landing right in my lap. Oh brother. Now I really didn't know what to do. I can just hear Buddy at the Exxon giving me all grades of it now. Benny Foushee don't know what to do. Got the little beauty right in his lap and he don't know what to do. I didn't even feel right touching her. I just patted her on the back real soft like I was afraid I would break her or something. Her shirt felt like it was silky cloth, real fine and cool. I'm glad it was just me and Polar, real glad.

"Does this mean our trip is over with, Tennessee?" I don't know why I had to go and say that. She wasn't talking back anyway, just sobbing like her heart was broken. I guess that is what happens to a rich girl when they run out of money to buy things. Their hearts break. Maybe that's what "broke" really means with a heart.

"I miss Lacey and Tracey," she whimpered.

"Who's Lacey and Tracey?"

"My Shih Tzues. My little doggies."

"Oh, yeah. I remember you told me their names."

I looked at Polar. Poor guy. He thought she loved him too. I wouldn't give you Polar for a dozen of those Shit Sues she said she bought from a breeder. Two dozen. Enough to pull a dog shed. He knew that. We set in the truck till, I'm telling the truth, I could feel the top of my jeans legs all wet from her crying. She was like that cactus, a ton of water inside. Now it came out and was soaking in my britches. She had to hurt inside, she cried so much.

Things started to get red inside my truck. It took me a minute to get it straight what was happening. The sun was setting. The sun would be setting behind that big cactus. And I left old Aunt Lucy setting out there in her rocker by herself. Bring her all this way and just leave her out there by herself. What in the world would I do if I went back and she was gone? Took off to jail by that ranger cop. Told to get out of the park because it closed at sunset. And her big black purse and Lucy Lucy ID card are here in my truck. That poor old woman. Can't half hear. All by herself. Trying to carry that heavy rocking chair. I'm worse than Uncle Tendall.

I sat Tennessee up in the seat. I guess I did it too fast because she started into coughing like she was choking. I started up my truck and took off. Not using good sense. Pulled right in front of a guy who blew his horn at me like he'd rather be punching me in the mouth. I don't know if Tennessee said a thing. I guess I wasn't listening and Polar was barking at the car that blew at me.

"It's OK, Polar. I'm the one did wrong. But I did a lot worse wrong leaving Aunt Lucy."

I saw the park gate. Nobody had put the bar over it yet. It was still red outside. I still had time if it really closed after sunset, like it said. Sunset. Not sun setting. That's what I'd tell that ranger cop. Then I saw her. I've never been so glad to see that old biddy in my whole life, even more than yesterday after she went in the wrong room. Rocking in that chair like her life depended on it. Black as the ace of spades up against that red sun, that little white lady. And there it was, the big cactus with the sun setting behind it.

Wow.

I jumped out and left the door open. I could hear Polar running behind me, still barking. It was a different bark now. If I was a dog, I'd be barking like that too. There was that old lady, in her rocker, in front of that big cactus with the sun setting. It was the prettiest thing I'd ever seen in my life.

"Aunt Lucy!"

I stopped on one side of the rocker and Polar was on the other.

"Benny Foushee. I have died and gone to Hell, just like I deserve to.

Ain't that the prettiest thing you ever seen in your life?"

I watched the red light reach around the green arms and I said, "It is, Aunt Lucy. It's the prettiest thing I ever seen."

"It ain't going to last. We got to watch fast once it gets started. That's what the book said."

"I'm watching fast, Aunt Lucy. As fast as I can."

"Turn around."

I heard it, but as usual, Aunt Lucy didn't.

"I said turn around."

I did, and as soon as I did, a white light flashed and I saw a thousand black dots.

Tennessee took our picture.

9

I heard Aunt Lucy mumbling and asked her what she was saying.

"Working on my story to tell Tendall. Got to get it just right. Working on my story," she told me, every time I asked, then went back to mumbling.

She could hardly make it back to the truck last night after it got black dark at the big cactus. Tennessee carried the rocker while I had to almost carry Aunt Lucy. Had to hurry out before they locked us inside.

After we left the big cactus place in Arizona, I didn't know what to do next. There was nothing further west that I really wanted to see except the Pacific Ocean some day, but that was a long way and Aunt Lucy was getting pretty worn out. She was still smiling about the big cactus; at least I hoped that was what she was smiling about.

I thought about asking Tennessee if maybe she hadn't seen the big trees in California yet, but she had probably already seen them three times like everything else. Since she ran out of money, she hadn't had two peeps to say to any of us and for sure she wasn't smiling like Aunt Lucy. Kind of quiet in my truck.

I saw this sign just outside the town we stopped in for the night: Old Yeller Uranium Mine. The sign was old and the road up to it was dirt. I didn't think it would cost money so I asked Tennessee if she still wanted to go see a uranium mine. She didn't answer, just shook her head.

"I thought you said you'd never seen one," I said to the air for all the answer I got.

In the morning after Tennessee finally came out of her room, I started driving us back towards New Mexico. Trying to keep the room as long as she could I guess because I know she used up the last one of those checks. I took a turn off on this little road instead of the one we got there on. Just so I could make the trip take a little longer. Nobody seemed to notice. Pokey. That was Mother's word. Pokey Benny. Back then it meant I didn't want to go back home; I guess it wasn't any different now except I knew who my reason was.

After we got burgers in this little town I didn't even see a name on, we stopped to let Polar go do his business. All three of us people took a walk to stretch our legs down by a animal watering hole beside the road. Tennessee's idea. I guess I did everything she asked. Polar was doing laps around the watering hole, following more scents than he knew what to do with. There were a lot of piggyback frogs watching us in the shallow water at the edge, not letting us change their plans. I was hoping Aunt Lucy's eyes were so bad she wouldn't see them to comment on it. I believe she saw straight through me, where my thoughts were dwelling. Though Aunt Lucy hadn't said so in those words, I was about to lose Tennessee.

"Look at that black beetle with his butt up in the air," Aunt Lucy said. "Looks like Tendall crawling off after that foxhole over in France."

"That's a dung beetle, Mrs. Williams." Tennessee surprised me when she spoke.

"Pow!" Aunt Lucy shot a hole in the beetle's butt with her finger. "Does he live in dung or eat it?" When she asked that, Tennessee's face turned as red as her lipstick. You'd think she'd be ready for Aunt Lucy by now, but I guess I'm not always either.

"Both, I think," she stumbled, then added, "I've seen a dung beetle rolling a ball of horse manure. Then it digs a hole to bury it. Juan says it's good for the soil. Look at all the different foot prints," she changed the subject real quick. I should learn to do that.

"Here's a Sears Roebuck clodhopper," I said, trying the Tennessee approach to changing the subject and pointing at my own footprint in the mud. And to be honest, to try to cheer her up. "And this one is a Afghanistan goof hound. Over here is the brown and black footed mud hen with toes that point in but some days they point out. Don't know about this one," I said looking at Tennessee's tennis shoe print and trying hard to make her smile again. I was kind of acting like Daddy for some reason. "Could be dangerous," I added.

"These are serious footprints, Benny." Tennessee scolded me for goofing off on our nature walk. Not much good at being a comedian. "This is probably the only watering hole for miles," she went on. "That's a coyote. And here is an elk. And this one is a mountain lion." She could be such a show-off sometimes. After she said mountain lion, Aunt Lucy turned around and headed back to the truck like she was hauling the U. S. Mail.

"Where you going so fast, Aunt Lucy?"

"I figure that thirsty sonavabitch might be hungry for a gristly old lady. I don't truck with no mountain lion." I had to admit that I could imagine a mountain lion come flying off the cliffs above us, like some kind of giant flying squirrel with fangs and claws. Too many Westerns as a little kid I guess.

Right then when I was imagining that, Polar froze. Except for one ripple that I saw go down his white back like a mole scooting underneath the ground. He stood still as a dog statue, staring across the water hole. When I went to ask him what was the matter, I saw it too, on the other side of the muddy water, something big and black that made my legs start shaking. Its head was big as a cow, but its sides were shrunken down to the ribs.

"Poor dog," Tennessee said calmly. "That's a pure bred Rottweiler."

I guess that was a dog name, but not one I'd ever heard of. Funny how a dog can tell a dog from another animal whether it weighs a pound or a hundred pounds. Polar kept watching it and whimpering.

"How come you know so much?" I asked Tennessee. She really was sort of a know-it-all.

"My father shows dogs," she answered. Father again. She pouted and for a second looked a little like Valinda.

The black dog had a rusty nose and rusty feet and muscles like a prizefighter. "What's he doing out here if he's a show dog? He doesn't look too healthy."

"That's what people do. Dump dogs in the wilderness. When they're not cute little puppies anymore."

"Look out, Benny. Mad dog!" Aunt Lucy screamed from up beside the truck, where she was tugging on the door to open it, without pressing the button down. She sure got to the truck fast for her. A chill ran up my back when she yelled that mad dog business. She was getting so crazy I didn't think I could listen to Aunt Lucy anymore, without working out my own opinion for my own good.

Before I could do anything to stop her, Tennessee walked around the water hole towards the dog. It had a collar with a short chain hanging from it. The chain had pieces of dead plants stuck in it.

"Mad dog! Mad dog!" Aunt Lucy was still hollering, over and over. I wish she'd figure out how to get in the truck or shut up one. The big dog backed up a few steps before it dropped down on its belly, looking more like a bear rug than a dog. I saw the hamburger Tennessee must've saved from the lunch I bought her, because she wasn't hungry as usual. It came out of her purse, out of its yellow wrapper, in the dog's mouth and down its throat in no more than five seconds. Tennessee must have picked up that food in the purse habit from Aunt Lucy.

The dog's black rear end went up in the air like a big old dung beetle, its butt wagging where it didn't have a tail. The giant dung beetle rolled over on its back and pointed at the sky with all four paws. "It's a female dog," Tennessee called out. "Doesn't appear to have puppies. Got a scar. She's been fixed. Probably because she wasn't perfect. She's got Dumbo ears. Her head is too big. Oh, and look. She has a little white dot on her chest. That's probably why she got dumped. Had a litter of puppies with white spots."

Now Tennessee was really showing off how much she knew. For all I knew, she could be making it up. Her not perfect dog still looked like a not perfect monster to me. I saw a dog looked like that in a movie once and it grew teeth like a vampire. I figured I better do something soon, so I wouldn't seem like such a wimp. Or forever hold your peace. Mother again. Why does she keep saying that to me when I still don't know what holding my peace means? It almost sounds dirty, but that sure wouldn't have come from Mother.

When I walked towards Tennessee and the dog, it dropped its head and wiggled behind Tennessee. I had seen that before. Uncle Tendall had that same effect on dogs. "A man must of been mean to her," I commented.

Tennessee looked up at me and I'm not kidding, she had a smile that made my feet and shoes melt into two big blobs. After yesterday I thought she might not ever smile again. Everything had me feeling so down in the dumps today. Then all of a sudden, she smiled and everything seemed OK.

That is until: "We'll take Shenandoah with us," she said.

When the big dog stood back up, Polar broke his freeze and ran between us with his loudest, meanest bark. I squatted down and patted Polar on the head. I swear, another look I'll never forget, only this one was on Polar. Maybe I had the same look to him that he had to me. I didn't know what to say to him. I could still hear Aunt Lucy up by the road, kicking my truck in the side because she still hadn't got the door open.

Don't you see, Polar, I do everything this girl tells me to do, I wanted to explain to him. I can't help myself. I hope he reads my mind and understands. What he can't understand is that I am really making a mess of things right now. And there was nobody to stop me.

Now I'm going to have five to get in my truck every time we stop, not four. And I have to buy food for another dog and rooms and food for Tennessee too. I asked Polar to ride in the truck bed. Shenandoah would have some company that might could teach her to have the good sense not to jump out while we were moving. For all I knew, the reason that dog was at that waterhole in the first place was she jumped out of somebody's truck. That business about the white spot on her chest sure didn't make sense to me. This guy at school's got a white spot in his hair that's a birthmark and I don't see his parents should have left him at a orphanage because of it. I think I'm trying to make a joke out of what Miss Know-it-all said and what she's done now isn't funny.

I drove on up the hill from the water hole real slow, looking at the big dog in my mirror. Polar was stretched out on top of all of Tennessee's bags, watching the big dog while she climbed around him like a cow on a merry-go-round. Her big feet could do a lot of breaking.

Tennessee didn't make another peep about the dog, acted like it was another bag of stuff she bought in a store. Just throw it in the truck. Except this bag of stuff had to eat and drink and go to the bathroom. I could sure make some comment that Daddy would come up with, like you get what you pay for, but I had to keep my mind on who Benny Foushee was. Not Daddy. If I knew anymore.

If you can believe this, just when I was feeling like my brain was in Mother's Mix Master, I heard this noise, right as we got near the top of the hill. Not from the dogs in back of me but the front, like somebody was under my truck hood with a sledgehammer. My stomach went sick along with my head.

"Pot's a boiling," Aunt Lucy shouted as I shut off the engine and watched the steam roll around the nose and across the hood. I did the quickest bootleg turn I ever did in my life to get my truck pointing back downhill before I lost my speed. In the quiet as we rolled down the hill, out of gear with the wind whistling around us, Tennessee asked: "Did I break this one too? I'm starting to hate cars."

I couldn't make talk with either one of them. They weren't worth a damn to me right now, to tell the truth. And both dogs barking their heads off as we squealed through the curves weren't any help either. Trying to keep my foot off the brakes in the turns so I wouldn't lose my speed. Trying to remember if at the bottom of the hill there might be a filling station. Trying to decide if I should stop for water for the radiator when we rolled back past that water hole I thought was behind us for good.

When it rains, it pours. I don't know who said that, Mother or Daddy or both of them. I been wanting time to stop for me and Tennessee. Watch out or you might get what you wish for. That sounded more like Aunt Lucy than anybody, but she wasn't saying anything now. I don't know if she even knew what was happening. Hot water hit the windshield like it was raining in Hell. Pots boil in kitchens not under hoods, Aunt Lucy.

I was doing all kinds of guessing about the motor. The one that made the most sense was the water pump. The thing that made the littlest sense was thinking I was going to find a water pump for a '65 GMC pickup V6 in no name town. About as likely as a Porsche fan belt. Speaking of fans, I really didn't even want to look under the hood and see if it went right square through the radiator when the water pump let go.

You can be feeling so good, like what it must feel like to be rich as cream, just tooling along down the road, getting off the beaten path, then bang, and you're going nowhere fast. Thanks, Daddy. Coming to a stop, nowhere fast, with nothing left but feet. Out of the corner of my eye, I could see those old feet I had with me, her shoes on the right feet in honor of our big day yesterday at the big cactus. She couldn't walk across the room anymore without leaning on me.

Aunt Lucy was watching TV, sitting in the bed in our room in Gold Cave, New Mexico. The woman at the desk told me the town name. Aunt Lucy looked as worn out as I've ever seen her. I had to ask her three times for the money for the room. Maybe she looked worse because I was worried about everything now. No matter how good seeing that big cactus made her feel, she couldn't leave her old worn out body behind.

When she started chewing something she pulled out of her purse, her mouth was on the wrong speed, real slow. She didn't have anything to say. I don't think she even noticed that her mad dog got in the back with Polar. And that it ate about half of Polar's bag of food that was meant to last till we got back. And that my truck couldn't just start up and take us back towards home any more.

Tennessee didn't ask for a room for herself, I know because of the money thing. She just wandered off. Something else to worry about. I could see her out the motel window, walking from store to store. Only this time it was different. I'm imagining what she was thinking, looking in the windows: I don't have any more money so I'm not going inside. She stopped near the street corner where there was a Indian woman with stuff to sell spread out on a blanket. Tennessee got down on her knees, picking up jewelry things. I wonder if she was just getting madder and madder, knowing she couldn't buy any more stuff, knowing she was as poor right now as that Indian woman. I could get her some money from Aunt Lucy maybe, but I had to ask her at the right time. I'm broke except for change. And with the engine broken, we might need all of Aunt Lucy's money to fix the truck just to make it home with the engine broken. That's what I got to get my mind on.

I watched Tennessee until she took off for a walk with Shenandoah and Polar instead of coming in the room. I guess she didn't plan to help me think through this. At least she'd be safe from anything smaller than a elephant. She didn't ask me to come along, which hurt right much, just went over and called the dogs out of the truck bed and left. I could sleep in the truck tonight if that was worrying her. Those guys at the Exxon would love to get their hands on that one. I'd never hear the last of it. I never had so much to worry about all at once in my life.

The dark skinned woman at the motel desk didn't even know what a car graveyard was. The truck had cooled off so I pulled the water pump off. You couldn't see the numbers until you did. The fan and radiator looked OK, but the pump was broken in two. Maybe Daddy would be a little proud of me for guessing what it was. Or he would say something unfunny like maybe you sucked a possum in the carburetor. I don't think they have possums out here, just possums with shells called armadillos that get squashed in the road as much as regular possums. I made black fingerprints on the rosebud on the soap wrapper. My hands wouldn't come clean with that little bitty soap. Every time I touched that busted water pump, I just got filthy again. I don't know why I kept picking it up and studying it; it wasn't going to heal up.

Me and Aunt Lucy got supper from the only place nearby for food. She seemed a little perkier, still mumbling her story for Tendall. When I asked her to let me hear it, she said it wasn't ready yet. She kept ordering beers because it was so hot and I kept sipping hers when nobody was looking. I took Aunt Lucy back to the room and went outside. Still no Tennessee but no dogs either.

I saw a beer light across the street. They sold it all over the place here. Not much else to do. It was so damn hot, even at night, and not getting dark fast enough. I decided to have a beer and think things through, try to get away with ordering one without dragging Aunt Lucy along to buy it for me. I got a five out of her purse when she was in the bathroom. That really felt strange, going in that purse and taking money. But she would have given it to me if I asked. But not been real nice about it, I have to admit.

A old sunburnt sign said "Must be over 21 to purchase alcoholic beverages." I sure felt old enough to have a beer and cry in it too, if you want to know the truth. I set down next to this beat up looking guy at the bar. The bartender put a draft beer in front of me without me asking. He winked at me and said something about old Cravon being my legal guardian. Guess I didn't look as old as I felt. I could tell right off that the guy beside me was just dying to have you tell him he looked like Willie Nelson. He had worked at it pretty much.

"Yeah. I'm a good friend of Willie's," he answered. "Folks say we look like twins." He pulled a medallion out from under his t-shirt that said it was OK for him to go back stage at a Willie Nelson concert. In front of him on the bar was a tube of toothpaste and a bottle of Mennen deodorant, both used, sitting beside his beer that was almost gone. I ordered him another one on me by pointing at his empty glass and at my chest, like they do in the movies.

"Think I ought to take the hint," Cravon nodded at me with a smile. "Woman behind the desk give these to me."

"Somebody probably left them in their room."

"Naw, son. You don't get it. She is telling me that I stink."

I shrugged and looked back at our beers that had arrived. I hadn't really noticed his smell. Probably from riding with Aunt Lucy; that could kill your nose buds for good. I must of hit his talk button.

"Lived up in Canada before I come down here looking for the Golden Canyon. Wolverines up there in Canada got claws long as my fingers. Grizzly takes four slugs from a thirty-ought-thirty to die. Hate having to kill them myself, but they get to coming after the livestock. Come after you too."

"Never seen a grizzly," put in Benny the babbler. "Don't even know what a wolverine is. Know what a wolf is, but never seen a real one that I know of. Had a uncle from up to Canada, uncle by marriage to my Aunt

Lucy but I never knew him because he died on the manure spreader before I was born."

"Where you from, boy?" He looked at me the same way that park ranger did.

"Summit, North Carolina."

"I been to North Carolina. Nice place. People real friendly. Ain't like that up in Canada. Keep to theirselves. My old lady worked in the office at a sawmill. Them union guys hired to drive the forklifts punch in and go to sleep on top a wood pile earning seventeen bucks an hour."

"What'd you do for a living up in Canada?"

"Lately I don't do nothing, which is why I'm down here. My old lady kicked me out. Got so I hated to leave the house. So frigging cold. Indians get drunk and freeze to death. They stand them up and stick a cigar in their hand and leave them till spring. I'm not lying. Don't even know what is dead till spring. Then everything starts stinking. Got wolves in packs, come over the fence after my dingo, but my old lady wouldn't let me bring him inside with her precious cats who sleep all over the house and piss all over my stuff. I'm on my way back to Mexico."

"Wolves got your dog?" All of a sudden, Cravon began to sob and drink his beer at the same time, slobbering it down his front like a drooling dog. He was shaking so hard his barstool was rocking.

"Sorry," I said. "Shouldn't have asked."

Damn. I wouldn't let some woman tell me I had to leave Polar outside. Wolves would never get my Polar if I had to keep him under the covers with me.

I paid for the beers, two for me and one for Cravon, and got up to go. Had to be careful. Things were a little spinney. I'm used to just being setting around somewhere when somebody gives me a beer, like down at the Exxon. When I told the bartender that the dark lady who ran the motel didn't know what a car graveyard was, he told me where one was walking distance.

"Hey, buddy," the bartender said after he gave me my change. "Don't let old Crybaby Cravon here get you down with his blubbering. Tomorrow he'll tell you about his stroke. I got to listen to him and smell him all the time. Crybaby plans on taking a bath next Saturday whether he needs it or not." That was one of Daddy's favorite comments. Probably piss him off to have somebody beat him to the punch with his cornball stuff.

Just when I was thinking nothing good was ever going to happen to Benny Foushee again, something good happened that I wasn't even ready for. It happened right when that bartender said that about the bath. I saw just what I'd been looking for. I couldn't believe it. Never thought I'd find the perfect present for Tennessee in a bar.

"What you think of that, kid? Got a old Mexican who comes in here who smuggles them into the country under his shirt. Actually I think he's smuggling his whole body into the country."

In a pie pan beside the cash register set these little chunks of dark wood covered with black bugs even bigger than the dung beetles we saw today. Only they weren't really like bugs exactly because they were on gold chains and had colored jewels sparkling all over their backs. A sign stuck in the pan said: "Want the perfect pet?"

"I never saw nothing like that," I said.

"Me neither, till he started bringing them in. You don't have to feed them or nothing. They live forever and they don't even take a crap. They just set on that wet piece of wood and every now and then they start wiggling. Give one to my girlfriend. She didn't catch on it was a real live bug till somebody told her her jewelry was walking across her shoulder. It started bunching up the cloth on her blouse thing and she like to had a heart attack. She don't wear the bug except when she's high as a kite."

"Can I buy one? I got somebody I want to give one to."

"Help yourself. Two dollars. Buck fifty for you. How about a buck since your pickup's gone bad on you?"

I fished four quarters out of my pocket and picked up the prettiest one of the bugs. It was covered with blue stones like Tennessee likes and it had a safety pin on the end of its chain. It grabbed a real tight hold on my finger. Probably liked it because of that wet beer I was holding a few minutes ago. Boy, I could just see it hanging on that charm bracelet. All by itself; don't need the safety pin. Put the rest of that stuff on there to shame. Twice as big. And it's alive. The bartender wrapped my bug and its piece of wood up in a paper towel.

"Don't lose his wood, now. It's special."

I was pretty stumbley when I got outside. There was a drug store. I went in to get my bug gift-wrapped. This lady said: "Little boy or little girl," when she handed me a white box filled with cotton. I said girl and she started unrolling this pink paper with baby elephants and baby rattles on it. Oh well. I put the bug under the cotton real quick and decided not to let her see what it was. She might not think that was a very nice thing to get for a baby. Might swallow it or something dumb like that, safety pin and all. Ethel did that and had to get a X-ray to see if the pin was closed which it was. Don't think you could swallow a open one. The lid wouldn't shut good so I took out the cotton and slipped his wood in the box. He already got kind of white fuzzy from the cotton.

Hope he doesn't smother in there. Two bucks she charged me for wrapping it. My last two bucks from Aunt Lucy's five. Cost more than the present. When I went back towards our room, the bug made a far away thumping like something live in a casket.

I saw a white dog face and a much bigger black dog face looking at me out of the back of my truck, pinched between all the black garbage bags that I stuffed full of Tennessee's stuff so there'd be room for the dogs. I looked like a garbage man now, I guess. Aunt Lucy's rocker was in its torn bag that I didn't even bother to take out for her tonight. I patted Polar and said hi to Shenandoah. Pretty stupid name for that cow if you ask me. I still wasn't sure she wouldn't take my arm off. Every time I gave her a bowl of water, she knocked it over and I had to grab up Tennessee's bags to keep her stuff from getting wet.

"Be back in a minute to sleep with you guys. Got to get a pillow if there's a extra."

I went in the motel room, trying to be real quiet so I wouldn't have to answer to Aunt Lucy. There was Tennessee, already asleep on the other bed with her arms around the pillow. Got to use that imagination again. Benny, the pillow.

Aunt Lucy was wide awake. The sound was off on the TV, but she probably didn't know the difference. The remote was by Tennessee's hand. I saw a gold dragonfly flapping its wings on her special things bracelet, getting ready to take off. Boy, was she going to flip over that jeweled beetle. I put the package it was in on the little table between the beds.

"The whale put Jonah, Down the hatch, But coughed him up, Because he scratched," Aunt Lucy recited.

"Don't tell me," I said real quiet. "Another Burma Shave."

"You don't believe that Noah's ark bullshit do you, Benny?"

I remember what brought this on. Before the big cactus, we had stopped at a huge dead cactus that looked like a old rotten boat washed up on a beach. It had a sign on it: "Noah's Ark." Then there was a black rock that Tennessee said was lava rock and it had a sign: Jonah's whale. A man in a black suit who looked like a undertaker in the movies tried to charge us for looking so we left.

"I reckon I never thought much about it."

"Time you started into thinking about things," Aunt Lucy said. "You're near about a grownup. Well, to look at you. And to smell your breath."

"You're one to talk, Aunt Lucy. You drank more beers that I did. OK. So Noah caught up a bunch of animals so they wouldn't drown, two by two, husband and wife of every animal. Two by two. Guess he didn't need to get a husband and wife fish. Can't tell a boy fish from a girl anyway."

"Shut up, Benny. You're drunk."

"Yes Ma'am."

"Noah's ark was bullshit."

"Yes Ma'am. You said that already. But don't say that around Mother or you'll end up sleeping in a row boat."

"OK by me. Better company out there. Now Noah, if he had good sense, would have said 'Lord? Ain't this a real good time to get rid of a few things? Like fleas and ticks and mosquitoes, huh Lord?' And the Lord he said, 'Good idea, Noah. I'll count on you to swat them last two flies too while you're at it. Never did know why my father in heaven made the little SOB's.'"

Aunt Lucy was pretty wound up tonight after hardly saying a word when we ate dinner. Since this was the first time we tried going the opposite direction of the big cactus, I thought she might be down in the dumps.

"Yeah, Aunt Lucy. And the wildcats ate the rabbits and the elephants stepped on the turtles. Noah's ark is bullshit."

She laughed. She always laughed when I cussed. "You said that already."

"Naw I didn't. You said it, twice, Aunt Lucy. I was just being agreeable."

"Remember, don't pay no mind to a couple of drunks, Benny."

"Yes Ma'am. But there must be something good about all the animal things He picked to put on that boat, Aunt Lucy. Or He wouldn't have made them in the first place."

"What things?"

Sometimes she made me feel so tired. "Fleas and ticks and mosquitoes and flies. They must be good for something. Something must need them to eat."

"To eat what? Why's that?"

"You're worse than a little kid, Aunt Lucy. Don't be so loud. You'll wake up Tennessee. I don't know. The Bible told me so."

"Shut up. I hate that song."

"The Bible told me so," I sang so she grabbed the Bible and threw it at me and started flipping through her *Arizona Highways* again. I already had to buy Scotch Tape to put it back together. She had definitely lost that Alamogordo pamphlet.

"What did you do with the money, your mama…" Aunt Lucy started to tease me about my singing when she noticed my present for Tennessee on the table. "That's a joke about spending your singing lesson money on something else. Who had a baby? Looks like you just spent your hard earned money on a going away present for somebody who don't need a thing." I kept quiet and didn't tell her I had to use her hard earned money to get it wrapped. I needed to confess about taking her five dollars without asking. She looked back at her magazine.

"Papa's brother Jacob got in big trouble. Made fresh this little rich girl over in Raleigh. They run him out of the state. Papa never did find him again."

"What's made fresh?" I asked. "Oh never mind. I think I know."

"Says here the big cactus makes forty million seeds and is lucky if one makes it. Know how they get planted?"

"No Ma'am."

I didn't even bother to brush my teeth. I grabbed up a bundle of dirty clothes and stuffed them in a t-shirt to make a pillow. I set on what was usually my bed real easy to listen to my bedtime story before I went out to the truck. Tennessee wiggled but didn't wake up. The dragonfly on her bracelet flapped its wings again. She looked pretty raggedy in those jeans, like she really was poor. I guess she was now. There was a little Indian bead bracelet on her wrist I never saw before, hiding underneath her special things bracelet.

"Bird crap and bat crap," Aunt Lucy went on, "Calls it droppings here. One place called it scat. They sure got a lot of names for shit. Says here woodpeckers are smart enough not to peck a hole in them big cactus, except in dry weather, because they'd bleed to death. Lot smarter than most people I know."

"Yes Ma'am."

"I know you're tired and ready to go to sleep, Benny. And you wish I'd shut up and do the same. I know I haven't said it out loud, but I'm much obliged to you bringing me out here."

I was dreaming. I had to be. Just so I was real sure I was dreaming, my mind made a big cactus that had a face in the side like a Aunt Lucy cartoon character and it said beep, beep, and fell over and smashed my truck. Then I pinched myself on both cheeks. I was awake.

"You're welcome, Aunt Lucy." I didn't know what else to say.

"Nicest thing anybody ever saw fit to do for me."

"Glad you liked it." I felt pretty awkward too. Guess neither one of us is used to people being nice to us. "I love you, Aunt Lucy." I kind of blurted it out without thinking about it much, doing what Tennessee wanted me to do even though she was sound asleep and didn't hear me do it finally. She probably won't believe it if I told her.

"Yeah, Benny. I think her trip's over too. But I think the little gal had the time of her life, getting away from that fancy family that made her put on a certain way. Don't think it was too smart picking up that dog, though. Them pure bred dogs are one dot short of a deck of cards."

It wasn't easy sleeping on that truck seat, I can tell you that. I think I could fall asleep easier sitting up driving than trying to decide whether to have my feet over the side, or my knees up under my chin. Last time I fell asleep good on a car seat was when I was about half as long. And those dogs were making all kinds of racket in the back, walking on Tennessee's bags of stuff and rooting under the rocking chair. I must have started dreaming because I looked out the back window and saw Ferrell's bicy in there beside the rocker. Must have been dreaming because he was in Wonita so far as I knew and we weren't back there yet. And I could have sworn the rocker was still in its bag.

I heard this rustling sound like a rat caught inside a feedbag and then I realized it must be the bug I got for Tennessee. When I gave it to her, she clapped so loud I thought she might bring out the motel manager to tell us to get quiet. She really liked it like I thought she would. It grabbed hold of that bracelet and wouldn't let go, holding on tight with its real feet. She threw away the safety pin on the chain in its back. It had even more blue stones than I remember and they were real turquoise she said, not just cheap glass. And one clear shiny rock out of the Cape May River sat on its head. The bug must have got that one from Aunt Lucy.

Well, you guessed it. It was a dream. I was the one having the dream and should have known right off that it wasn't really happening because I had left the bug all wrapped up in the motel room beside Tennessee's bed. I dreamed that Tennessee decided to sleep out there with me. It was OK she said because the dogs were doing it too and they were boy and girl. And one thing led to another in my good dream. So you can figure what happened. Yeah. It happened. And the next morning, I wished I hadn't used up so many of my quarters buying that bug, because I needed them to finish drying my jeans after I washed them at the Laundromat down the street along with all the dirty stuff in my pillow bag.

I couldn't walk back to the motel to get more money wearing this black garbage bag around me so I put my jeans back on half wet. At least I had a clean t-shirt that was almost dry. I tried to think about old Crybaby Cravon and his dingo the wolves ate or Ferrell with his burned up brain. There had to be worse off people in the world than me but I didn't know any right then.

Right before I got to our room, I saw one worse off. That Indian woman with the jewelry on the blanket. She got in my way. She had her hand out, begging for money.

"I don't have any money," I said.

She stuck her hand in my stomach, poking.

"No money," I repeated and turned my wet pockets inside out for her to see. I pushed her out of my way, not mean like, but I wanted her to leave me alone.

When I went to the door of our room and knocked real easy, Aunt Lucy opened it and asked me for food which I didn't have. I've got nothing and everybody is begging me for something.

Tennessee's bed was empty. Her present was still sitting on the little table beside the bed where I left it, like I needed anything else to tell me it was a dream. I felt so sad. Like I just drove my life square in a brick wall and my truck wouldn't even run. Well, I guess I ought to be happy I didn't make a rich girl fresh like in Aunt Lucy's story about Papa's brother. That'd be just my luck first time.

Tennessee had this magazine called *Glamour*. She must have bought it before her money ran out because I didn't get it for her. She was turning the pages slow and not looking up at us at all, almost like she was by herself at the food joint. I offered to buy her some food, but she said she wasn't hungry, that she just wanted coffee. I got it for her when I got mine and Aunt Lucy's breakfast and she just let it sit there and get cold. She was still mad at me I guess because I wouldn't give her the money she asked for a bus ticket home. I told her I was driving her home, that it was my duty, soon as I got the water pump I found at the junkyard on. My hands looked too black to pick up my food, much less touch a girl like Tennessee.

Then out of the blue, right in front of three other people eating and the Indian guy doing the cooking, Aunt Lucy said real loud: "I picked up the phone and Tendall hollered: 'I can't get my pecker out, Lucy.'"

Oh brother. Here we go again. I heard her right, and it was too late to shut her up. Tennessee kept turning pages, but she had to have heard Aunt Lucy.

"Tendall hollers when he's scared," Aunt Lucy kept going. "A wise man whispers." I couldn't help but think about her hollering 'mad dog' and kicking my truck if you want to know about wise. "So I said to him about his pecker," she went on, "'Tendall, did you try unbuttoning your britches?' He gets mad as a hornet, yelling at me how he's got enough sense to unbutton his britches. That the reason he can't get his pecker out is his pecker ain't there. And I told him, you're expecting a little too much of your big sister to expect her to come over and find your pecker for you, Tendall."

"He must of been drunk, Aunt Lucy," I whispered. I felt my face get hot but I didn't have a sunset to duck behind this time.

"I don't believe so, Benny. I don't believe so. I said to him 'What do you find when you unbutton your britches, Tendall?' You know what he said? 'Cloth. Appears to be polka dotted cloth, Lucy.' So I said: 'Let me think on this a minute, Tendall. Your underdrawers is probably made out of polka dotted cloth, because I seen what Mona give you for Christmas. And your pecker ain't.' Then he gets mad as a wet hen, so I slammed down that phone and traipsed right over to his house and I like to have split my sides laughing.

"I told him, 'Tendall, pull down your britches and step out of them,' and he did. 'Now, if you ain't peed in them already, pull off your underdrawers and turn them around. You put your underdrawers on backards and your britches on frontards, you old fool. That's what happened to your pecker.' Just look at what a big sister has to do for you, Benny. Next time you're being so mean to Ethel, you think about Lucy and Tendall and how you might get your underdrawers on backards someday."

I couldn't say a thing. I was so embarrassed, my face burned like I'd gotten blistered in the sun. Not a peep out of Tennessee. Not even a giggle. For sure not a clap. It was like we weren't there for Tennessee but the other people were laughing at Aunt Lucy.

"So Tendall turned around real quick so I wouldn't see his little tallywack, like I cared if it looked like a pink worm hanging out of a crabapple. And what do you know? That's when I seen the pucker in his butt." Aunt Lucy was quiet a minute and then she asked: "Do you know what I'm telling you, Benny Foushee?"

"No Ma'am, I guess I don't exactly."

"I'm telling you that's when I seen where he got shot over in France. A bullet hole, right in the butt. Looks like a belly button in his fat ass." She began to cackle: "So I went: 'Pow!' at him with my finger and liked to have fell over laughing. Tendall Foushee, war hero. I asked him, 'What was you doing when you got shot, Tendall? Trying to wiggle in a foxhole already full up with yellow blooded Frenchmen?'

"And Tendall starts begging me, 'Don't tell Rupert. Please don't tell my little brother. Dressing up like a soldier like his big brother makes him so proud.' And I told him, 'Tendall, I believe your peanuts done gone to vine. Your little brother don't dress up like nothing but a plumber, last time I looked. I believe your remembering is leaving out a few years.' But I give him my word. Shouldn't have. Don't know why I did. Little as the sonavabitch ever done for me. I didn't tell Rupert. My word is good. I did that for Tendall and he never give me air in a jug a day of my life and wouldn't right now if I was blue as a redskin pancake. What do you think of that, Benny?"

With my brain half there, I asked her: "How long ago did Uncle Tendall get his underpants on backwards?" Tennessee was already out the door, getting the dogs out of the truck. Aunt Lucy was quiet a few seconds. "Don't recollect. Now you weighing on my old memory. Not long before we left for out here, is the best of my recollection. Right before he told that D-Day story for the umteenth time. The day he brung up that milk snake. That was it. He done peed in his pants, and who you think watched him put his dirty clothes in the dryer instead of the washing machine, and had to straighten him out? Now who you think needs to get moved out of their house?"

"You think Uncle Tendall is slipping pretty bad, Aunt Lucy? Or was it just that one little mistake?" Aunt Lucy started laughing her mean laugh. I watched Tennessee and the dogs, just half listening to Aunt Lucy. Someone was coming down the sidewalk towards Tennessee. It was Crybaby Cravon. He stopped when he saw her.

"Tendall was fixing his sweet taters and he turned them on sixty minutes meaning sixty seconds. In that microwave thing he got at Wal-Mart. Opened the door and out come all these pieces of glass and his taters burnt like black rocks. I was fixing to kid him about them sweet taters one Sunday, ask him if they was as good as the one his big sister fixed him on the motor on the way to Wilmington."

"Guess Mother isn't going to be missing you too much. Not with Uncle Tendall around. I got to go, Aunt Lucy. That water pump isn't going to put itself on."

She was reaching in her purse for her wallet to pay for breakfast. "I owe you five bucks from last night," I said quick before she noticed it.

"You owe me ten bucks," she answered, looking in her wallet.

"Five," I said again.

"Ten," she said as she spread her wallet and thumbed through her bills. I refilled her coffee at the counter and spilled it on my hand before I got to her with it.

"A watched pot never boils but a watched cup always spills."

After that I quit hearing her. I left her talking to the air inside the burger joint.

Crybaby was still there, talking to Tennessee now. He wasn't so old, his hair red as clay in the daylight.

"Benny," Tennessee said. "This is Cravon Nelson. He said he'd be glad to take me home. He's leaving today in that direction."

Crybaby saw me then. His eyes narrowed to slits. I couldn't help myself. I went after him. His eyes opened to two blue balls floating in red when I grabbed his shoulders.

"I believe you're going to Mexico," I said to Crybaby. "I believe you're packing up right this minute."

"Hey buddy. Calm down. I didn't mean no harm. Calm down. Just giving a hand to the little lady. Didn't know she was yours." When I let go of him, he backed up, losing his balance on the step to the bar where we were last night and falling into the door. He tried the handle even though there was a closed sign. It opened and he went inside.

I turned back around to where Tennessee was. It was like the ground had opened up. She was gone again. Polar let out a loud yap and jumped out of the truck bed. He knew where she went. It couldn't be far. Shenandoah came behind me, her breathing sounding more like a cow than a dog as I followed Polar on the weed filled path. Tennessee didn't get far. She was sitting on a giant rusty can, turned bottom up, her back to me. She didn't have on the straw hat. As Polar sat beside her, she put her hand on his head. I could hear her crying again. When I walked around in front of her, she would only look at my feet.

"Don't you give me a lecture on bad people," she whimpered.

I didn't know what to say so I just said: "OK."

"I know the difference. I can take care of myself. Leave me alone."

"OK."

"Stop saying OK."

I came so close to saying OK again, I almost had to stick my fist in my mouth to stop it. I squatted down on the other side of her and to my surprise I was as lucky as Polar. She put her other arm around me. Me and Polar sat there a while and didn't make a sound until she had cried herself out again. I sure was glad I had Polar to tell me what to do. He had a lot more work to do teaching Shenandoah who was digging in the trash pile, getting ready to cut her paw on busted glass.

Tennessee let go of both of us and clapped her hands hard, not her happy clap. She yelled "Stop!" like that dumb dog was heading off a cliff. The big dog fell down on her knees in front of Tennessee like she was bowing to the princess. Guess that makes three of us but I sure didn't mind. I almost reached over to hold Tennessee's hand that was on her knee but my hands were too filthy with engine crud to touch her. I saw she had on two of her butterfly rings that were opening and closing their wings like they were getting ready to flap off. And that Indian bracelet under her special things bracelet I don't know where she got the money to buy. I almost couldn't wait to give her her present.

10

Aunt Lucy told me to get her rocker. After I dumped out Shenandoah in the truck bed and set the chair in front of our room in Gold Cave, New Mexico, I turned Aunt Lucy's body so she would fall back in the seat. When I handed her her battered magazine, she didn't start reading like she usually did, just stared up at the mountain behind the bar. Up high was a uranium mine with yellow rocks around it that I don't think she could see. I cleaned her greasy glasses on the bottom of my t-shirt like I usually did but her expression didn't change when I put them back on.

Tennessee jumped up backwards on the railing in front of Aunt Lucy, rubbing Polar's head with her feet when he came up to her, so I set down beside her. When she came out to talk to me while I put on the water pump, she asked me to tell her the story of how I got Polar. I guess Shenandoah was the first stray animal she ever picked up. I told her how I stopped on the highway on a rainy night to let Polar in my truck. Only problem was it was prom night and my then girlfriend Valinda was in my truck in her new Dayglo pink prom dress. Tennessee seemed to like my funny story: end of girlfriend, beginning of good dog story.

I'm not so sure she's going to be that lucky with Shenandoah. I never saw a dog could eat that much. And that dog always gets her feelings hurt when you ask her to quit doing something she shouldn't.

"Mrs. Williams, what do you want more than anything in the world?" Tennessee asked Aunt Lucy out of the blue. She was back wearing that stupid hat and sunglasses disguise. I don't even think Gold Cave had a policeman.

"I wish Obie could see that big cactus," Aunt Lucy said without missing a beat. My first thought was how much trouble it would be to take two old Aunt Lucy's to see the big cactus. Mother would call me selfish for even thinking that. I'm getting a little better at keeping my mouth shut. "It would have pleased him," Aunt Lucy went on, starting to rock hard. "Something to talk about in our old age. If he had got there. Me and Papa set on the porch when the work was done and he talked about seeing the big cactus. Tendall would go off to the pool hall. Papa promised he'd take me to see it one day but he didn't get to. Benny, bless his heart, did it for him."

Aunt Lucy reached out and patted her hand in the air, which would have patted me on the head if I'd been three feet tall and standing beside her. I heard Tennessee giggle at that.

I was trying to pick the black out from under my nails with my pocketknife. Mother would have been harping on me how rude that was to do in public. Daddy did it. Wish he was here to take a look at my repair. I put on a rusty old pump from the junkyard that looked almost as bad as the one I took off only it wont broke in two. When I announced, that I thought it was fixed, nobody seemed to care. I don't believe they caught on to how much trouble we'd been in. I sure didn't feel like bragging on my repair just yet.

"Mrs. Williams, why didn't you and Obediah have any children?" Tennessee asked another one of her questions.

"Because we didn't know how to do it."

That made Tennessee giggle even louder. She probably shouldn't have asked it. It just popped in her brain. I bet she believed Aunt Lucy would be a better mother than hers was.

"Neither one of us knew anything," Aunt Lucy kept on. "It just never seemed to work. I was mighty old before I got hitched. I never felt bad about it, to tell the truth, because I didn't see no need of children for me. Able to go here and there and never have to worry: now where is that baby? I had to fret all the time with Rupert when I was near about a child myself. You two don't know what I mean. Men don't know what I mean. Obie didn't know what I meant."

"I know what you mean, Aunt Lucy. You mean once you have a kid, you have it the rest of your life until it is old enough to take care of itself."

"You're not near as dumb as you look, Benny Foushee."

"Thank you."

After that the kid takes care of you, I thought. Every minute. All day and all night.

"I think he got tired of just me, though. Obie, I mean. A person thinks you're the cat's pajamas the first couple of years. Then you got to remind them you heard that story already. Or you got to sit and listen to them tell somebody else the story you heard too many times. Then Obie gets his stupid overalls caught." She blinked like the slide show in her head needed to go to the next picture. "Obie's boat broke in two."

Aunt Lucy said that before. I didn't have any idea what that came from. "What kind of boat? Did he drown?" Tennessee asked. She sure isn't afraid to ask questions. I wish she hadn't.

Aunt Lucy rocked hard now, talking in spurts that we were meant to put together like a jigsaw puzzle. "Obie seen in the paper, boat come out from Canada, where he come from, split in two. Storm in cold water. Cracked apart like kindling. Men made rafts out of cabin roofs. Drank all the liquor, floated off on the barrels. Ten of them, never turned up, dead or alive. No time in a war. No time to rivet them right. Little over a month, whole boat done. Slam, bam, thank you ma'am. Obie took it all on hisself."

Aunt Lucy was getting all worked up over her thoughts. Her jigsaw puzzle didn't have a picture on the box to go by. To tell the truth, I think her puzzles were starting to miss some pieces. Uncle Tendall told me once that Uncle Obie was the reason for a bunch of soldiers getting killed. I didn't know how that could be since Aunt Lucy said he wasn't a soldier. Uncle Tendall lied a lot anyway.

"Tendall come back from that war hotter than a billy goat in a pepper patch," she went on, "strutting with his Purple Heart. Little Rupert begged to wear it, but Tendall wouldn't give it to him. Give him a pin with wings and a parachute he got at the five and dime. That poor little fellow wore that parachute pin ever where he went. Even slept in it. Thought his big brother was really something."

Aunt Lucy made a big sniff, wiping her nose on the back of her sleeve, making a little blood spot where she nicked herself on one of her pins. "Tendall started in on my Obie, who hadn't been allowed to serve accounting his eyes was so bad. Tendall didn't come upon many men shorter than him, but Obie was, bless his heart. 'Why don't you sue the city for building the sidewalk too close to your ass?" he mocked Obie. That hateful Tendall made fun of him every way he could, mocking the way he talked funny. Even had Aunt Agnes saying he wont one of us when he was working to feed every one of us."

I did hear Uncle Tendall throw off on Uncle Obie's way of talking, how he said "Eh?" after everything. And he called him a sawed off runt on a few occasions.

"Do you mean he made a boat that sank, Mrs. Williams?" It wasn't like Tennessee, to keep asking what she shouldn't of Aunt Lucy.

"It was in the papers. Tendall read about the welded boats breaking up. Read it out loud to Obie and made him cry. Obie was just doing what the government told him to do. They wanted the boats too fast to rivet them. Tendall gets the idea for Obie to weld a handle back on Papa's old rusty manure spreader. Just meanness. Obie didn't want to do it, but Tendall dared him."

"Stop it, Aunt Lucy. Stop telling it right there. I don't want to hear what happened because I've seen that manure spreader and I know what kind of wrong thing it can do. Daddy told me enough times, so it wouldn't hurt me. We ought to get rid of it. We never get rid of anything. I don't want Tennessee to hear stuff like this."

Aunt Lucy ignored me. I could put a bag over her and she wouldn't shut up. "Obie wont shy about work. But he wont suited for farming. Tendall wont suited for work period. Good for nothing more fancy than chopping up cigarettes at Liggett and Meyers. He couldn't hit water if he fell out of a boat."

"I'm sorry, Mrs. Williams. I didn't mean to make you mad."

"If there was really a god in heaven, he'd a took Tendall and left Obie. Obie had a skill and a heart good as gold. Sorry piece of junk manure spreader Papa give Flonnie Glover a dollar for. 'Too old and brittle, needs sanding,' Obie said about fixing it, but he done it anyway. Come winter his weld broke like mud. Obie lost his glasses and bent over..."

I got up and pulled Tennessee up by the hand, maybe too hard because when she stood up, it made her start coughing right at first. I pulled her along behind me. The last thing I heard Aunt Lucy say to the air was: "Drove it clean inside his brain…" Now she's blaming Uncle Tendall for killing her husband. It was an accident. She has to fix blame for every single thing.

Polar stood up to follow us, but I told him: "Stay Polar. You already seen where I'm going. You and Shenandoah stay with Aunt Lucy." He took one little step and I said stay again. He minded. He always did even if he couldn't understand. I didn't want him running in that mine anymore where there might be a bat. And I wanted him to keep an eye on Aunt Lucy.

"Where are you taking me, Benny?" Tennessee asked. "I won't bug her with anymore questions. I didn't make her mad on purpose."

"To see the uranium mine," I said out loud. Something you've never seen, I said inside to my brain: I am taking you away from hearing something else to break your heart worse than a little animal hurting even. "It's right over us," I told her. "I went up there after I finished the truck."

I tugged Tennessee along, up the path to the mine entrance that was cut in the hill. I turned every few steps to check on Aunt Lucy who rocked slowly in her chair, under the cover at the front of the motel. She appeared to still be talking. Polar and Shenandoah were listening. They were hearing about those belts that slipped off that turned the sharp blades that busted up the cow piles.

"Come look here." I pointed Tennessee over to the edge of the cliff. "See. There are those layers you told me about. Like a cake with a lot of different ingredients." I was trying to impress her. Seemed to work. She was smiling.

"Yes. And do you know where man came in this picture?"

I should have known she'd nail me on something. I shook my head. "Right at the top," she said, pointing across the canyon. "Remember what I told you about the river cutting the canyon, that down at the bottom are the oldest things? Pretend this canyon was made in a day, twenty-four hours. People would be in the last minute at the top."

Now she was making me feel like a little kid, a stupid little kid at that. "You said it took millions of years. That Adam and Eve are buried over there a few feet down. I mean over there in the Holy Land."

"I didn't say Adam and Eve. I said man."

"They were the first man and woman."

"No they weren't. Never mind."

I really didn't want to piss her off now. "I'm sorry Tennessee. I'm just saying what my mother would have said. I'll listen to you from now on. She gets all her stuff at church."

"See the white place down there?" she went on. "That is when this was covered by the ocean. You can find seashells in the rocks. And that dark stripe over there is when the dinosaurs lived. Over seventy million years ago."

I sure wasn't going to ask about Noah with the ocean way down there and the first people way up there. Even Aunt Lucy said Noah was bullshit.

"We better get a move on it," I put in. "Don't want it to get dark and us walk right off the edge, end up down there a billion years ago." She let me pull her away from the side and back on the trail. When we got to the mine entrance, I let go of her hand to go check to make sure nobody got my present. It was still there, stuck inside the springs of the car seat I found for us to sit in at the door to the mine. The view was real good from there. Could see Aunt Lucy with the dogs and the sunset too.

"Have a seat," I said. Tennessee hesitated. "Don't worry," I added. "I put one of the motel towels on it so you wouldn't get dirty and beat on it in case there were snakes. The view is real pretty from here." I'm afraid I sounded like I was trying to sell her something. When she set down, I set down real quick beside her. "I wasn't meaning to jerk you up so hard, but Aunt Lucy has some terrible stories, two of them I know of, and I don't want you to hear either one from her."

"Is that true, Benny? That cold water makes a welded boat break in two?"

"You sure can ask a lot of questions."

"I want to know a lot of things. I want to be a teacher."

"Well, it's true. Cold can break a weld. I seen a weld break last winter on a old fender that Buddy at the Exxon did."

"Saw a weld break."

"Saw a weld break. Getting like a teacher already, that's for sure. I want to be a truck mechanic. NASCAR trucks at the races. Don't need grammar. Bet you can't teach me nothing about that."

"Anything."

"Anything about that."

"What do you want more than anything in the world, Benny?"

"You just asked Aunt Lucy that question. Are you doing riddles again?" Tennessee didn't say anything. I had to quit fiddling around with this talking. I was getting nervous. "To answer your question," I said, "I guess I want to get Aunt Lucy back home alive." After I said that, I wasn't sure I was honest that that was what I wanted more than anything. I knew it ought to be if I was a good person. I'd like to fix Tennessee for asking that so I asked her right back: "What do you want more than anything?"

She didn't even think. Before I hardly got it out, she answered: "I want to be a boy."

So Benny just had to come up with something dumb to say to that: "Well, even if you hadn't ran out of money, run out of, you couldn't buy that." I needed to just shut up and do what I planned. I reached under me inside the springs where I left the present. "Here, I got this for you."

She looked at the wrapping paper kind of funny.

"I messed up with the paper."

We both laughed kind of uncomfortable. This wasn't going as well as I had hoped. When she tore the paper off, the wind took it out of her hand. She set down the box and went chasing off after it. "Let it go," I yelled. "The present is in the box." I almost couldn't stand the wait.

"I don't want to litter," she said softly, catching the baby paper and balling it up in her fist which seemed pretty silly to me since there was enough litter and stuff around the front of that mine to make a junk yard and trash pile rolled into one. She took her present box out of my hands, handing me the paper ball when she set down. That old bug was rustling inside the box. I had been a little worried that he might of smothered in there. I watched her face when she took the lid off the box. She let out a little gasp like there was something in there wasn't supposed to be. She kind of froze so I figured I better say something.

"It's to put on your bracelet."

She looked at me and then back at the bug. That old bug had ideas of his own. He was out of that box and headed down her pants leg with that chain dangling after him like he escaped from the road gang. I picked him up real fast. Didn't want him to scare her. His feet kept running. He didn't act this alive in the bar. Must have gotten bored wrapped up in that box. He grabbed holt the end of my finger like he was hanging on for dear life. Tennessee still hadn't said anything.

"I got the one with the blue stones because you seemed to like blue," I said, holding the bug up. "You do, don't you?"

Finally she said something: "Yes. I like blue."

"He doesn't have to eat. He is at a time in his life when he just wants to sit on this wet piece of wood every now and again that's in the box with him. Kind of like Aunt Lucy in her rocker, but different in that he won't be any trouble." I was talking too much. "Not like a dog," I heard myself say which I probably shouldn't have considering what she did picking up that dog.

After what seemed like a million years, she reached over and got the bug from me, holding on the jewels on his back actually, not him. She moved him real slow through the air, his gold chain with the safety pin hanging down. She lifted up her other arm, still like slow motion, the one with the bracelet on it. He did just what I thought he'd do. Soon as that old bug saw that bracelet, he grabbed it. Tennessee let out another little gasp. He grabbed on to that gold horse like he planned to ride it. With this little gold cross in one hand. Or I guess you'd call it a foot.

"Onward Christian soldiers," I said. "Believe he's too big to ride that little horse."

All of a sudden Tennessee started laughing. She was just plain busting up laughing. I had really hoped for a clap but I guess she had her hands full.

"Boy, I'm glad to hear that laugh," I told her. "I was starting to worry you might never even smile at me again. Do you like your present? I mean do you really like it? Don't just act polite and try not to hurt my feelings."

"Benny, you're crazy. You're completely crazy," she said.

"Yeah, I know."

She unhooked her bracelet and let it drop in the box. I thought that old bug would be dying to jump back on his wood, but he decided to go from charm to charm. Special thing to special thing. She put the lid on. We both could hear all the different things jingling inside the box. "Boy, listen at that," I said. "Bet he's the first Mexican bug to get to play with fancy stuff like that." I waited a second but went ahead and said it: "Me too. Having the time of my life being with Tennessee Gentry." She didn't say anything but at least she was still smiling. "I'm sure going to hate taking you back home, Tennessee."

I kind of blurted it out too fast I guess. I was thinking about moving closer to her when I said that but I swear, she had already moved further away so I would have to go twice as far. Guess I ought to take the hint. I got me an old dog named Polar and now I bought a bug and both of them just go right after what they want. Me, I just set here. And forever hold my peace.

After that we watched the sun go down. And she had to tell me about all the yellow rocks around the mine, that yellow was the sign they had uranium in them. I just half listened. I thought about asking her if she wanted to go in the mine a little ways, but I didn't have the sense to remember my flashlight. Daddy always remembers to bring a flashlight. I didn't like thinking about the bats that might be in that mine.

Polar was still setting down there beside Aunt Lucy like I told him to. Shenandoah looked like a cow laying down with her head against him. I figured we better head back down the hill before the sun was so far gone we couldn't see the trail. I just wanted to stay for one more thing. No sooner than I thought it, there it went. I saw it. So neat. Polar did just like the cliffs and turned red.

"Red dog," I said to Tennessee.

That did it. At least I got one of the little claps. Then Aunt Lucy's face and hair went red like she caught on fire.

The next day we drove back through Wonita, New Mexico. A city limits sign on the west side of town showed a big airplane flying over a cactus, so I guess Pete the barber's story must of been the truth. When I stopped again at the long stoplight, I checked out the filling station. The wrecker was there, but I didn't see the Porsche anywhere. On the other side of the street, Ferrell was back in the barber chair and Pete looked out at the parking lot. I waved at them when the light changed and they waved back, out of politeness, not like they knew me. I bet Ferrell would recognize Tennessee without her straw hat and sunglasses. Her blond head was asleep in Aunt Lucy's lap. Tennessee's hat was on the old lady's feet, ready for her to grab soon as she woke up. She usually had little pearls on her ears that looked like drops of water. Today she had long beads hanging down that matched that Indian bracelet.

The highway patrol probably checked the license tag on the Porsche and called Tennessee's daddy. He must be worried sick by now, but I'm sure not going to mention him. To tell the truth, I was feeling really worn out. I didn't sleep too good in the truck last night. Felt about like I got run over by somebody else's truck when the sun came up in my face. I wanted to go as slow as I could, which wasn't like me. I usually wanted to get somewhere new as fast as I could go, even if I was just going to mess around when I got there. I felt like that old rusty water pump on my truck, like I might break in two any minute.

I had to take Tennessee back home today, that's what was wrong with me. There wasn't any use pretending that we weren't almost there. I found Taos on the map and it was up north from Wonita. She reminded me again this morning that she wanted to go home. I couldn't tell if Aunt Lucy was going to miss her or not. Tennessee fell asleep with her head in Aunt Lucy's lap like she was her little girl. They talked all the time like two girls when Tennessee was awake, if you can believe that. I felt kind of left out. And she wasn't wearing her special things' bracelet. Just that

Indian bead one like the new earrings. I wanted to listen to her leather suitcase to see if the bug was thumping around in there.

Even though Tennessee hadn't said a dozen words all morning to me that I could recall, as soon as we got past Wonita, she all of a sudden started yelling at me: "Benny, did we pass it already? Benny, you should have awakened me. Benny, why didn't you wake me up when we passed the Porsche? I know it was before now…" Fussing at me bad as Mother.

"Whoa. Hold your horses." I hated to shut her up with her finally deciding to talk, but she was getting all in a uproar over nothing I could do anything about. She didn't care one hoot about that car when I tried to do something.

"It wasn't there, Tennessee. I paid special attention to where you left it and it wasn't there."

"Oh no. Oh no. Oh no."

"Is your record broken?" Aunt Lucy asked.

"Aunt Lucy. Don't pick on her. Tennessee, remember, I told the filling station in Wonita about it the day you left it. The car is gone. Your daddy probably came and got it."

"Oh no. Oh no."

"Is your record broken?"

"I bet he won't even be mad," I said after I told myself I wasn't going to mention him. "I bet he's worried sick about what might have happened to you. Finding your car broken down and worrying some bad person got you."

"Two bad people got you," Aunt Lucy put in.

Tennessee didn't have any more 'oh no's' for me after that.

"If I was your daddy, I sure would be worried," I added, just begging for trouble.

"You're not my father." Now I made her mad even though I knew better than to mention him. He was father again, not dad. "He didn't want me. He wanted a little boy," she added with her lip out.

I didn't want to think what I was thinking right now, because I would probably regret thinking it later on but I was starting to feel like I did the night I took Valinda home from the prom. I know I would be sorry I thought it, because I shouldn't feel that way at all about Tennessee. I know with Valinda, I just wanted to dump her out and drive off. It's like being mad because it's raining. Not a damn thing anybody can do to stop the rain and you're not the only one getting wet. What in the world did a pretty girl want to be a boy for?

"I want a credit card just like my mother has," Tennessee went on. "Then it doesn't matter if I don't have any real money. Sometimes she doesn't even have enough real money to get me a pop. So she gets money at the ATM."

"Where did you get the money for those earrings?" I asked her. She turned away and looked out the side window. I heard the glass roll down and back up. When I looked at her, the long earrings were gone.

"Where are your earrings?"

"I didn't like them. They were too big and tacky. Stop! Stop, Benny, right here," Tennessee yelled.

I did. I did everything these women asked me to do, I guess. Polar and Shenandoah hit the back of the cab. Poor old dogs don't have brakes as good as my old truck even.

"What for?" I asked. She sure wasn't going to be able to find those earrings she threw out. I think she took them from that Indian woman is what I think and didn't pay for them.

"Here. Turn in that parking lot," she pointed ahead. "We went here from school. This is really cool. You wait and see." I pulled in the parking lot of the Dead Horse Mesa Trading Post. I didn't know what she was going to use to buy more stuff with. And with her big, black dog in the back, we were flat out of room.

"What you want with a dead horse?" Aunt Lucy asked. "They'd probably give it to you since it's dead already. Sell it to the glue factory since you ain't got no more money." I knew I shouldn't have told Aunt Lucy that Tennessee was out of money.

"I'll get money from my father to pay you back," Tennessee answered. "It won't cost much. I want it to show the girls at school. They won't believe what I did." Aunt Lucy got out mumbling something about not walking around the block to see a dead horse. I think I was the one ought to be mumbling about being in a bad mood.

Inside the Dead Horse Trading Post was a place to get your picture took, pretending to be the Wild West, which they seem to like to do out here. I saw Miss Kitty from *Gunsmoke* and Marshall Dillon. Even a cardboard horse with a hole in his head big enough for a people head to poke through. We finally got all the cardboard people we wanted all lined up. Aunt Lucy was Miss Kitty.

"You look mighty good to a old cowboy after a hard day on the range, Aunt Lucy. A real old cowboy." I tried to be cheerful.

"Shut up and poke your head in the gunslinger. You can't hold a candle to Marshall Dillon yourself, smart ass."

It sure was hard to get everybody situated right for the picture. Polar's horse kept falling over because he thought I wanted him to crawl through the hole instead of sticking his head in it. It wasn't something that was easy to explain to a dog. Glad we left Shenandoah in the truck. She didn't mind worth a damn, and she wouldn't stick her head in anything but somebody's crotch. Me, it made me about a foot taller to be Marshall Dillon, taller than Daddy even. I had to stand on a box, but I wasn't the first one since the box was already back there.

Another problem was Tennessee kept changing her mind which person she wanted to be. I was kind of hoping for one of the saloon girls or even the schoolteacher because I could really brag about knowing her if my friends saw that. She had such a nice little shape for real she didn't even need to stick her head in a cardboard cutout.

There was a short woman with a little tiny waistline, holding a shotgun by the barrel like some women would hold a broom. "Annie Oakley," Aunt Lucy told me when she saw it. "Papa throwed a hundred clay pigeons for her at Pinehurst when she was a old lady. She got every one of them." I hated to say it but I didn't know whether to believe her or not anymore.

Tennessee studied the Annie Oakley cutout. I was sure disappointed when she settled on this little kid instead, little boy at that. Awful pretty little boy. I should have guessed that was what she'd pick. The guy took a bunch of pictures. Aunt Lucy grumbled and paid him his money to get a copy for us and one for Tennessee.

"You sure these won't fade away before we get home with them," I asked him. "They look awful brown."

"That's sepia. That's done on purpose to make them look old. Guaranteed for five years."

"I ain't lasting five years," Aunt Lucy said.

The man laughed at that. "I guess I ain't got to give you a guarantee, Granny," he said.

"If you was my grandson, I wouldn't admit it."

"Aunt Lucy, hush. Do you have to get us in trouble everywhere we go?"

"He's a smart mouth. Shouldn't make fun of his elders. Not good for business." I turned her around and shoved her towards the door.

"Don't forget your damn dog," the man yelled.

With that Polar let out a bark loud enough to make the wind chimes in the place start jingling, then he took a leap off the stool he was on and sent that old horse over like somebody shot it. I don't know how many things got busted, but I heard more than a few go flying. I lifted Aunt Lucy over my shoulder like a sack of potatoes and went fast as I could for the truck. Polar and Tennessee beat me there because Aunt Lucy was heavier than I thought to tote that far. I pushed and Tennessee pulled on her till we got her in the truck. The photographer guy was cussing at us from the open door. Good old truck started right up.

"Benny the Kid and Ma Barker," Aunt Lucy grunted as we headed down the highway, rocking on the truck seat. "Shot up another saloon. Robbed another bank. All in a day's work. Should have spared the horse though, Mr. Kid. Then they might of named the place Benny the Kid Trading Post." Aunt Lucy was back to life and Tennessee was sitting beside me. Finally she was laughing and clapping like she was at a stage show. We were all laughing. Except Polar who had wiggled in the cab with us, but dogs do kind of smile. Polar's not used to doing bad and getting fussed at. Shenandoah was still riding in the back, too dumb to know what had just happened. I know what they mean when they say that sometimes you laugh to keep from crying. I saw a sign. We weren't but nine miles from Taos where Tennessee said she lived.

"Shit. There it is," Tennessee said. Sounded more like Aunt Lucy.

I'm telling you I never saw nothing like it in my life. Anything. Looked like a house made out of a bunch of pink boxes. I mean a bunch of them, a really big bunch. Went halfway down the side of one of those mesas. Looked like what they teach you in Future Farmer's about contour plowing, only here you grow pink boxes. Even the rocks in the driveway were pink. Cactus were all over the place. They stuck up around the pink boxes, shaped just like the big cactus we went all that way to see, only nowhere near as big. Could of fooled somebody in a picture though.

"That's where you live?"

"Yes. I hate this fucking house. I liked our last one much better that had the stable near the back of it. Had a real barn. My room is over there." She pointed at one of the boxes.

"Don't count your chickens," Aunt Lucy said. "Don't take much for your folks to decide on renting your place out." Then she added, "Maybe they adopted a boy since you been gone."

Aunt Lucy could be pretty mean. I hope Tennessee understood she was just being funny. Well, maybe she was being funny. Tennessee didn't say a word. She was staring at the big iron gate made out of black metal and gold where you could see right through a picture of a dog howling at the moon. Tennessee reached in her purse and took out this little thing I never saw before. She pushed a button on it and the gate started opening.

"How about that?" I couldn't help but say. No use at this point trying to hide I was a redneck. Then she pushed another button and the big pink box at the top of the driveway opened. There it was! The little silver car I first saw her standing behind. I sure felt a big relief, I don't mind admitting it. "There's that little car. Safe and sound," I said out loud. "The Porsche got back before you did. Boy, there are enough cars in that garage to start a car lot."

"He's home."

"Who? Oh, you mean your daddy."

"There's his Ferrari he drives to the office."

"Aren't you glad to see the Porsche is OK?"

"Um," she grunted. Didn't sound very glad. I thought she was real worried about it a while ago. I've been worried about that car since we left it.

A short dark man in blue jeans and a cowboy hat came running towards us.

"That your daddy?"

"No," she replied, like I was the dumbest person who ever walked the face of the world. "That's Juan. He keeps the cars clean. He exercises my horse and feeds the dogs when I forget."

The dark man was mad, jabbering at us in something other than English. He had on muddy cowboy boots with sweat showing through in a ring around his hat. Tennessee crawled over Aunt Lucy and hopped out of my truck, slamming the door. As she did, her big black dog jumped out of the back of the truck, and rolled over in the grass like she was making herself too big to pick up.

When the dark man saw Tennessee, you would have thought he was her daddy, he was so glad to see her. Damn. He ran up and hugged her. I never had the nerve to do that. She had the leather suitcase with the long strap over her shoulder. It swung around and hit her in the behind when he hugged her. I saw the top of the envelope with her copy of our wild west picture inside, stuck in the outside pocket on her suitcase. I sure wish she'd left that suitcase in the truck. I'm still living in a dream world, as Aunt Lucy would say.

The guy named Juan came to the window on my side and started jabbering at me. I couldn't understand a word. He was pretty upset with me. Maybe I was parked on top of his garden hose.

"Juan. He's an American. He's my friend. Mi amigo. Did you think he was a gardener because of the truck?" Tennessee giggled.

Amigo. Mi amigos. I remember that from a cowboy movie. Juan didn't look any too friendly to me.

"I thought he was kidnapper, Miss Tiffany."

I thought her name was Gentry.

"He gave me a ride after the Porsche broke, Juan. That's Benny Foushee and Mrs. Lucy Williams. And Polar. My friends. Mi amigos. And this is Falling Rock, my new dog."

Falling Rock? What happened to Shenandoah? Juan frowned at the dog and held up his hand to the window to shake. Juan Sanchez, he said. His hand was pretty awkward to reach, but I tried to shake it. He didn't stop frowning.

"Tiffany!"

Another man. OK, tell me this one is not her daddy. He had on blue jeans too, but they had creases. And a white shirt. Tennessee backed up a little when he came towards her, but he grabbed her and hugged her anyway. But it wasn't hard to tell, she didn't like it. Behind him came these two little bedroom shoe dogs. He turned Tennessee around and pretended to smack her behind, but he didn't really hit her.

She pushed her daddy away and started dancing around in this green patch of grass with the two little white things bouncing up and down around her like she was dribbling two fur balls. Polar started to growl. I didn't like to think what Shenandoah might do faster than any of us could stop her.

"It's OK, buddy," I whispered. "I guess that's Lacey and Tracey." He whimpered. I was waiting for Shenandoah, alias Falling Rock, to go swallow them whole. But she was just making herself lower, going from a piece of furniture to a rug.

"Shut up, mutt." That was Aunt Lucy to Polar. She hadn't said a word since we got here. "We better get out of here fast, Benny. I don't like the looks of this. Kidnapping is a pretty serious crime."

I couldn't say anything. I didn't know what to say to anybody. Not even to Polar. Or what to do. I was still dreaming that Tennessee was getting back in my truck and leaving all this pink house stuff behind. She called it her "fucking house." That's pretty strong talk, real strong for her.

I didn't know what the heck I'd do with those fur balls though, if she brought them with us. They looked pretty spoiled rotten. I watched Tennessee throw her suitcase on the ground and get out the two collars with the blue stones and put them on the fur balls. As soon as she did, they stopped bouncing and started rolling on the pavement, growling and snapping like they had snakes around their necks. Tennessee took the collars off real quick and dropped them in the driveway. Then the dogs started bouncing again.

Her daddy came walking towards us. His feet looked too small to stand on. He had on black loafers with a gold thing across them that looked like it came off a miniature bridle.

"Look out, Benny," Aunt Lucy warned. "He could have a gun."

I had to make myself look at his face, not his feet. "Hope I didn't mess up your car," I heard Benny Foushee saying. "I changed the fan belt, but it broke again." There went Benny Foushee talking to her daddy like there was nothing wrong with me.

"What? Oh no, no. The spare was dry rotted. Probably in there since 1956. I had the car flat bedded to Santa Fe for repair. Are you a mechanic?"

"Kind of. Don't do foreign cars at our shop." If you could call a filling station a shop.

"Let me pay you something for attempting to repair the car. And most of all for bringing Tiffany home. There was no sign of foul play the police said. The service station in Wonita said she was with friends, but I've been worried sick. She never phoned."

He took out his wallet while he was babbling, babbling kind of like I do. The wallet was made of the same nice looking leather as his shoes only without the horse bit. He started pulling out money that looked like it had just been printed. "I need to notify the police that she's back again. This is getting embarrassing with her. If anything bad ever does happen to Tiffany, no one is going to believe me."

"How come you call her Tiffany? She said her name was Tennessee."

He finally got a little expression on his face. "And once it was Shenandoah. And Savannah. Can't do anything to please her. Not even name her. I tired half a dozen nicknames and even offered to let her pick her own nickname. My wife, ex-wife, named her. After her favorite store in New York."

"You named her after a store?" I said.

"Could of been worse," Aunt Lucy piped in. "Could of named her Piggly Wiggly."

He smiled at that. "No chance that would be Darlene's favorite store. She's not in to cooking what she purchases."

I saw Tennessee—Tiffany—walking back towards the truck with her two fur balls bouncing along behind her. Her daddy was holding a bunch of money in his hand. I saw Tennessee's eyes find that money. She stepped right on those collars with the stones like they were worms. I didn't know that the eyes in the truck with me were looking at that wad of money too. And I don't mean Polar.

"Please," her daddy said, "I don't know how much my child has cost you. Or how much inconvenience she has been responsible for, but this might help ease the pain."

He held out the stack of money towards the truck window. When he did that, Tennessee went back to playing with her bedroom shoes, ignoring all of us. Even Shenandoah. Falling Rock. Tiffany.

"No need to do that," I said. The words weren't half out of my mouth before Aunt Lucy was in my lap, grabbing the bills like Polar chomping a fresh ham bone.

"You lame brain," Aunt Lucy mumbled.

A woman came out on the porch as dark as Juan. Tiffany went running to her, the dogs bouncing along behind like they were on strings. "Miss Tiffany. I am missing you so much." The little dogs ran in the house while they hugged. Before Tiffany went inside the door of the largest of the pink boxes, with her arm around the brown woman's waist, she yelled out: "Bye Benny and Mrs. Williams and Polar. Thank you for being so nice to me. I'll send you the photos when I get them developed." And then she was gone, like the little fruity looking guy that goes back inside Mother's kitchen clock.

I felt too heavy to move. I don't think my one-ton truck could carry me without busting the tires, I mean it. Polar was still whimpering over Lacey and Tracey. I wish sometimes I could be that honest. Then suddenly he went squirming out the open window before I could grab him and took off, tearing around that fancy yard. Shenandoah jumped up and took off after him, kicking up green chunks from the yard with her huge feet. Oh god. If those bedroom shoe dogs come back out, those two will swallow them like meatballs.

"I'll catch those two crazy…"

"Photos of what?" her daddy asked me, ignoring the dogs that were wrecking his yard.

"Our trip to see the big cactus," Aunt Lucy answered the question for me, because I sure couldn't find any words for that. "I give her our address last night," she added. I didn't know Aunt Lucy did that. Tennessee's - Tiffany's daddy was frowning.

"She went on vacation with you?"

"Yep," Aunt Lucy answered. "She had a big time."

"Did you know her before? I mean how did you meet her?"

"Picked her up off the road," Aunt Lucy said. With that her daddy groaned, backed up and gave us a short wave.

"Thank you. Thank you for keeping her safe." He looked at me, a sad look. "I don't know what I'm going to do. I couldn't admit to her mother she was gone again. I was praying that she would come home before Darlene got back. I had to notify the police. But I don't know how to keep her at home."

"Put her in a bird cage," Aunt Lucy offered, "and snip off her flying feathers." Sometimes Aunt Lucy sounded stupider than I did. But that answer made him smile pretty big. First time I saw that.

"Oh," I finally found my voice, "What about all the stuff she bought? Where do you want me to unload it?"

"Please. Please. Keep it. It was her Europe spending money I'm sure. Too late to take that trip now."

"But it's all hers."

"Shut up, Benny. Much obliged, Mr. Gentry. We'll give the stuff your daughter bought to folks for presents when we get back to North Carolina. Uh, don't look now but them two sorry dogs are leaving you a couple of presents out there on your grass."

I couldn't believe Polar. He had lost all his raising, as Mother would say. Taking a crap right on the guy's perfect lawn. Then he peed on one of those fancy cactuses, showing off to Shenandoah who was squatting in a flowerbed. Bad company. I know Polar wouldn't have behaved like that if Tennessee's dog hadn't done it first.

"I'm sorry, Mr. Gentry. I'll go clean up the mess those dogs made," I offered.

"It's Mr. Barrow. No, no, son, don't worry. Juan will get it. Homer Barrow." He held out his hand for me to shake. It was cold and hard as a wheel bearing. "North Carolina." He kept talking. He was a babbler too. Acted kind of lonesome. "I have a small division in Raleigh, North Carolina."

"Summit is twelve and a half miles from Raleigh."

"That's interesting," he said in a way that said it wasn't in the least interesting.

"Tennessee never said you had a business in North Carolina."

"Tiffany," he corrected. "She could care less what I do."

"She thinks you could care less what she does." Oh boy. I was getting brave, but I didn't know what I had to lose anymore. "Ask her to show you the picture we just got took. It's in her suitcase. We got one just like it. Then you'll see. She thinks you wished you had a boy instead of her." My brain sure wasn't in gear, but my mouth was going a hundred miles an hour with no brakes. That really changed the look on his face. He started coming at me.

"I got to get going," I said, and started the engine.

"No, wait," he said, but I was already in gear and backing out of the driveway. I cracked my door and Polar jumped from the driveway in my lap and wiggled between me and Aunt Lucy and I swear if he didn't have those two little jeweled collars in his mouth. Thank the Lord those two fur balls weren't still in them.

I should of turned the truck around and gone out frontwards, but I didn't want him to catch up to me. I was looking at him still standing there when I slipped and drove right over a bunch of flowers beside the driveway. I heard the little white fence around them crunching under my back tires. Juan will really be pissed now. I could back better than that, if

I hadn't been rushing.

"I done that once," Aunt Lucy mumbled. "Only time I ever drove. Knocked down a fence with Tendall's fliver. Get out of here Benny."

Aunt Lucy was stuffing all that money in her big black purse, the crisp green bills in there with her limp lettuce from lunch, stuffing it away like she stole it. When I got backed up to the iron gate, right when I let out a big groan because I was trapped like a rat, it opened up for me and I didn't even have the thing with the button that Tennessee used. I turned the truck around after I got it outside and looked in the rear view mirror. The gate closed behind me.

But it made a mistake. It closed her big black dog who was chasing us down the driveway on the outside of the gate. Shenandoah took a flying leap in my truck bed and did a somersault right into all the bags of Tennessee's stuff. Too tough to hurt. First thing, that dog started making giant daisies on the back window at Polar.

I heard Polar whimper, but Aunt Lucy said, "Don't go back, Benny. He's calling the law. We'll give the dog to Tendall. Act like we bought it for him. She don't want him. Probably just busted half the stuff she bought. Things like that dog get dumped off for a reason."

When I tried to look back one last time at that pink box house, the bright sun messed up my rear view mirror. As we left Taos, Aunt Lucy recounted the money in her lap. Hard to believe how much she had. It had a hundred on every one. I never even saw anything bigger than a fifty and that was once at the Exxon and the boss didn't want to take it. That Yankee General Grant, I think. Aunt Lucy was smiling from ear to ear. It kind of hurt my feelings, how happy she was over that money.

"I got enough money here to go to the moon," she said. "Except I'd die before I got there." I hated it when she brought up dying. Talked too much about dead people on this trip, at least to my mind.

"What you like best, Aunt Lucy? All that money he gave you or the big cactus I took you to see?" I needed to make some talk. I was driving but I didn't know where I was going.

"Don't put me on the spot." She took the bills and spread them in a fan in her lap, straightening each one real careful. It looked like the fan Mother took to church folded up in her purse in the summer, only this fan was made out of money instead of an ad for Hudson Funeral Home.

"What you doing, Aunt Lucy? You so rich, you can make a fan out of money to take to church on a hot day? If you were a smoker, you could light a cigarette with one like they do in the movies. I dare you to light one of Uncle Tendall's cigars with a hundred dollar bill when we get back."

She put a lump of snuff under her bottom lip. "I ain't going to church no more. Money's the root of all evil, just ask your mama. I'm going to rent my house back now." I shouldn't have said anything made her think of Mother.

"Wonder if that would have been enough money," I asked, "to last her all the way to North Carolina with us? That would really fry her daddy, if she did that. Came running back out of that house and left with us. Not enough money in the world to do that, I reckon. Do you think I should have said that about him wanting a little boy to a important man like Homer Barrow? He'll think about it, I bet you." For once I answered my own stupid questions before Aunt Lucy got a chance. Then all of a sudden, she wadded up that fresh money and stuffed it in her purse. She didn't say a word to answer me.

"What are you thinking now, Aunt Lucy?"

"I'm thinking when you ain't looking forward to doing something come tomorrow, money ain't worth the paper it's printed on. Don't let me slip and eat it for lettuce, Benny."

"I kind of miss that little old girl already," Aunt Lucy mumbled, as we weaved back through the mountains towards the interstate. "Got a lot more room on the seat though. Unless you decide to put that other sorry dog in here too."

I was trying hard not to think of Tennessee. I could smell my truck starting to get hot. Every time after I came over a top, I took it out of gear and let it coast down to cool off. I got to change the oil tomorrow. Least I could do for my truck. I put it through a lot. I hated giving it a rusty old water pump instead of ordering a new one like I would if I was home. Should have changed the oil yesterday so I could have kept Tennessee longer. One thing's sure: nobody on the face of the world would pick up the bunch in this truck now like I did her. We'd all end up hanging around a water hole with our tongues out like that black dog back there.

I didn't have enough to go on about Tennessee, no longer than I got to know her. She did have me confused. Her daddy might not give her any more green and purple checks, try and see if he might can keep her at home. He seemed like he cared about her to me. Maybe didn't pay enough attention to what she liked.

"The hills look like that cake Tennessee ordered at supper that time," I said, just not able to help myself. First time I'd said her name out loud since we left her house. I couldn't make myself call Tennessee Tiffany. I knew a Tiffany at Summit High. Well, I knew who she was. She was as snooty as her name. Tennessee was never snooty. Be easier to call her Piggly Wiggly than Tiffany, she was so cute.

"You remember, don't you Aunt Lucy, when she got three forks because the slice was so big and you ate almost all of it? German chocolate cake was the name of it," I stumbled. Wish I could stand it quiet, but I couldn't seem to.

"Never had it," Aunt Lucy said.

"I saw you eat it."

"Don't know that I ever had German anything. Old folks don't like Germans much because of the wars. Has that got coconut? I hate coconut. Your mama always acted like coconut was from Jesus."

My head was starting to hurt. Swarms of bugs flew straight at my windshield like a snowstorm but they splattered white guts that didn't melt. When I went around corners, the guts turned red as the cliffs when the sun went through them. I couldn't keep my mind on what Aunt Lucy talked about. She was going on about the Anasazi Indians, another thing Tennessee taught us about. But Aunt Lucy was doubting they went to the trouble to put fancy colors on baskets when they were starving to death.

"Aunt Lucy," it was me talking, getting ready to ask for trouble. If there's one thing I learned this trip, a person can't make himself keep his mouth shut, no matter how much he wants to. I wasn't one bit sad about those old Indians dying in the woods or freezing to death or getting dumped out through the floor; I didn't even know them. "Aunt Lucy, don't you reckon there has got to be more to life sometimes than just making do?" My voice cracked and my eyes stung. Now why did I have to ask that? "I don't want to just get by, Aunt Lucy. Make do. Maybe those Indians wanted to wake up in the morning and have a real pretty basket to eat their ham and eggs out of. Or blue pancakes, if that was what they were having that day."

"Benny, you think that's why there's pretty baskets in the back of this truck? You think your little sweetie was buying them pretty baskets to feed you breakfast out of?"

"To tell you the truth, Aunt Lucy, I don't know half of what she was buying, she bought it so fast." Aunt Lucy didn't have reason to be mean to me right now. "You said Grandpa got you a goldfish for Christmas. You didn't eat that fish even when you were half starved."

"I put her in the well when Tendall got drunk and broke her bowl. That fish was special. Came up in the bucket on occasion."

My eyes were starting to mess up. I pulled off the road at this turnout, looking out the window on my side to hide my face from Aunt Lucy. This was the last lookout place before the interstate it said, so it was going to be ugly outside soon and flat. It got too pretty outside to talk about to Aunt Lucy. The black limbs were piled high with white. It was snow for sure. I guess I ought to worry about my poor old tires that were about to give out completely, but I couldn't make myself think that like Daddy would.

Snow came sifting down when the trees wiggled a little after the stacks got too tall. My words would just blunder through the sight anyway. I didn't have nobody to impress anymore with what I had to say anyhow. Anybody. To tell the truth, I was crying like a baby on the outside now, but Polar was making more crying noises than I was. I don't think he ever seen me cry before. Saw. I don't much. First time I ever let a girl make me cry, I can tell you that.

"Benny Foushee. Benny Baby. There ain't a damn one of them Anasazi left, honey. They all died off. Like the dodo bird. Which had two left feet, I might add." I felt a hand reaching around Polar to pat my shoulder, a hand that wouldn't have the strength to take the lid off a jar for herself.

"Aunt Lucy. What if we decided right now not to go back to Summit? Just stopped right here and used all that money to build a little cabin out there on that mesa. People in Summit would think we died out west."

"So Benny Foushee is all ready to build him a house out here now and raise a family. And when old Aunt Lucy kicks the bucket, dump her out through the floor like them Anasazi." She was making fun of me mean now.

"I didn't say nothing about raising a family."

"Anything. Naw. All you said was you was hurting to leave that pretty little girl behind. I ain't dumb as you think about that, Benny. You're too young to know what's good for you and what ain't. That man who give us that money would pay somebody a lot more money to kick Benny Foushee out of there for good. Don't you know we're trash, honey? That little girl just climbed on the first roof in a flood. She didn't give us the time of day in her own fancy yard. You ain't never going to be able to build a house big enough to put all her stuff in it anyway."

"I guess I know it. Why did Mother marry Daddy then, to your way of thinking? Mother's not trash."

"Because Rupert Foushee was about the most handsome man ever born in Summit, North Carolina. Looked like Tyrone Power."

"Who's that?"

"The handsomest man ever born anywhere."

"If my mother's not trash, I'm only half trash."

That made Lucy laugh and start singing "Half Breed". "And you can't carry a tune in a bucket and you don't sound a bit like Cher. I'm not trying to be funny, Aunt Lucy."

"I know you're not, Benny. And I'm a mean old biddy to pick on you when you're hurting. I just can't help myself. It's my nature to be the tail end of hard times."

"I bet I look about as much like that Tyrone Power as Junebug Mule."

"Don't go fishing for a compliment. You might catch a toad frog. You'll look a sight better. Soon as your pimples clear up."

"I'm going to be a good mechanic, Aunt Lucy. You just wait and see. If we hadn't come on this trip, I think I would have gotten my name on my shirt at the Exxon before summer was up. If I get really good, I'll get on a racing team and wear a uniform."

I looked at Aunt Lucy because she didn't say anything. Her eyes were shut. She was not even listening. Just as well. She doesn't appreciate being able to work on cars. She doesn't know I got us out of this mess fixing the truck. Daddy might even be proud of me there.

I pulled back on the road, going real slow. I couldn't tell if shiny spots on the pavement meant water or ice. I couldn't have told you if it was winter or summer outside if I didn't know already. I didn't have any business even thinking about building a house there, no more than I know about anything.

Polar was turned around in the seat, nose to nose with Shenandoah through the glass, so I stopped again before we left the turn off and let Shenandoah inside. I swear she was trembling like she was freezing. She hadn't got half as much hair as Polar. I de-double-dare Aunt Lucy to say a thing about letting that dog inside now we got more room on the seat.

Actually Aunt Lucy didn't make a peep about Shenandoah. Acted like it was going to be such a big deal if the big black dog ever got inside the cab. Then when it really happened, she woke up and fussed about a cold fly slipping in.

I got to admit that of all the people I know, Aunt Lucy knows more about hurting inside. She knows how I feel now without me having to tell her. Tennessee wouldn't be hurting for me unless I turned into a gopher and a hawk got me.

11

As well as anybody in the world, I ought to have known they'd make Aunt Lucy and the dogs get out of the truck before it went up on that grease rack in Texas. And I shouldn't have been studying how black my oil was when it ran out. I mean I should have been watching out after Aunt Lucy.

Polar started barking. By the time I got there, Aunt Lucy was beating on Shenandoah for rooting at her on the ground by the gas pumps, acting more mad than hurt at first. When I tried to pull her up she said, "Leave me here a minute, Tendall." She gave me this goofy grin and said: "I'm looking for the set." She couldn't remember the rest of her little joke about dropping the setting out of her ring. Or who I was to boot. "I smelled a melon so I might as well pollinate," she said instead. That was something to do with bats and the big cactus. She smiled up at me again. "Fill me up with water, and take out my wrinkles."

I hadn't seen her on the ground since she fell out of her rocker at home. I had been so careful with her. I couldn't believe I let this happen. And on cement. This nice lady helped me get her back up, feeling Aunt Lucy's hips and arms like she knew what she was doing. The lady took her to the Ladies room, which I sure appreciated. She patted my arm after they came back and had tears in her eyes. "Reminded me of my mama," the lady said. I knew Aunt Lucy would pipe up with something to embarrass me: "I'm sore as four boils. You ought not treat me so bad, Tendall."

After that Aunt Lucy got like a stuck record, telling me to hurry the trip up, even after I explained to her my oil was black as tar and I didn't want to blow my truck up. She didn't say much else, just hurry up. She didn't even notice me going into her purse and getting the money to pay for everything now. I could have been a pickpocket and got away with it. And now she had started in to calling me Obie.

I didn't want to take the time to do laundry so I put my sweat pants and my cleanest t-shirt on her while she sat in the bed in Arkansas. I jumped to catch her when I saw her hair move because I thought she was falling over. "Let me do my own hair," she squeaked. I hadn't touched her hair or her. She blinked at me and started doing her combing, just as normal. I felt a little better, seeing those old white fingers tying up that hair as smooth as ever with the loose hair she pulled out of her comb.

That night I noticed that Aunt Lucy's bare right arm was red and blue: red from the sun and blue with bruises like polka dots. "Aunt Lucy, your arm looks like Uncle Tendall's Sunday necktie."

"He don't have no white tie. Not that I recall."

"I meant your arm's red with blue polka dots on it. See." She frowned at the inside of her hand. I sure felt bad letting that happen. "I didn't know what you were fussing about," I kept babbling. "Grasshoppers were hitting the windshield. I thought you were just imagining they were hitting you when you said ouch. But they must have been hitting your bare arm. I should of shut your window. Look like blue nail heads."

She echoed: "Look like blue nail heads."

At supper near Memphis, we went inside a little café. I ordered a tuna sandwich for Aunt Lucy. She always seemed to like tuna, chicken with a kick, she called it. I didn't know what a fish kicked with. When I put her food in front of her, she didn't look down. Or sideways or up at me. She didn't look, period. I couldn't see anything in her eyes, like trying to look through a dirty windshield. Her glasses were gone.

"Food, Aunt Lucy." My voice made her jump like she stuck a bobby pin in a socket.

"Too thick," she said, her voice low, like it was thrown from the man two tables away. She tried to put the fat sandwich in her mouth, opening as wide as she could. I don't know why eating places do that to sandwiches. Keep fat people from fussing, I guess. I saw red splashes, falling in her plate, coloring her French fries red.

"Aunt Lucy, put it down. Quick!" I said, way too loud.

She put the sandwich back on her plate. Red dripped from her chin on her food like water off a roof.

"Don't you feel that?" I whispered this time. She didn't answer me. "You cut yourself, Aunt Lucy," I said so the people at the other tables couldn't hear me. "With the toothpick. Take the toothpick out before you try to eat it. Grab the end with the colored plastic and, never mind." I reached across and pulled the toothpick out myself.

She picked up the top slice of bread and began to eat it.

"Wipe your chin, Aunt Lucy." As soon as I said it, I knew I shouldn't have. She wiped her bloody chin with the white bread.

I slid my chair around beside her, cleaning the blood off her chin with my napkin, pressing it against her face hard, trying to stop the blood. It kept coming after I lifted the napkin, as thin as Kool-Aid. "Aunt Lucy, let's go back to the truck. We're going to make the other people in here sick."

I don't know why I kept trying to talk to her because she wasn't answering. I lifted her up from the back by her elbows then wrapped my arms around her, holding that napkin on her chin while we inched to the truck like I was taking her prisoner. In my clothes, her body felt as thin as her dresses blowing on a clothesline at home, like she wasn't in her clothes anymore.

"Watch her for me, Polar." I heard something crunch under her feet. I couldn't make myself look. It had to be her glasses. I forgot she kept them in her pocket and my sweat pants didn't have a pocket.

I went back in the restaurant. I ate my cold burger, real slow, like I used to do at home when I didn't want to do my chores. I needed to think. I was starting to feel really scared. Scared I was doing the wrong thing, but not knowing what the right thing was.

"Hey, bud. When did your grandmama have her stroke?"

I jumped when this man who was beside my table spoke to me.

"Aunt Lucy's OK. She didn't have a stroke. She didn't sleep too good last night. Lot of noise from the trucks."

He started nodding his head in that way people do when they think you are somewhere in left field. Then he turned away. I felt even more scared and now I was starting to shake. I made myself stay there until I finished my last fry. I pulled Aunt Lucy's blood splattered plate over to my side of the table. I didn't want to look at it before I finished mine. The talkative guy had left. Nobody around me, just some new people who never saw Aunt Lucy. It looked like ketchup anyway. She hadn't used any ketchup. She likes a bottle and they didn't give a bottle here. I took every one of the little plastic ketchup packages at our table and emptied them across her food. Ketchup on tuna fish. Kind of goofy to do that, I guess, but it covered the blood. I wrapped her placemat around it all. I watched that enough to know how to do it.

When I got in the truck and put the package of food in Aunt Lucy's lap, her eyes were still blinking. She was stretching my t-shirt she was wearing, winding the bottom around her fingers. I took her food back out of her lap and put it in the big black purse before the dogs got it.

"Much obliged," she said. Clear as a bell. She'd be OK soon. I kept telling myself that, but I couldn't make my shaking stop. But she'd be OK. That night in the motel I got out her tuna sandwich and fries from the purse and broke it all up in little pieces. She opened her mouth and held her head back like I was feeding a baby bird. Only you don't go in a purse and get false teeth to stick in a baby bird's mouth when he can't seem to chew his food. But she ate it all, which was my first good feeling in a long time. She had one lens left in her glasses.

"You'll get your strength back, Aunt Lucy. You're tough."

"Tough as a woodpecker's lips," she answered. Anybody knows woodpeckers have beaks. But it was nice hearing her talk, even if it was something goofy. And saying one of those corny country people things. Tennessee called them expressions. I can't remember the word she put in front of expressions, sort of like colorful but fancier than that. Tennessee never used expressions to say anything that I recollect.

"Airplane hit the big cactus," she said when I came back from the bathroom and turned off the TV with the remote thing. Crazy again.

"The big cactus is not that tall, Aunt Lucy."

After she started snoring, I said something I had to say out loud. I had to hear it out loud, not just think it. But I didn't want her to hear it. "Don't die, Aunt Lucy. Please don't die."

I went out to the truck to talk to Polar. I sure needed to. This area looked kind of bad, but I dare anybody to try to steal the stuff in my truck when they see those two in it. Polar was in Aunt Lucy's rocker that was sitting up, still in the black bag, trying to get as far away from Tennessee's black dog as he could. Aunt Lucy hadn't asked for her rocker since we were in Gold Cave where my truck broke.

"I hate to say it, Polar. I'm starting to wish we never left home. We went a long way just to get some new stories to take back home, don't you think?" He whimpered a little. He was seeing things the same way. He came over to lick the side of my face and put his chin on my shoulder. That was unusual for him. He wasn't much of a slobberer.

"Don't know if you paid attention to the story when Aunt Lucy was telling it, Polar, but Uncle Tendall left this old lady, even though she was just a young lady then, in a parking lot. Just drove off and left her, long before she was a lot of trouble to look after. When she could still do something to help you, like fix a potato on the engine. He could at least have took her back home, when they ran out of money, don't you think? The way some people are is starting to make me mad. Good and mad.

People don't always do the right thing, even when they make their best effort, as Mother would say, but Uncle Tendall wasn't even trying to do right."

I just couldn't stop talking. At least there was nobody around to think I was nuts. "We just got to make it back home, old feller. Taking care of me and you is easy. I know you'd rather be back home, not have to get in this truck every day and ride. And sleep back here with that big old dog hogging the room. Not that you ever fussed about it.

"I should of thought twice before I did this, Polar. We'd all three still be setting on the porch. All because I got a truck and know how to shift gears and put gas in it, I got us in all this trouble. Maybe after I get us back home, I'll think better of all this. But having Aunt Lucy this bad off is worse than anything ever happened to me. Right now, if you let me pick what I'd rather have done, which you can't, I'd rather be home in Summit sleeping in my own bed and eating what Mother cooks and going to work at the Exxon tomorrow and never even seen that big cactus. I wish I'd said that to Tennessee when she asked what I wanted more than anything in the world. She deserved it."

Polar looked at me like he wanted to help. Shenandoah was trampling all over the bags in the back like she didn't have a brain in her head. Hard as I tried I couldn't call that big black dog anything but Shenandoah, which was one of the fake names Tennessee, or whoever she was, even called herself. I hadn't been able to call her dog a new name any better than I could call Tennessee Tiffany in my mind. Tennessee switched the dog name to Falling Rock, just like that, which was really a dumb name for a dog and a better name for a Indian or a road sign.

Aunt Lucy was still calling me Tendall and Obie. But she wasn't meaning to be changing names. I think people who lie a lot get like Tennessee, if you want the truth. It gets real easy to make stuff up. I was trying not to feel mad, but it really kind of came over me. It started happening when I was in the grocery this morning, buying a king sized bag of dog food because Shenandoah ate more in a day than Polar needs in a week. When I got back to my truck, I threw the bag over and beat on the tailgate until my fist hurt. When I quit, Polar started licking my hand. While Aunt Lucy still had a brain, she would have told me a dog lick would heal a sore.

All day long I had to look at my skint knuckles and try to come up with why I did that. Nothing came up I could say in words, but my mad hadn't gone away. I needed to get Polar to lick my brain. Or my heart.

12

"We are back in good old North Carolina, Aunt Lucy. Can't you imagine the look on Uncle Tendall's face when he sees the dog we got him? He can hunt mountain lions with this one."

Aunt Lucy set up and looked out the truck window in the dark, I hoped trying to figure out where we were, looking through her one good lens. "Did you hear me? That's North Carolina out there in the dark."

I got us going before daylight I was so excited about being close to home. "Aunt Lucy, I don't want to wear this NASCAR truck t-shirt for about a year, I'm so sick of it." I tried again to make talk. "Almost as sick as I am of that dress you got on."

Aunt Lucy laughed a little. Maybe not at me, maybe at what she was thinking. It was pretty funny what I did with her dress yesterday. I washed it out in the motel sink and tied it to the antenna like a flag and put her back in it this morning. I went through Tennessee's bags until I found some of that expensive perfume and sprayed it on Aunt Lucy's backside. She didn't even notice it but I sure did. I sure wanted the folks at home to think I took good care of her. Well, I tried to.

"Know why I told you Tendall shot your dog, Benny?"

I couldn't believe it. Aunt Lucy was talking again. And to Benny. She hadn't made a lick of sense since she fell down in Texas, but now her voice was as clear as when she told me about Bear the first time.

"No, Aunt Lucy. I guess not. So I'd quit looking for him?"

She echoed me: "So you'd quit looking for him." Damn me. I shouldn't have given her the answer. I should have made her use her own brain.

She reached in her purse and got that flashlight. I hadn't seen her use it since the day we left. She shined it out the window but all the good it did was bounce off her window glass on her face.

"We're back in good old North Carolina," she said. Was she just repeating me again? Maybe wearing that old dress she was used to might of made her head work better. Along with all that tuna fish and McDonald's fries. Something did. You could hardly tell where that toothpick stuck her when I painted her lipstick on.

She started to laugh real loud. "What you thinking that's so funny, Aunt Lucy?"

"The look on Tendall's face when I start telling him about where we been. He ain't never been even close to the other side of the Mississippi River. If I can get him to hush his mouth and listen for a change."

"Boy, you had me worried, Aunt Lucy. You quit talking to me much at all, way back in Texas. I mean you started acting like you didn't even know who I was. You kept calling me Uncle Tendall. And you called me Obie even."

"When Aunt Agnes ain't seen you in a spell, she says every name she knows till she hits on the right one."

"Aunt Agnes has been dead about three years, Aunt Lucy."

"Then I guess she's quit saying names, ain't she?"

Uh oh. Aunt Lucy's mad at me already, but she did need to learn to remember when people were dead. I think that's important no matter how old she is. Maybe I need to work on getting happy that she's mad again. It was almost like she woke up from a dream and remembered who she was. I don't think she looks any worse for the wear, as Mother would say right now. I think she would anyway. I'll know soon.

It was well past daylight when I saw the Summit city limit sign. Nothing had changed except somebody didn't get the American flag all the way up the pole. There was a "Help Wanted" at the hardware. Might check that out. Keep my fingernails clean, as Daddy would say. Or was that about dishwashing at Sudie's Café? The café appeared to be closed which means it's Sunday. But I was planning on getting home in time for breakfast today. Big breakfast on church day with grits and sausage. Maybe Mother wouldn't make us go to church our first day back.

I couldn't wait for old Ethel to see all the stuff we brought. I bet the clothes won't be big enough to get on Ethel's big toe. I hope Aunt Lucy will keep her big mouth shut, and not fess up that Tennessee meant to buy all that stuff for herself.

"I feel a little scared, Aunt Lucy. How about you?"

"What you scared of, Benny? We didn't do nothing wrong. We are coming home with more stuff and more money than we left with. And one more stupid mutt. Might be hard to explain the money and the stuff. Not the mutt. Any fool can pick up a mutt. Just ask Benny Foushee."

"She couldn't help being so tender hearted."

"Yeah. So tender hearted she dumped her tender heart on us. That's rich people for you. You have to finish up their good deeds for them."

"I think she liked us a lot, Aunt Lucy."

"We'll see how many pictures she remembers to send us."

"Bet you a dollar she remembers."

"You got a dollar left? Here have a hundred."

Aunt Lucy threw a hundred in my lap. I left it there because I figured she planned to grab it back. Instead she picked it up and stuffed it in my jean pocket before I could get out Indian giver. She started singing. She still couldn't carry a tune in a bucket, Daddy's saying; all the way out west and back with no improvement.

I had rushed so hard to get back home, but when I got on the road up to our house with Aunt Lucy acting like she got back most of what sense she left with, I couldn't help slowing up. I knew how long it took to do this road at the speed limit. Seven minutes and twenty-seven seconds from the resume safe speed sign. And I knew soon as I slowed up some

SOB would start tailgating me, some SOB just like Benny Foushee usually. Damn car right on my bumper.

I wanted time to take in things near home. Study what wasn't the same. I never left this long before. So far, except "Help Wanted" at the hardware, everything was like we left it. Except the trees had started turning. Kind of brown looking, not real pretty. Been a hot, dry summer here too. Takes the red color out of the fall leaves to have a summer drought. Wonder if Tennessee knows that? They don't know much about colored leaves where we been. She might have read it in a book.

Can hear the tar sticking to my tires. Lot slicker tires than when we left, for sure. May pops. May pop any minute, Daddy would say. But I can walk home from here. And carry Aunt Lucy on my back if I had to. I watched Polar in the mirror who was starting to get antsy too. Shenandoah hasn't learned where she lives yet, but she's about to find out. Polar's so smart, he's getting ready to start barking. He knows he's almost home.

"What's the first thing you want to do when you get back, Aunt Lucy?"

"See if Elijah's still alive."

"Thought you said you didn't like him that much."

"I don't."

"I want to go get a drink out of the refrigerator. And make me a sandwich. Or better yet, let Mother make me one with everything on it. Sweet gherkins. That's what I've been missing. Having my own refrigerator."

Aunt Lucy grunted. "And help yourself to some macaroni and cheese. And finish it off with a big bowl of banana pudding. But be sure and get a big dish of green beans that somebody I know cooked till they turned gray."

I didn't pay any attention to her talking mean about Mother. "Then I'm going out in the barn and get my tools to tighten a bunch of stuff on the truck. Mainly that door handle on your side that you been yanking on too much getting in. And there is a rattle up under the dash I got to find. Wash off bugs we've collected from one side of this country to the other. Then wax it. It deserves it. Didn't even pop a tire. Knock on wood," I knocked my head, "but I can walk home from here. Never thought I'd be able to say that again. I can walk home. That sounds so good. There it is, Aunt Lucy! There's Mother and Daddy. On the front porch, dressed for church. And Ethel."

"Tendall must be on the commode."

Mother was the first one to see us coming. Or the first one to care I guess. She stood up and started down the steps, really hurrying. I got out with Polar and Shenandoah hitting the ground, tearing around in circles, going everywhere. Mother looked kind of surprised.

"Hey, Mother. How you been?"

"Not too good, Benny. Things are not too good," she said. Her voice was the same as always. Mother, the worrywart. She ran up and grabbed me and started hugging me so tight, I couldn't help but hug her back. Nobody to be embarrassed in front of, just family.

"I've been so worried about you, Benny. I've been worried sick you were never coming back. You haven't been driving near long enough to take off on a trip by yourself."

"We just pretty much went straight to the big cactus and back, Mother. Like I said we were going to. Took a long time to get there. Had a little engine trouble. Didn't hit nothing. Anything." I patted her back. She sure felt big and solid to me and she wasn't really that big.

"You should have sent us a card. Or called us collect." She finally let go of me. "You don't know, Benny. You don't know what has happened."

"Here, I got this for you." I pulled out the silver dog collars with the blue stones that I put in my pocket this morning. I stuffed Aunt Lucy's hundred dollar bill back in real quick. "I got one for Ethel too."

I didn't know Ethel was already there until she snatched that collar like it was a hunk of red meat. "Are these real turquoise or fake?" she asked. "Sterling silver," she read off the inside of the collar. "Probably real," she answered her own question. Ethel slid it over her fat hand and struggled to clip it together. First time I'd seen it as a bracelet.

Mother held hers, rubbing her fingertips on the blue stones. "Thank you, Benny. It's very pretty and I know you must have paid dearly for it. Oh Benny. You shouldn't have allowed that old fool to talk you into doing that. Look how your face is broken out. You've been eating too much fried food. And you're skinny as a rail. Have you and Lucy been sleeping in an alley somewhere?" She reached up to put her hand on the side of my face. Kind of shocked me. I guess women don't show me much affection.

"I knew you wouldn't stay mad at him," Ethel grunted. "He's like that guy in the Bible. Prodigal son."

"Looks a little better on you than it did on the dog," Aunt Lucy said to Ethel as she shuffled past. Aunt Lucy had gotten out of the truck by herself and was heading to the steps.

"Where's that sorry brother of mine?" she hollered so loud that Mother clamped her hand over the bracelet, like somebody was trying to steal it. Daddy was coming down from the porch. For once in a long while, I didn't have to run help Aunt Lucy up the steps. She was kicking at the bottom step like she wanted it to move out of her way. Mother's eyes were fluttering back and forth from Daddy to me, but she had grabbed my arm and wasn't letting go.

Daddy put his arm around Aunt Lucy's shoulders. He was so big, she looked like a little girl from behind, her nightgown hanging out under her dress. I guess he was a handsome man although I never saw Tyrone Power in a movie. Daddy picked Aunt Lucy up over the steps to the porch with her feet paddling in the air. When Daddy set her feet down, she plopped down in the first empty chair, which was where Uncle

Tendall usually was. She wiggled backwards, feet straight out. I hoped somebody would notice her shoes were on the right feet.

"Where's my useless brother?" Aunt Lucy shouted.

"He's gone, Lucy," I heard Daddy say. "About a week ago."

"Gone where?"

"Gone to his Maker," Mother whispered before Daddy answered, not loud enough for Aunt Lucy to hear. "We pray he has."

13

Getting used to the good part of being back home came pretty easy. Mother really knocked herself out in the kitchen for me, making everything I liked. And I wasn't the only one had to look after Aunt Lucy now. The bad part of being home was harder. I never thought we wouldn't all set out on the porch and talk on Sunday. As many times as I made excuses so I could go to the filling station and work on my truck where Mother couldn't see me. Now no Uncle Tendall. No more parachute caught on the church steeple. No getting to hear Aunt Lucy brag to him about seeing that big cactus he never saw. I never figured on anything happening to him.

When Mother sent me to the closet under the steps to get a jar of chow chow for my greens, I did get a real funny feeling I didn't use to have. I've been in that closet more than a hundred times I bet, before I knew that was where my grandpa died, beating his head on the bare wall behind the rows of colored jars. When I shut the door and tried to imagine being Grandpa closed in the dark, I made a whole shelf of yellow tomatoes turn as gray in my brain as a black and white movie. Only me and Aunt Lucy know. Uncle Tendall is gone. If I don't tell somebody someday, it is like a page got torn out of the Foushee family history book.

I finally decided to not say a word to Daddy about Grandpa. I figured it wasn't the same as Aunt Lucy telling me the truth about Bear so I'd quit hoping to find him. It was like her telling me about Grandpa and putting nightmares in my brain for the rest of my life. My daddy has no need to know. He told me his daddy's heart quit, just like Uncle Tendall, and that the men in the family, meaning me and him I guess, should watch their hearts. When I try to imagine my heart quitting, a part of me just falls off, like my arm died and I can't carry in wood anymore and just get sent out for eggs and tomatoes. I can't imagine hearts really. There's an arm of a great uncle over in the graveyard but the rest of him died somewhere else. My daddy's daddy's whole round skeleton didn't get buried in the graveyard either and is lost in the pinewoods for good. Except in my mind and Aunt Lucy's mind. And hers is going fast.

A couple of days ago, I was watching Aunt Lucy go down the hall to the bathroom. Her dress was stuck to her back with blood dots that looked like nail heads where Elijah dug in his claws when she tried to carry him up to our house. He jumped off her back and went right back to her old house. Aunt Lucy walked with one foot on its side instead of its sole. I didn't offer to help because I figured since she was having to try so hard to walk, it might jar a little of the rusty crust off her brain. To tell the truth, I'm afraid every time I go off somewhere that I'll come back and she'll be dead like Uncle Tendall. Wouldn't surprise anybody if she died, I guess. There is a big difference between hearing about somebody who died like Grandpa and knowing the person alive who died, if I'm making any sense.

She is doing a lot of rocking these days and not much talking. She doesn't say her Burma Shaves and funny expressions anymore. I kept trying to think of them to remind her. I told her a funny new one I heard at work: "Gone like moth piss on a sixty watt bulb" and she looked at me like she didn't understand a word I said.

She's eating pretty good and not complaining too much about Mother's cooking, but she just keeps getting a bigger watermelon in her belly and nothing anywhere else. Like she's storing up all that food Mother cooks that she doesn't like for later. One day her body doesn't want to work all over, and the next day, her mind gives up on her for a while. Then most of her comes back. But not all, if you want the honest truth. She is older than Uncle Tendall was when he died. Mother keeps reminding me: "She's had a hard life, Benny. There's no cure for old age."

Mother did something I couldn't do. She pulled all those clothes layers off of Aunt Lucy, down past that nightgown to buck-naked and threw the whole smelly mess in the washing machine. Then she got Aunt Lucy in the bathtub and scrubbed her. Mother did something else I couldn't believe. She threw Aunt Lucy's purse in the garbage can. I could of washed it out with gasoline or something. I warned Mother that the you-know-what was going to hit the fan when Aunt Lucy missed it. And the big surprise? Kind of sad, to tell the truth. Aunt Lucy never said a word about it being gone. I guess she's got no need of it now to carry her food, now that we're home. She carries her extra food in that watermelon belly.

And if you're wondering about all the money in the purse, she had me put it in a envelope. She told me to write WILL—OPEN AFTER I PASS on it and stick it in her magazine box. I probably ought to check and make sure she hasn't moved it somewhere else and forgot where she put it. I did see Uncle Obie's glasses, her bag of colored rocks, that stupid pamphlet I thought she lost and her *Arizona Highways* in the magazine box. Maybe she hid the other Cape May diamond in with the polished rocks. That would be like her. I think I know her pretty good, but I got to admit I missed on the purse.

Somedays when I go to see Aunt Lucy in her bed in the storage room where she stays most of the time, she sets up just to listen to me. I like to help her over in her rocker because it seems like that is where she looks better. But when I've got something to measure her by, I do notice how little she is getting. The rocker was showing its worst for wear too, as Mother would say, the paint flaking, almost all of it worn off the rockers. That old rocker had rocked all the way across the United States whether she was in it or whether it was in its bag in the back of my truck, filled up with dogs. It even rocked in the desert sand where it wasn't allowed. Got its picture took. Taken. Mother would love to throw it out with the old black purse, I know her. She will when Aunt Lucy is gone but I can't stand to think about that.

I've been trying some of my stories out on Aunt Lucy, hoping I'll make both of us feel better. I made up a pretty good one about Ferrell, the crazy cowboy whose Indian mother was too close to the bomb test. He robbed a bank with a water pistol and tried to make a getaway on his bicycle in the modern world. Aunt Lucy laughed and called me Papa but that was OK. I reminded her about Ham the space monkey who died in North Carolina but got buried in New Mexico beside his wife. Aunt Lucy said, "Bury me in New Mexico, Obie," and I said OK, but I had my fingers crossed where she couldn't see them. Probably didn't count anyway since she called me Obie. I sure hadn't forgotten how much trouble agreeing with her got me in.

I put a crazy story together about the dead cow table and the mad blue bird, where my hero Jack sold the dead cow table before it got rotten for some cactus seeds and planted them to climb higher than the mad blue bird could fly. It was so tall that when Jack got to the top, he found out what he thought looked like a elf owl from down low was really this giant owl who ate Jack up in one bite and spit him out in a big owl ball and he rolled along with the tumbleweeds. Aunt Lucy piped up: "That's a pretty good one, Tendall, for you."

"I'm not Tendall. I'm Benny."

"Is that so?" she said real mean.

I didn't mind her calling me Obie and Papa because she loved them both, but I'm not letting her call me Tendall no matter how mad she gets when I correct her. She never messes up and calls me Mona so no matter how nutty Aunt Lucy got, she still knew I was a guy.

Now here's a story I can't get going in my mind. I tried to see that dark woman in the pink house in Taos, New Mexico, up a ladder, cleaning off the boiled egg stuck on the ceiling. Or that dark man, Juan, painting over the spot the egg did before her daddy got home from work. I couldn't see any of that good enough to tell it. I think it was because I couldn't picture Tennessee running water in a pan inside that pink house and putting the egg in the water and turning on the stove. I don't even know if her stove was gas or electric or something else that rich people might have. I've never been in a house like that and she sure didn't ask me and Aunt Lucy inside.

I could sort of hear the phone ring in the pink house, like on the soap operas that Ethel watches. Mother too, peeping up from her sewing machine at what she calls the stories. Funny, Ethel and Mother call them stories. I call them soap operas and have no idea in the world what that means except that's what Daddy calls them. People singing and making bubbles? I don't know why. So Tennessee's story might go like this: The phone is the golf pro so the man with the little feet with the bridles on his shoes gets real mad and he and Mrs. Gentry argue. I could hear the TV people arguing better than I could picture Tennessee's mother and daddy. I guess her daddy, I mean her father thought the golf pro might be stealing his wife away. Maybe he really did. Didn't interest me. My stories keep coming back to a old woman who can't seem to get her shoes on the right feet except by mistake. Don't think they'll be wanting my stories for television.

To tell the truth, there is a story I can never make myself tell to Aunt Lucy and I'm not sure why I hold onto it so tight. It is even one she knows her side of already. It is the big cactus story. I'm not understanding why I can't tell it. I wonder if Tennessee told anybody that story about the old lady in her rocker at the cactus she came two thousand miles to see. Tennessee seemed to only want to tell sad stories. I wouldn't want for me to tell Aunt Lucy's story for her because it would steal her thunder. As Aunt Lucy herself would say: Don't steal my thunder, Benny. OK, then you tell it, Aunt Lucy. I'm saving it for you. I want it to cover over Grandpa's story like plowing a field and starting it with fresh seeds. Not like throwing a bed quilt over his story so all the bad stuff can crawl out from under it again.

Aunt Lucy would do the telling better than me but that's OK too. Maybe that pretty little blond girl was gone to her like the frost off her window when the sun hit it. She never makes mention of her. I can't bear to ask her if she remembers Tennessee. No matter what her answer, yes or no, it would hurt too much so I'm just not going to bring it up.

I do find myself talking about Tennessee to everybody else though. Even embarrassing myself in front of Ethel. I try hard to remember what her hand felt like or her silky shirt when she was crying in my lap, but I've got nothing to touch to remind me of it. I think girls are better than guys with those keepsake things. I don't think a thing but the real thing would help me right now.

Every time I mention something about Tennessee, Mother has to come up with something about Valinda. And then Ethel pipes in how she heard Valinda might get married to Howard Pedigrew, like I care. Sounds like one of their stories. Their soap operas. I ought to tell how Buddy at the station told me about how Howard Pedigrew came by to borrow a sack of tools so he could walk in his house in front of his parents and carry the tools down low so they wouldn't see where he creamed in his gray Sunday pants. That's my Valinda soap opera.

Something that I did think about a lot: Valinda was just like that dress she paid so long for on layaway to wear to the dance. Hot pink she called it. Day-glo if you ask me. And Tennessee was that red flower corsage I bought that Valinda told me clashed with her dress. Valinda is a loud gaudy color and Tennessee is a perfect red tomato. That's how they are in my mind and you can bet I won't tell another soul that. They'd say that was how a girl thinks. I told Polar so I could hear it out loud, I thought it was so cool. That night in the rain, Tennessee might have even let Polar in on her side of the truck. Maybe we would have decided not to go to that stupid dance. Or laughed about the paw prints on her dress. I never saw her in a dress. Tennessee would have said: "Benny, you're completely crazy," and clapped her hands. No matter how much she hurt my feelings, she was just being like a rich girl. Didn't mean to be hurtful. It was how she was raised, as Mother would say.

Ethel and I had words about that, as Mother would say. I need to stop saying that, as Mother would say. The words started when Ethel wore the dog collar I gave her to church with her fat covering so much of the silver, it looked like she had blue bumps on her arm, then Buddy at the station's mother told her it was pretty.

"Benny bought it when he ran off," she said real loud.

When me and Ethel were in visiting with Aunt Lucy before Sunday dinner, I told Ethel: "I didn't run off. I went on a trip with Aunt Lucy and we came back."

"Run off. Run off at the mouth," Aunt Lucy mumbled.

Ethel grunted at me, which was her way of saying I wasn't telling the truth.

"Why would I run off?" I asked her. "I like it here."

"Why would a fancy rich girl want anything to do with a pimply pizza faced ner-do-well?"

"I'll do well. Your face looks like a lemon meringue pie. I'll do well when I get good and ready."

"Ner-do-well white trash," Aunt Lucy said. "I prefer key lime myself."

"Aunt Lucy hasn't got a brain in her head but she knows her place," Ethel said and handed me the bracelet back. "You didn't buy that," she snorted. "That rich girl bought it. Lerner Jewelry told me it was real. You think you're too good for people around here."

"I thought you told me I wasn't good enough for Valinda. You're just jealous because you never got past the Burma Shave signs."

"I don't want to go past the Burma Shave signs."

"And you're proud of that?"

"Turnip greens for lunch. With my new chow chow."

I realized Mother was at the door when she spoke.

Aunt Lucy said: "If turnips were swords, I'd have one by my side."

Mother took the bracelet from my hand as Ethel left and dropped it in her apron pocket. She lifted one of Aunt Lucy's arms and I lifted the other. After we balanced her, Aunt Lucy took off for the table.

"Ethel didn't mean that," Mother whispered. "She was real proud of your gift. I'll give it back to her later when she calms down. It's that time of the month." Mother's face got red and she held her hand to her mouth. "I'm sorry, Benny. That slipped out."

"I know what you mean, Mother."

She patted my arm before we caught up to Aunt Lucy, ready to catch her if she toppled. Ethel was already there, pretending to be praying.

"Now I lay me down to sleep," Aunt Lucy said.

Mother pinched my arm and winked. I tried to wink back but I'm not very good at it.

"You've grown up a lot this summer," she whispered.

I looked everywhere for that camera, thinking maybe Tennessee left it in the truck by accident but she didn't. I was getting real worried, hoping she hadn't forgotten about sending the pictures of Aunt Lucy and the big cactus. I don't think Tennessee realizes how you can't mess around very long with old people like Aunt Lucy. She didn't see what happened to Aunt Lucy on the way home. And look how fast Uncle Tendall was gone.

I was really curious to hear how Tennessee's daddy and the girls at school liked the bug I give her. Gave her. I need to be around people who don't destroy the King's English, as Mother would say, instead of them, those rednecks where I used to work. People at the hardware store are a little better. Not much. I bet folks can't stop talking about that blue jeweled bug in Taos, New Mexico. I told the other guys who work at the hardware about the bug. They said they wished I'd got them one for their girlfriends. A girl couldn't help but go crazy over a jeweled bug on a chain, was what one of them said. I think he might have been pulling my leg, as Daddy would say. I told him he didn't know Tennessee. She was different. I think most of them were pretty jealous of me and my adventure out west. I had to kind of make fun of Aunt Lucy around them. Sort of hard to explain to other people why I like her so much. Love her, I guess.

Sure wish I had a better picture to brag about than that one with Tennessee's head in the little boy cardboard thing. Can you believe I'm so stupid that's the only picture I ended up with? Didn't do her justice, as Mother would say. I look at that picture a lot with all of us in the Western store that got took, taken, the day Tennessee left us for good. Even though it was guaranteed for five years, I'm afraid it's starting to get fainter. Maybe in five years the paper will be all white. Maybe in five years she won't even look like that anymore.

I went to the Public Library and looked up Cape May diamonds and bug jewelry in the World Book and wrote down a bunch of stuff to talk about after she writes me. Mother keeps harping on me to join the National Guard when I turn seventeen and I keep forgetting to look up how because I don't really want to. But I'll do it for Mother. Those bugs like I bought are really famous over in Egypt, as important as a cross to a Christian, which I wouldn't say around Mother. And that ball of manure the dung beetle was rolling? I'd like to tell pretty little Miss Know-it-all that a egg was in that turd. She didn't know that. It's real hard to figure how those Egyptians come up with this, but that horse turd with the eggs in it was like the moon and the sun to them and the beetle was rolling it along to change night and day. That happened because some Egyptian saw a bunch of baby beetles coming out of a horse turd and made all that up about the sun and the moon. Got to have a better imagination than I do. Not sure how the Mexicans and Egyptians got together either, but that old beetle I gave her was going to live forever. Eternal life, better than a mummy even.

Having the postcards I bought at a filling station with pictures of the big cactus weren't near as cool as it looked with Aunt Lucy, sitting in her same old rocker she's in right now, right in front of it. I won't ever forget it. But I was there. Won't be any pictures of Tennessee being there because she was the one doing the taking. What an idiot that I didn't even ask to take a picture of her with that same camera. I took Aunt Lucy's magnifying glass to study her face on top of the little boy's body. Maybe she'll send me a school picture when she sends the others. I need to quit thinking about it so much because I just get mad at myself all over again. Nobody's fault but my own. All that buying she did, I got to admit she never bought anything for me except a meal or two. Guess I'm selfish to even think like that. What I want so much that I'd never ask for anything again is the pictures of Aunt Lucy at the big cactus. I'll admit that.

The honest truth is it's getting real important for Aunt Lucy to see those pictures. Even if Tennessee don't, doesn't care about me. I called the operator, but she said Homer Barrow's phone number wasn't listed. And there was not a Tiffany Barrow either. I need to get over to Raleigh and look for a company called Barrow. Things are getting away from Aunt Lucy fast. Things that just happened. On Sunday Daddy took her over to the church graveyard to see where they buried Uncle Tendall.

"Obie ain't going to like it," she whispered to me on the way over, "if he's next to him. He'll turn over in his grave to look the other way." That made me feel a little better to hear her talking mean like that.

When we got there, I could spot Uncle Tendall's place easy. The red clay was just starting to sprout wild grass and good grass hadn't grown all the way across it yet. First thing Mother and Ethel did was go rushing over and start pulling the wild grass like their lives depended on it. And Mother told Daddy to bring some good store bought seeds to plant on it, next time we came. He just nodded his head. He misses Uncle Tendall the most. It is hard for me to feel what he does because to be honest, I think less of Uncle Tendall now than I did before the trip. Not to speak ill of the dead, as Mother would say, but I mean to speak ill.

Daddy let Aunt Lucy go over to the grave by herself. Her foot looked a little better, almost straight. Every time she messed up her shoes, Daddy changed them now and she didn't even get mad.

She made a beeline towards Uncle Tendall's grave, probably because she saw the new little American flags sticking out of it. Mother told me the veterans' association had paid for the gravestone: 82nd Airborne - 1944. I noticed right off that the stone looked just like the ones they put over the guys who really died in the wars. Instead of sitting in their Lazy-Boy watching wrestling on a butt with a bullet hole in it. I bet the undertaker saw that.

Aunt Lucy went right by Great Aunt Agnes' son Buck who got killed in Korea. Aunt Lucy told me nothing was in that grave but bones could have been a pig's; that they told Aunt Agnes they found Buck so she would stop fretting. Not long after they found his bones, she did quit fretting and died herself and got put beside his bones, be they right or wrong. She might have been better off hoping he was still alive.

Aunt Lucy walked past Uncle Obie's grave that didn't have a stone paid for by the veterans. Maybe she forgot where it was because the wild grass had taken over. She stood a long time at Uncle Tendall's grave, talking. I couldn't hear what she was saying from where I was, but she did sound mad. I didn't want to butt in. Maybe she was mad at him for dying before she got back, just like Tendall got mad at their daddy for getting killed.

I couldn't hold back asking her when she was back in her rocker: "Did you tell Uncle Tendall about the big cactus, Aunt Lucy?" That made her look at me hard, her cloudy blue eyes squeezing into two thin little slots. Then she answered me, as clear as the black-headed jaybird that squawked over our heads when we were in the burned out place in New Mexico, with a voice that didn't sound a bit like Aunt Lucy.

"What big cactus?"

I think you can go the rest of your life, wishing you had done this, and wishing you hadn't done that. I'm going to try and not let that happen to me, at least much as I can help it. Young as I am, I already got a few things on my list. But that hurt me awful bad.

Now I've got to come up with a way to remind Aunt Lucy about that big cactus that will make it all come back to her as clear as it is to me. Maybe I'll tell her about the little owl that was living in the hole way up at the top. Remind her how she told me about the famous woman who carried the little owl in her pocket. That ought to blow the dust off her brain. Ask her to help me remember that famous woman's name I forgot already. Name was some kind of bird too.

I've been wondering if I ought to go in Aunt Lucy's magazine box and pull out the *Arizona Highways* again. But what if all that did was make her start asking me to take her out there all over again? I don't think my truck would make it even with the four new tires and the new water pump I got with the money she gave me. They would put me in jail in modern times if I buried her in some strange woods. I think her seeing the big cactus is over with, if you want the truth.

Don't know if Polar remembers the trip or not. Well, he does, but not the same as me. Anything I ask him to do with me is OK with him. I see him running through the woods around here until he just falls down tired with his tongue out and I know he's the happiest thing living here. With Shenandoah running along behind him who Mother complains is eating us out of house and home. Uncle Tendall just didn't get it, saying a dog didn't have any right to live if he didn't want to hunt. Trying to feel like a man saying that a dog was only worth something if he did what he was told by a man. Worst of all trying to make what he the man did OK by blaming the dog. About the worse insult somebody could say to me was I reminded them of Uncle Tendall, but I can't say that because Mother would fuss at me for talking ill of the dead.

I'm seeing how Mother and Daddy are real different from Uncle Tendall. Mother talked real tough about putting Aunt Lucy in the county home and taking Shenandoah to the pound, but they're both still right here and she feeds them both just like they were worth as much to her as her best hens. And Daddy just says corny things and does what Mother tells him to do. That's the way I am with women too. Except Ethel. If Ethel told me grass was green, I'd argue with her.

I can't talk about a lot of things with Mother because I don't want to hear what the Bible says about right and wrong. I want to find out the difference myself, if you know what I mean. Sometimes a mistake has got to be owned up to. Lots of times I can feel like I made a mistake taking Aunt Lucy all the way out there to see that big cactus without asking anybody if it was OK, especially since I knew they'd say it wasn't. That maybe going to the big cactus made her get old faster. But other times, I just say to myself that I did right. Tennessee told me I did right and she's the only other one who saw Aunt Lucy in her rocker with the sun setting behind that big cactus. There might not be a right answer in Mother's book, but seeing Aunt Lucy at that big cactus is my right answer. I had Tennessee on my side and she'll probably never say two words to me again.

Daddy the cornball would probably come up with a Burma Shave:

Benny Foushee
Toted Aunt Lu-cy
Across the desert
In his GMC.
Benny Foushee
Discovered Tenn-es-see
But he didn't lose
His vir-gin-i-ty.
Hang on Sue Faye
For another day

His chin's too smooth
To waste the blade.
Burma Shave.

I put up too many signs. And the rhyme's not too good. Aunt Lucy's right. They'd never hire me.

I've tried to do a story in my mind about what happened to me. It almost comes out like something to sing like a country song, but there is sure nobody around here to sing it to. Soap bubble opera. They'd all get a big laugh out of that. I put in a part in the song about waiting for the mailman and every time I work on it, I almost start to cry again so I have to quit. I sure wish those pictures of Aunt Lucy and the cactus would get here so I could do a happy ending for my story. Right now making up a happy ending makes me even sadder than what is really happening. Just can't kid myself there to tell the truth.

Aunt Lucy knew we needed to rush home from the big cactus. Maybe that was why she pushed me so hard. She felt what has happened to her coming on. Uncle Tendall died so fast nobody got to tell him goodbye.

Well, Benny Foushee is just going to try to be glad I went to all that trouble to take Aunt Lucy to see the big cactus. Pure and simple, as Mother would say. It was the nicest thing anybody ever did for her; Aunt Lucy told me that back when she still could remember that I did it. And it won't be the dumbest thing I ever do for somebody, I can tell you that. That's just the way I am.